ISBN 0-373-70704-5

A FAMILY OF HIS OWN

"It's one o'clock in the morning!"

"What's the matter? Why is Jason here?" Ginny
continued. "Is he sick?"

Her husband pulled on a pair of pants, then paused.
"Lovesick."

Ginny laughed. "What? Who?"

"Laura, of course. But I don't think he knows what's
hit him."

Ginny tried to muffle her laughter. "So he's getting
drunk? Why?"

"Because my dear brother hasn't a clue what's happening to him. All he knows is he feels like hell, kind
of sick inside for no reason. But wait till he realizes
what's going on and tries to deny it. He'll make
everyone within five miles of him utterly miserable."

Ginny groaned and stuck her head under a pillow.

D1173041

ABOUT THE AUTHOR

Evelyn A. Crowe worked for twelve years as a media director in an advertising company before turning her hand to writing in 1983. Her decision to change careers was certainly a stroke of good fortune for Harlequin readers, as Evelyn's bestselling books are favorites with readers around the world.

The many fans of Evelyn's last Superromance novel, *Fathers & Other Strangers*, will be delighted to learn that *A Family of His Own* is a spin-off of that book.

Books by Evelyn A. Crowe

HARLEQUIN SUPERROMANCE
112—SUMMER BALLAD
160—CHARADE
186—MOMENT OF MADNESS
233—FINAL PAYMENT
262—TWICE SHY
294—A WILD WIND
362—WORD OF HONOR
570—REUNITED
646—LEGACY OF FEAR
667—FATHERS & OTHER STRANGERS

Don't miss any of our special offers. Write to us at the following address for information on our newest releases.

Harlequin Reader Service
U.S.: 3010 Walden Ave., P.O. Box 1325, Buffalo, NY 14269
Canadian: P.O. Box 609, Fort Erie, Ont. L2A 5X3

Evelyn A. Crowe
A FAMILY HIS OWN

Harlequin Books

TORONTO • NEW YORK • LONDON
AMSTERDAM • PARIS • SYDNEY • HAMBURG
STOCKHOLM • ATHENS • TOKYO • MILAN
MADRID • WARSAW • BUDAPEST • AUCKLAND

A FAMILY OF HIS OWN

CHAPTER ONE

JASON VAN DER BOLLEN tilted his chair on two legs, letting the back rest against the kitchen wall, as he closed his eyes and sighed with contentment. He'd just eaten his fill of buttermilk pancakes drowned in butter and maple syrup, lots of crisp bacon, fresh orange juice, three cups of hot, strong, black coffee, topped off with a homemade blueberry muffin the size of his fist. It was a great breakfast. Now all he wanted to do was let the morning family chitchat between his brother, a very pregnant sister-in-law and his nephew float around him like a sweet dream.

Feeling like a lazy, contented cat, he opened one eye and grinned as he watched Ginny struggling to get out of her chair. It was hard to believe they'd only known her for a little over a year and they'd all come together in the most absurd set of circumstances. So many things had happened. The most important was his brother's good fortune in marrying Ginny.

Jason gazed at Ginny and realized he loved her. It shocked him that he actually cared about someone other than himself. Oh, the love wasn't a sexual thing. Jeez, Matt would skin him alive and stake his sorry hide to the vineyard gate as a warning to any other males with such ideas. No, no. He loved Ginny like a sister.

Life was perfect, he thought. Well, almost.

Jason's grin grew wider and his bright blue eyes had that mischievous sparkle Ginny knew never to trust. "Wipe that goofy smile off your face, Jason,'' she said testily, automatically rubbing at the small of her back. Then she crossed her arms over the large mound of her stomach, tapped her foot and glared.

Jason's grin grew even wider. Her ever-present shadow, an ugly mutt by the name of Dog who'd become overprotective lately, snarled and snapped his teeth at him.

''I was just thinking how lucky you and Matt and Austin are.''

She'd expected one of his usual sarcastic comments, was ready for it, but was thrown by the longing in his voice. Jason was lonely, she realized, and hot tears immediately pooled in her eyes, blurring her vision.

Austin and Matt paused as they cleared the table, gave each other a knowing look, then quickly glanced away to keep from laughing. ''Now look what you've done,'' Austin said. ''I explained to you about women's crazy hormones when they're going to have a baby. It's kind of like PMS, only a hundred times worse.'' Austin gently patted his stepmother's arm. ''Don't pay any attention to Uncle Jason, Ginny. He's getting old and having trouble with his own hormones. I think he's been bitten by that nesting impulse again.''

Ginny wanted desperately to laugh. Her men were so obsessively protective she didn't have the heart to belittle their good intentions or their feelings. ''Well, he needs a female to nest with.''

Jason frowned. They'd been teasing him ever since he sold his investments, the wine-and-cheese shops in Austin and other businesses he owned, and decided to take up the land his father had left him. That land was directly across the highway from the family vineyard, and he intended to ranch it. Well, not ranching in the traditional sense. But he'd surprised them by showing he was capable of renovating and remodeling the old stone barn into a home.

"Women—" he gave a dismissive wave "—are not my problem. There're always plenty to pick from when the time's right."

Ginny opened her mouth, glanced at Matt, then pressed her lips together. She wanted to ask Jason about love, but realized by the shake of her husband's head and the sparkle in his dark eyes that her question would only start a long-standing argument.

Jason was one of those beautifully handsome men. Tall, well built, with light blond hair and laughing blue eyes. But even if he'd been unattractive, he would still have had women falling all over him. He was one of those people who never met a stranger; he had a charismatic personality, loved to laugh and have a good time. Furthermore, Jason really liked women. He was fascinated by them and truly enjoyed their company. And he always had plenty of company.

"What I need is some muscle. A little help with putting in the kitchen cabinets." He was disappointed that Ginny hadn't made one of her usual knife-edged comments after his statement about women. He and his sister-in-law often wound up in a heated but good-natured exchange he found stimulating. Then he reminded himself of her condition and realized that the closer she got to her due date, the more prone she was to bursting into tears. He looked forward to these mornings with his family and didn't intend to start anything—with either Ginny or Austin—that would get him kicked out by his brother.

He smiled sweetly, brought his chair down on all four legs and picked up one of the books Austin had brought home. His nephew was an eleven-year-old genius attending the University of Texas, studying something Jason couldn't even pronounce and living with the dean's family during the week and coming home on weekends and vacations. Summer break had sent Austin home for a couple of months, and Jason looked forward to spending time with his nephew.

"What are these, Einstein?" Jason tapped a stack of books. "Surely you're not going to study this summer. I thought you were going to help me."

Austin slipped back into his chair and dug one of the books from the stack, then held it up. "It's about home birth. I thought since Ginny's decided to have my sister here that Dad ought to be apprised of what to do and expect."

Matt paled, which made his eyes look larger and darker. He ran a suddenly nervous hand through his long black hair. "The doctor will be here, Austin." But his interest was piqued, and he set down the stack of plates and picked up a book. *"Name Your Baby."* he read the title aloud. He picked up another. *"From One Month to One Year. What All Fathers Should Know.* This is great, son." He began thumbing through one of the books. "We'll start going through them tonight."

Jason loved just to sit back and observe the three of them. He almost laughed out loud when he listened to Matt run through the titles. He thought his brother was teasing but quickly saw Matt was as serious as Austin. A painful lump lodged in his throat and he had to swallow a couple of times to force it down. Maybe it was time to leave.

Then something about Austin's behavior caught his eye. He studied the way the boy kept glancing from his father to Ginny as if struggling to make up his mind and weighing his options at the same time. Fascinated, Jason cupped his chin in his hand and waited, knowing Austin was too much like him to be quiet for long. His nephew was cooking up a scheme, and he'd be damned if he'd miss what was about to happen.

"I've asked a friend of mine from school to spend the weekend," Austin said loudly and to no one in particular. When he didn't get an immediate response, he quickly gathered up the remaining dishes and carried them to the sink. "You said I could have anyone I wanted. Anytime."

The kid was going to blow it, Jason thought. Whatever he had up his sleeve, he was going to talk too fast and too much, dig himself a deep hole that his father would only push him into. Jason shook his head in mild disappointment.

Austin snapped his lips shut and shot his uncle a fierce glare, then shifted his gaze to his father, saw his own face mirrored there and averted his eyes. When he glanced at Ginny, he'd arranged his features into as sad and pitiful an expression as he could manage. "Her name's Laura and she'll be here this morning." His best defense, he decided, was to distance himself from the adults, but before leaving, he said, "You'll like Laura. I do. I mean..." He quickly disappeared up the stairs and headed for his room.

Ginny glanced around, and when no one spoke, she said, "Laura? A girl?"

Jason whistled softly. "And the kid's only eleven years old. Must take after me, after all."

"Jason," Matt said, irritably, "Austin's too young to be interested in girls. Not that way. And she must be a contemporary of his, so she's too young, too."

Ginny pulled out her chair and sat down. "I don't know. Did you see the way he was smiling? But, Matt, you're right, he's too young to be thinking girls and sex. Isn't he?" She directed the question at Jason, the expert.

"Nonsense," Jason said. "I had girls, including older girls, chasing me when I was younger than Austin. And she must be older, because I haven't heard about any female geniuses attending the university.

"Jason..." Matt growled warningly.

"You don't think?" Ginny shook her head. "No. He's far too young, isn't he? When do boys...?" She let the question dangle and waited for an answer.

Jason laughed. "No male is too young when it comes to a persistent older female. Actually, I believe I was about Einstein's age the first time—"

"Dammit, Jason, don't you have something to do?" Matt glared at his brother, then rose and squatted down beside Ginny's chair. "Now don't get all upset. It's not good for the baby."

"I'm not up—"

But Matt didn't let her finish. "Come on, I'll help get one of the guest rooms ready, then finish the dishes." He glanced across the table. "Or maybe Jason will do them?"

"Yesterday was my turn. Besides, I have to get to town and pick up some supplies I ordered." Jason knew when he'd worn out his welcome and he quickly started for the door, only to have his exit hampered by Dog's vengeful snapping teeth. He danced around the animal and out the door. "How about coming over later, Matt, and helping me with the cabinets?" Not waiting for an answer, he kept walking.

TWO RIVERS WAS a farming community set in a triangle of equal distances between Austin and San Antonio, with the small town of Fredericksburg not far away. Most of the Two Rivers' townspeople were artists and craftsmen who sold their products to the merchants in Fredericksburg.

After Ginny's arrival more than a year ago, the face of Two Rivers had changed dramatically. The townsfolk, as in most small towns, were a close, suspicious lot, but once they met Ginny and fell in love with her, they counted her as one of their own. Ginny had paid them back for their love and protectiveness. As a corporate lawyer, she'd advised the local artisans and the town elders to incorporate, so they could obtain much better prices for their merchandise.

Now Two Rivers was becoming a bustling community. The town council used some of the town's earnings to refurbish the facade of the buildings on Main Street. The co-op was making money, and some of the young people, who had moved away because they couldn't practice a trade there and make a living, were returning. They rented the empty storefronts along the main drag and set up their businesses. There was a new energy in the town, new life. Jason had to admit it felt good, right somehow.

He parked the vineyard truck at an angle on Main Street and sat for a moment, absently watching the two old people seated on benches outside the general store. For as long as he could remember, those two had sat there arguing with each other and with anyone who stopped to pass the time of day. They were fixtures. As he watched, Mister spat a stream of tobacco into a brass spittoon, never once taking his eyes off the piece of wood he was whittling.

Jason crossed his arms over the steering wheel and rested his chin on his folded hands. How many times in his lonely childhood had he walked to town and sat at the old man's feet, watching those talented hands work a block of wood? Mister was a master carver, creating animals so perfect you expected them to come to life, jump from those gnarled old hands and run away.

Jason grinned as his attention shifted to Miss Rosemary. She had to be in her late nineties, and he couldn't remember ever seeing her when her hands weren't busy. Though he knew nothing about tatting, lace-making, knitting or crocheting, he was aware that, like Mister, Miss Rosemary was an artist and that everything she made sold at outrageous prices.

For as long as he could remember he'd wanted one thing—to get away from Two Rivers. His father, he knew, hadn't cared about him one way or the other. He was just the result of an act between him and his mother. The only thing his father had cared about, deeply loved, was the vineyard, which he'd guarded like a jealous lover. During his lifetime, he'd refused to share the vineyard or winery with his first son, Matt, and he wasn't about to share it with his second, either.

Jason's one driving passion back then had been to make something of himself on his own, without his father's interference or wealth. Of course, that was more easily dreamed about than actually accomplished. After all, he was accustomed to having money and privilege. Then, once he was away at school and later college, he'd found women, or they'd found him.

Oh, he'd made good money on his own through his investments and business deals. But now, after having sold everything, returning to Two Rivers and investing every penny into his new venture, he realized that he'd never felt so good—so happy and content. Hell, he didn't even miss the women, except maybe when he was alone in bed at night. He chuckled. Ginny would be appalled, but with a snap of his fingers he could have as many women as he wanted. Anytime. Anywhere. Anyplace. Women were never a problem, not for him.

Jason jerked out of his daydream, stepped from the truck and, stopping only long enough to pass a few moments with Mister and Miss Rosemary, wandered into the general store. "Annie," he called, heading for the room at the back where a group of elderly local women did their quilting. He lingered at the door, then shaded his eyes and said, "So much beauty could blind a man."

Half of the eight women giggled like little girls, the rest grumbled under their breath, but they were all smiling. They were wise to Jason Van der Bollen, but that didn't mean they were immune to his charm.

"Where's Annie?" Jason asked, then jumped when a firm hand patted him on his butt. He swung around. "You better watch yourself, Annie. You know I'm partial to redheads."

Annie grinned. "Is that why you can't stay away from Ginny?"

Jason leaned against the door frame and gave her his most beguiling smile, aware that the store had big ears. "I love Ginny like everyone else does. The fact that she's a good cook, always welcomes me at her table, has tamed my brother, made my nephew a happy little boy again and has red hair helps. But, Annie, no one has that carrot shade of red like yours." Then he lowered his voice, but not so low that everyone couldn't hear, and said, "And I dearly love carrots."

Annie nodded and smiled as if all her worries had disappeared. "The eight gallons of stain you ordered came in. That seems like an awful lot, Jason."

He waved to the women and followed Annie to the front of the store. "I'm putting all hardwood floors in my place."

"How are the girls?" she asked. "Are they—" She didn't get any further, for the town alarm sounded and everyone rushed to the radio receiver. Jason was amused. He hadn't thought the old gals could move so fast.

As they gathered around the radio listening to Foster Schneider, who lived outside of town beside the main highway, Jason began stacking the heavy gallon cans by the door, keeping an ear tuned to the radio, wanting to make sure everything was all right.

Over a year ago the town had set up an elaborate alarm system to protect Ginny. A few years ago, his sister-in-law had testified at a trial, which had resulted in her being put in the FBI's Witness Protection Program for her own safety. She'd left the program, but the threat was still there. Now, any stranger coming down the old highway, from either direction, was spotted by Foster at one end or Tom Klein at the other. As the town watchers, they sat on their porches and kept an eye out for unfamiliar vehicles. When they saw one, they'd jot down the license number and other general information and relay it to Annie's general store. By the time the car was within the town limits, the license and description had been relayed to the sheriff's office and checked out.

Jason was stacking the last of the cans when Annie called him. He strolled over to where everyone was gathered. "What's the problem?"

"The sheriff usually pops over when we advise him we have an incoming, but he's out of range of the radio right now. If the car stops in town, would you go see who it is and what they want?"

"Sure." Jason left the store and stationed himself beside Mister. He didn't have long to wait. "Looks like something out of the seventies—an old VW van. Yellow or white. I can't tell." He shaded his eyes, trying to make out how many were in the front seat, but the morning sun shone directly on the windshield. He watched as the van came closer, then slowed down and turned into a parking space only a couple of feet from his truck. He cringed when the front bumper and grill ground against the high curb.

The old gals had clustered by the front door and were clearly nervous, and as he pushed away from the wall he noticed that a couple of men from the stores across the street had come out to stand on the sidewalk. He waved to them as he headed for the van. When he was closer his radar told him it was a woman behind the wheel before he actually saw her.

He patted the side of the mint-condition classic, but his attention was riveted to the shapely pink lips and small chin behind the sun visor. He stepped off the curb, misjudged its height and stumbled off-balance. He reached out to grab the door handle for support, but the door suddenly swung open and he was knocked backward, flat on his butt.

Jason threw back his head and laughed, and was still laughing when a booted foot stepped on his ankle. Reflex made him jerk his own foot back just as another boot came in contact with the ground. Suddenly, somehow, his legs were tangled up in another pair of legs, and a second later he grunted in pain as a small body landed on him. Hard.

Laura Ghant had never been so embarrassed in her life. She'd just clobbered a man with her door, knocked him down and almost trampled him to death. Then, as if that wasn't bad enough, in her effort to help, she'd lost her balance and fallen on top of him. "I'm so sorry."

The baseball cap pulled down over her eyes obstructed her vision, but she could feel the trembling of the man's body under her. "Please forgive me." One of her hands was wedged between them, but as she tried to push away, she heard a moan. "Sorry," she whispered. She was afraid to move again, even to shove back her cap, afraid she might hurt him. "Uh, if you're not hurt and can move," she said, "could you roll a little to the right, so I can free my arm?"

When he finally moved, he rolled the wrong way. Her right arm was still pinned. God, he was shaking again and she was really scared. Had he broken something? His legs were wedged between hers in such a way that she couldn't bend her knees or get any traction with her toes on the ground. She was afraid she might injure him further by putting her hands on his body for leverage. But she couldn't lie there and do nothing, so she gently lowered her hand.

"Don't put your hand there again. You could ruin me for life."

Laura almost jumped out of her skin. She tried rubbing the bill of her cap against him in an effort to dislodge it from over her eyes.

"If you'll stop wiggling," he suggested, "I might be able to get my legs from between yours."

Was that voice tinged with laughter? It damn well *was* laughter. "Ouch!" she said. "If you'll just roll to your left, I can free my arm and sit up."

When he actually laughed out loud, it was a deep, rich, infectious sound. If he could laugh like that, she figured he wasn't hurt. Not caring whether she scraped her arm or not, she yanked it free, then put both hands against the man's chest and pushed.

"Hey, hey, hey," Jason gasped. "Watch it." Any other protest quickly dried up and trailed away as he looked at the woman straddling his body. "You've got to watch where you put those hands, lady."

"Then don't just lie there like a bump on a log," Laura said, trying to sound serious but having trouble checking her own laughter, which now threatened to bubble up. She'd made enough of a fool of herself without adding to it. "You might give me a little help here."

It only took a quick flick of his eyes to total up her assets. She was small, not so much in height but in build. Delicate and neatly packaged. The tight, faded jeans hugged the slim curve of her hips and showed off her shapely thighs. Her arms were raised, and the pull of the turquoise cotton tank top didn't come close to hiding the high, firm breasts.

It was his turn to say, "Ouch!" He followed that with, "I'm not a horse. How about not digging the toes of those damn boots into my sides like that?"

"Listen, you big oaf, you almost broke my arm."

He rather liked his position at the moment and watched in amused silence as she tugged at the baseball cap. "I have plans for this body, you know, and it needs to be treated with tender loving care." He could tell by the way she bit her lip that she wanted to laugh but was fighting it.

Once the cap was yanked off, Jason's smile grew. She wasn't his type; nonetheless, he thought she was cute. Her short, curly, light brown hair was half plastered to her head and half sticking out in all directions where the cap band had ruffled it. Her face was a mix of embarrassment and amusement as she stared at him. Then just as he was about to say something, he saw the way her pretty hazel eyes darkened to a deep green, and her shapely lips folded together in a tight line of anger.

She started to say, "If you hadn't..." when she suddenly got a good look at the man she was straddling, and the rest of her words dried up in her throat as effectively as if she'd just stepped out into a sandstorm.

For the length of a couple of jarring heartbeats, she stared, denying what she was seeing. She couldn't believe her eyes. This man was no stranger. Memories she'd deliberately pushed as far as possible to the back of her mind came gushing back in vivid clarity. She went hot with shame, then cold with a deep, fearful dread. She didn't want to touch him but couldn't sit there letting him look her over with those eyes she remembered all too well.

Laura placed both hands on Jason's chest and pushed hard, ignoring the groan and gasp as she stood up. She tried to turn around too quickly before she'd cleared his body and almost fell over him again in her effort to get away.

Jason grabbed her ankle just as she was about to plant a boot in his groin area. "Hold on a minute, will you?" She hopped a few inches away, then he let go and quickly rose. He couldn't figure out what had come over her. One minute she was laughing, or trying not to, then she was acting as if he were some sort of hideous monster. And by the way she was glancing around, he figured she was looking for help. He tried to alleviate her fears. "I'm Jason Van der Bollen. I live here." That got her attention. He gave her one of his most charming smiles as he dusted himself off.

A multitude of emotions ran through her—shame, then shock and finally relief. He didn't recognize her, didn't know who she was. Thank heaven he didn't remember her. Jason was staring, and she knew she had to say something or look like a bigger fool than she'd already made of herself. "This is Two Rivers, isn't it?"

"The very place." Something peculiar was going on. When he moved toward her, she jerked and tried to hide the movement by dusting the dirt off her own clothes. "Who you looking for?"

"Well, the directions I had said to turn left at the third road before you get to Two Rivers, but there isn't a road."

"You're right, there isn't one." He watched the nervous way she combed her hair with her fingers. She tapped her cap against her leg before carefully fitting it back on her head.

"I must have gotten the directions wrong. Maybe he said the third road after you go through town."

Jason's interested gaze sharpened as he studied her. The third road out of town was to the vineyard. "This is a small town, so if you'll tell me who you're looking for, I'll tell you if your directions are right or wrong." He suddenly had the strangest feeling that he knew what she was going to say. He also would have bet his life he knew her first name.

"I'm looking for the Bolt place. Austin Bolt. Do you know him?"

"Sure do." He was going to laugh again, so he bent down, picked up a rock and pitched it across the street while he got control of his emotions. It was then he realized that practically all the townsfolk were watching them. He just couldn't take the chance of anyone spoiling his fun. "What's your name?"

The abrupt question caught her off guard and she blurted, "Laura Ghant," before she could stop herself.

Jason bit the inside of his cheek to keep a straight face. His nephew had a lot of questions to answer, and he didn't intend to miss them. He stepped up on the high curb. "Your directions were partly right. The Bolts live off the third road out of town." He gave her a halfhearted wave, crossed to his truck and climbed in.

Feeling unreasonably disappointed and insulted, she stood watching as Jason drove off down the highway. Then she opened the van door, got in and backed out into the street, heading off in the same direction. Who would have thought that, after eight years, she'd come face-to-face, literally, with the man of her dreams and nightmares? She was so lost in thought she almost missed the entrance to the third road.

She slowed as she traveled the long drive, taking in the beauty of the grapevines that went on forever on both sides of the road. When she came over the rise, she braked for a moment and stared at the huge two-story granite house sitting in a pool of green grass and old oak trees, surrounded by a stone fence that set it apart from the rows of grapevines that ran almost up to the fence. For some reason, she hadn't expected the grandeur or the obvious wealth.

JASON HAD BEEN GLAD the sheriff wasn't anywhere around as he'd raced down the highway as fast as the old truck would take him. By the time he'd pulled to a bone-rattling stop behind the house, he could hear the van coming slowly up the lane and he made a dash for the back door. He wasn't about to miss what his nephew was up to, and he had a feeling Laura's visit was going to be the highlight of the summer.

He was almost beside himself with laughter as he skidded to a stop in the middle of the kitchen. Then, ignoring Matt's and Ginny's startled glances and Dog's snarl of displeasure, he yelled, "Austin. You better get down here. Your girlfriend's arrived."

CHAPTER TWO

LAURA YANKED OFF the baseball cap and pushed her hair into some semblance of order as she followed the sidewalk to the door and knocked. A vicious-looking dog stood firmly planted on the opposite side of the screen door, snarling and barking with such volume he could have awakened the dead.

She was amazed that with just one soft command from the pregnant woman who approached the door, the animal immediately stopped and walked away. "Mrs. Bolt?" she asked. Austin had told her that his stepmother was expecting, and it looked as if it was going to be at any moment.

Laura was just about to introduce herself when Austin appeared in front on his stepmother, quickly opened the door and invited her in. No sooner had she stepped into the kitchen than she spotted Jason Van der Bollen leaning against the refrigerator, his arms crossed over his chest and a smug smile plastered on his face. She didn't have time to wonder what he was doing at the Bolts' as Austin grabbed her hand and pulled her forward.

"Ginny. Dad. This is my friend, Laura Ghant."

Matt Bolt rose from his chair and nodded politely.

Laura waited for Austin to go on, but when she glanced at him she realized her young friend seemed to have run out of words and was staring at his father. She smiled at Ginny Bolt and received what she thought was a thoughtful, rather measuring kind of look. When her gaze shifted back to Austin's father, she was momentarily speechless. He was the most strikingly handsome man she'd ever seen. Tall—well over six feet—and of obvious Native American heritage, which showed clearly in his high cheekbones, full, beautifully shaped lips, shoulder-length hair the color of coal and the blackest eyes she'd ever seen. At that moment those dark eyes were studying her with an intensity that made her nervous.

She broke away from that assessing gaze, let her eyes wander around the kitchen, deliberately passing over Jason, and settled on Ginny and Austin. Everyone seemed to be waiting for her to say something. "I can't tell you how excited I was when Austin—" She got no further as Austin interrupted.

"Dad," the boy said. "I met Laura at school."

Matt glanced at his son, then at his brother. Jason was enjoying himself entirely too much. "I assumed that, son." He nodded again at the young woman and wondered just how old she was. Twenty-three, maybe twenty-five? he thought. But too old for his son, that was for damn sure.

Something was terribly wrong. Laura could feel the tension in the room rising like mercury in a thermometer. For a moment she thought she'd stepped into the middle of a family argument, but it seemed all their attention was directed at her. Her gaze shifted to Austin, but the boy's eyes were glued to his father, and she saw something all too recognizable—guilt and fear. He either hadn't told them she was coming or the reason she was there. She opted for the latter.

She figured it was better to jump right in and see what happened rather than just stand there while everyone stared at her. "I can't tell you how—" once again Austin tried to interrupt, but she wasn't having any of it this time and gripped his shoulder in warning "—thrilled I was when Austin invited me to see your cave paintings."

If the silence had made her apprehensive, the roar that followed her statement reverberated like a shock wave. Glancing around, she noted that Ginny had sat down with a great sigh of relief. Jason was laughing so hard he seemed to have trouble catching his breath. The noise was from Matt and Austin, each speaking at once, each trying to out-talk the other. Matt, because of his size, was winning the volume department, but Austin was giving it a good try.

Laura quickly realized that the gist of the heated discussion was the cave paintings. It took only a minute to figure out that Austin had never asked permission for her to see and document them. At the first lull in their argument, she stepped in. "I'm sorry. I can see that Austin's played a trick on us and that you're reluctant to let anyone see the paintings. But Mr. Bolt, if the caves are in the condition Austin has described, then it would be a shame if they were destroyed before they were documented. I wish you'd consider letting me see them."

"Who the hell are you?" Matt demanded.

"Matt..." Ginny said. Matt recognized the warning note in her voice and immediately responded by sitting down.

"Dad, please. Laura works in the university's archaeology department. She has a masters in archaeology and is an expert in Native American cave art and history." Austin quickly rounded the table to stand between his parents, yet closer to Ginny and out of arm's reach from his father. "Dad, you can't let history be destroyed. It'd be criminal." Austin gave Ginny a soulful, pleading glance that never failed to work. "Talk to him, Ginny, please."

"You leave Ginny out of this, young man," Matt snapped.

Austin, Laura quickly saw, was the mirror image of his father, all flashing black eyes, deep scowls and righteous indignation that made their mouths tighten and thin. She looked on in amazement, watching Ginny's expression soften with love and concern as she turned her gaze on her husband. Matt's frown melted away as their eyes met.

Laura didn't know whether to be amused or angry at the way the child manipulated everyone. But then she couldn't be too upset, since their goal was the same. "I really am an expert, Mr. Bolt. I've been in dangerous situations before and I know how to take precautions. Please, before you make up your mind, just let me take a look at the caves and judge for myself."

"They're unsafe, Laura," Matt said. "Has Austin told you where they're located?" He didn't wait for an answer but went on, "The caverns are used to store and age the wine and champagne we make. It's very important to keep a constant temperature, to preserve the atmosphere. I can't have a bunch of college students—" he saw the way his son glared at him "—or experts tramping in and out."

"No, no, no. Mr. Bolt, there'd be only me and the lights...."

"That's another thing, there's no way to run electricity to the caves."

"All my lights are battery-powered and have special filaments so they don't put off any heat. There'd be no danger of a change in temperature."

Matt ran his fingers through his hair and looked at Ginny for help.

"I think you ought to let the professor do it, Matt."

Laura had forgotten Jason, and by their surprised expressions they had, too. She didn't care for his use of the designation, especially as he seemed to be laughing at her. "I don't have a Ph.D. Yet."

"Oh, don't mind Uncle Jason," Austin said, grinning as he realized he'd found an ally. "He's a big tease."

"Uncle?" Laura hadn't intended to sound so shocked but didn't know how to cover her mistake. Jason was scowling and the others were looking at her curiously.

It was Ginny, with a thoughtful glance between Jason and Laura, who came to her aid. "I think our guest is confused about the relationship." She waved between Jason and her husband. "Matt and Jason are half brothers. Same father, different mothers." She laughed as Laura's puzzled gaze bounced from one man to the other, then back to her. She fully understood what was going on in Laura's head. Matt and Jason were dramatically opposite. Matt was dark, with an erotic sensuality. Jason was light, with a hedonistic sexuality that drew females in droves.

Ginny wasn't surprised to see Laura's gaze linger a second on Matt. After all, her husband was damn sexy. What did surprise her was the way Laura seemed to dismiss Jason as unattractive and of no interest to her—which couldn't be right because no female could resist her brother-in-law. "It's a long story, but Matt changed his name from Van der Bollen to Bolt when he was about eighteen."

"I see," Laura said, but she didn't really. "Mr. Bolt."

"Please call me Matt. I'm not an old man yet. Though—" he aimed a hard look at his son "—Austin's working at putting gray in my hair."

"Matt, then." Laura continued hurriedly, "If you would just let me see the caves and determine if there's anything to be done to save the paintings... If not, then I could give you a rough estimate on how long it would take to document them."

"Da-a-d." Austin drew the word out but immediately shut up when his father sent him one of his quelling looks. He sighed and moved closer to Ginny.

Jason observed his nephew's maneuvering with amusement. Austin was a genius with a frighteningly high IQ. But his nephew was no egghead. He liked to tell people that Austin was street smart and people wise. If he really wanted something and intellectual reasoning didn't work, he wasn't above using his considerable charm and cunning. That he had Ginny wrapped around his finger went without saying, and when all else failed with his father, Austin wasn't above enlisting Ginny's help to get what he wanted.

Matt always protested afterward that it wasn't fair to have his son and wife gang up on him, and now that Ginny was so pregnant, Matt couldn't refuse her anything when she turned those soft brown eyes on him. Jason thought it was all a game—one he never tired of watching. Yet he knew that Matt would never give in to Ginny or Austin if he thought any harm would come to them. The Indian caves, he thought, were a closed subject, so he was surprised to see his brother wavering in his previous decision.

Jason grinned. Matt's vacillating amused him, and he decided the subject needed his two cents' worth of reasoning. "How can you say no, Matt? Isn't your own Indian heritage screaming at you?" Jason ignored Matt's scowl and said to Laura, "My brother's mother was a Mescalero Apache." He turned back to Matt. "Maybe those are Apache drawings."

"I don't think so," Laura said. "The Apache rarely ventured this far into Comanche territory for very long, and they weren't normally cave dwellers, either."

"See, Dad? Now we have to know what tribes. I've always thought that some of the drawings were a lot older than the others."

Laura could barely contain her excitement. Austin had shown her some of the drawings he'd done from only one visit. He'd also shown her a set of drawings his father had done when he was in his early teens. She had a gut feeling about what she'd seen. Jason was talking and she forced herself to concentrate on what he was saying. Like Austin, she'd found an ally but was suspicious.

Jason pushed away from the refrigerator to move closer to Laura. "It's science, research and history you're blocking, brother. What if there's something really important down there? You ought to let the professor at least take a look and give you her expert opinion." He glanced at Laura. "You *are* an expert, aren't you?"

"Yes," she replied sharply. "If you doubt me, I'll be happy to give you the dean of archaeology's number." She paused and frowned. "I forgot—the Dean's in southern France with some of his colleagues. They're in a small town called Vallon-Pont-d'Arc studying the cave paintings recently found there. Actually, there's no one in the archaeology department this summer but me. But you could always check with one of the regents."

Jason didn't like her tone. It was decidely hostile. "Maybe I will," he said, giving her one of his most charming smiles and wondering why she was staring at him with such a cold expression. What was with this woman? he wondered.

"Uncle Jason," Austin said, "I can vouch for Laura and her credentials."

"Children!" Matt growled, suddenly fed up with the whole subject. "Listen, Laura, I'm not against you personally, and if Austin says you're qualified, then you are.

But the caves are dangerous. They're crumbling and falling in. I can't let a young woman…" His words trailed off as he received identical scowls from Ginny and Laura and amended his statement. "I just don't feel comfortable about letting you or anyone else go down there."

He noticed Jason's smug look and realized championing her efforts was just his brother's way of getting Laura's attention. "But I might have a solution." He gazed at his brother and smiled. "Jason, since you're all for the caves being evaluated, then I'll let Laura take a look at them only if you accompany her every time she needs to go down."

Jason knew he'd just been neatly hoisted on his own petard. Over Austin's yell of triumph and Ginny's laughter, he didn't miss Laura's scowl. Into his nephew and sister-in-law's pleasure he dropped a bomb. "I can't take the time, brother. You know that."

"Oh, I think you can, brother." Matt rocked his chair on its back legs, looking very pleased. "You can't disappoint Austin."

"But the girls…"

"You'll have plenty of time for them *and* your work." Matt shifted his attention to Laura and Austin. "You do realize that even during the hottest days it gets very cold down there. You'll only be able to stay a couple of hours at a time. If you think the caves should be documented immediately, how long do you estimate it will take?"

"I wouldn't want to make that kind of prediction until I've had a chance to see the caves." Laura couldn't believe her good luck, even if it was partly ruined by having to have Jason tag along. "But usually something the size Austin has described shouldn't take more than two or three weeks. A couple of hours a day actually *in* the caves should be enough."

Matt nodded. "See, Jason, you can give up a couple of hours each morning for two or three weeks."

"Oh, no, you don't. Where did I say I'd do this for weeks?" He held up a finger. "One day."

"But you're so concerned about science—" Matt grinned and jeered "—research and preserving history. Surely you're not going to tell your nephew and Laura that now, because you don't want to give up a few measly hours, those things no longer matter?"

Jason caught Ginny's eye and gave her the same pitiful, pleading look for help that Austin had recently employed but only got a shake of her head. Traitor, he thought, and as if she'd read his thoughts, her mouth twitched several times before breaking into a smile. "Why don't we let Laura here take a look-see at our ancient artistic renderings and find out what she thinks before we make any definite plans?"

Jason deliberately resisted the urge to look at Laura. There'd be delight brimming in those pretty hazel eyes, of course, and victory on those kissable lips. He chalked his wandering thoughts up to too much manual labor and having to watch Matt, Ginny and Austin's happiness. Laura was not his type.

Laura was still a little shell-shocked but exhilarated nonetheless. It had all happened so fast. And she knew she'd won only because these two men seemed to thrive on one-upmanship. She was even willing to forget for a time that Jason was going to be by her side. After all, there was no use in spoiling a victory. Ever since she'd seen the sketches Austin had done, she'd known the cave drawings were something special, but she'd kept the knowledge to herself, letting her bosses leave on their trips without a word. She needed a discovery. The glory. She needed a dig of her own so she could write and publish her own paper.

"When can I see the caves?" she asked. For all her contrived nonchalance, she couldn't hide her excitement.

"Yeah, Uncle Jason, when do we get to go?"

"Not you, Austin," Matt said. "You know you're not allowed in the caves."

If he hadn't been eleven years old, he would have cried with disappointment. Instead, Austin's eyes narrowed a fraction, then he turned his back on his father, gazed at his stepmother and whispered, "Why can't I go if Jason will be there? It's not fair, Ginny. You know it's not fair. Talk to him, please."

Ginny obliged. "Matt, if Jason's going to be there..."

Jason saw the capitulation in Matt's expression and the heavy, slow sigh of resignation. He himself had been on the receiving end of those looks from Ginny and Austin, and knew there was no point trying to argue with either of them. But he also knew that if Matt hadn't agreed with the injustice in his denying his son, he would not have relented.

Until about a year ago, Matt had never been a real father to his son. His ex-wife had taken Austin to California when the boy was just a baby. Matt seldom saw them, only sending money to pay for his son's expensive education. Then, after Matt had been critically wounded and forced to retire from the Houston police force, he returned to Two Rivers only to learn that his ex-wife had been killed in an airplane crash and now he had a ten-year-old to contend with. Matt couldn't be condemned for being overprotective, but he was learning, if slowly and with Ginny's help, not to hold on too tightly.

"Dad?" Austin asked. "Please. I'll be careful."

Laura knew how much Austin wanted to see the cave paintings again. It was all he'd talked about from the moment he'd come into her office with his arms full of sketches. "I'll watch out for him, too," she offered. She watched as Matt reached into his shirt pocket, withdrew a rubber band and pulled his shoulder-length hair back into a ponytail.

"Okay," he conceded, then went on before Austin could shout his victory, "But don't think you'll be going down there every day. You're home for the summer and you have chores."

"You got it, Pops." Austin and Ginny slapped their hands together in a high five and laughed at the face Matt made at being called Pops.

"And remember we're going to start reading about home delivery tonight," Matt warned his son, now a bundle of energy darting around the kitchen.

"When are we going?" Jason asked.

Laura looked at Jason and was reluctant to even speak to him. "Right away, if that's possible." She started toward the door. "I'll just need to get a couple of lights from my van." She held the screen door open to let Austin go out, then quickly followed, letting the door slam in Jason's face.

Jason stood with his nose pressed to the screen, watching as Laura and Austin headed down the walkway. Then he turned and grinned at Matt and Ginny. "She's positively mesmerized by my charms, isn't she?"

Ginny laughed as she struggled to get up. She accepted Jason's helping hand, and when she was finally standing, she said, "Laura seems to feel about you the way Dog does. I wonder why?" They all laughed when the subject of their conversation stuck his head out from under the table and growled at Jason.

"I don't know," he said, truly puzzled by the dislike and animosity he sensed when Laura looked at him. He shoved the door open, pausing only to say, "But it might be interesting to find out."

He deliberately dawdled as he made his way down the walkway, and once he reached the old VW van, there was no one in sight. At the sound of muffled voices, he headed for the back of the van to look inside.

Austin stuck his head out. "Uncle Jason, you've got to see what Laura's done in here. I swear she has everything an archaeologist could ever need, all neatly stored away. It's really cool."

"Well, Einstein, if you'll move your carcass, I'll take a look." Austin scooted aside, and Jason stared at the cavernous interior, impressed. Every available space on the walls was used to hold what appeared to be an assortment of children's tools: small shovels, pickaxes, gadgets and gew-gaws he knew absolutely nothing about.

Laura was seated in the rear of the van, her cowboy boots thrown aside as she tied the laces of her running shoes. She gave him a quick glance, motioned for him to move, then hopped out of the van and picked up a canvas backpack. "I'm ready." She elbowed Jason out of the way, slammed the van doors and locked them. "Have you got the other light, Austin?"

"Check."

"The extra batteries?"

"Check."

"Okay." She finally faced Jason. "We're ready to go."

Why was it, he wondered, he felt like the odd man out?

Laura was too excited to concentrate on anything except getting to the caves. Yet, as they walked the well-worn path, she was once again aware of the rows upon rows of grapevines that went on for what seemed miles in all directions. But she forgot about that when the path took a sharp turn and they began walking straight toward the rear of the property. They walked so long in silence she was about to ask how much farther when the path took another sharp turn, this time to the left. When they came out from under a stand of oak trees, she spotted a large stone building.

"That's where my dad's grapes are taken to be mashed up. Then the juices are extracted, blended and fermented, and finally they're bottled and corked. He has a real neat high-tech laboratory, too. I'll show it to you later."

They came upon what looked like the front half of a building protruding from an outcropping of the granite hillside. She stood gazing at the wide double doors studded with crisscrossed iron work and heavy hammered hinges. "Those are impressive," she said, then jumped and half turned when she felt Jason's hand on her shoulder.

"They're rather weighty, too. If you'll let me by, I'll open them."

Laura stepped aside, scolding herself as she did. She had to stop being so prickly, stop letting him get under her skin every time he said something or looked at her. He was going to start wondering why she was acting crazily. She was afraid if he thought about her too much he just might remember, and she couldn't face him then.

Her fears were swept away by a gush of cold air that raised goose bumps on her damp skin. She followed Jason and Austin through the doors into darkness, and was forced to stop and let her eyes adjust to the lack of light. When Austin's hand grasped hers, she grinned and held on to it tightly.

"Dad thinks it's real fun to scare people in here," Austin whispered. "Calls Ginny and me sissies." Laura squeezed his hand in sympathy.

"You two stay put," Jason said, "until I find the light switch."

"No need." Laura turned on her light, and the brilliant illumination caught Jason and paralyzed him for a second like deer caught by headlights on a dark road. He shaded his eyes as he fumbled for the switch. That damn woman, he thought. One of those self-sufficient, I-can-do-it-myself-thank-you-very-much types.

He switched on the lights and reached for the inner doors to the wine cellar, then stopped when Austin said, "Those doors are over two hundred years old, solid oak and probably as hard as petrified wood. My great-grandfather had them brought over from France—from the Benedictine abbey of Hautvillers. It's the same place where the monk, Dom Pérignon, made champagne back in the seventeenth century. Dad's father sent him to France every summer to learn the wine business, and now he's making Texas champagne, Texas Joie—Texas Joy."

Jason was proud of Austin, and a little surprised. His nephew had obviously taken an interest in the winery. He wondered if Matt was aware of that interest and if he was willing to take the time to teach his son. But he knew the answer. Matt would share anything he had with his children.

As soon as Jason opened the doors, Laura felt another drop in temperature. There was a wonderful fragrance about the cold she'd never experienced before. As she and Austin passed Jason, who pulled the doors shut behind them, she freed her hand from Austin's and looked around in awe. The wine cellar was cavernous, dark, dry and cold, the atmosphere almost cathedrallike.

"This way." Jason touched Laura's arm, and when she didn't jerk away or jump, he congratulated himself that his plan to put her at ease was working.

The dim illumination of the overhead lights wasn't enough for her inspection. She switched on her own light again, letting the powerful beam play over the giant oak casks on her left, following the long rows until the casks became smaller, stacked four high. Then she turned to her right. There was rack upon rack, stacked as high as her own height, of bottles lying on their sides in neatly tilted pockets. A little farther down were rows of strange A-frame racks, filled with dark bottles pointing at a severe downward angle. "Why are those bottles like that?"

Jason grinned—they did look odd. "Those are champagne. And the weird racks are for riddling."

"Actually, they're not called riddling racks, Uncle Jason," Austin said. "Riddling refers to the mechanical method, and Dad is doing it the way they do in France—the hand-rotation method called *remuage*. *Remuage* is done about once a week for months and months. It's designed to work the sediment toward the cork where it can be ejected. Did you know that the pressure in a bottle of champagne is six atmospheres or ninety pounds per square inch? That's about three times the pressure in a car tire."

"Austin..." Jason warned with a laugh.

"Sorry. I guess I get carried away."

"Don't ever apologize for being enthusiastic or smart, Austin," Laura said, shooting Jason a look of distaste.

"That's not what I meant...." Jason watched as they walked past him. He didn't understand why he kept sticking his foot in his mouth. He was never clumsy or uncomfortable with women, but this one sure as hell made him feel like an awkward adolescent when she looked at him with those big hazel eyes.

Laura abruptly stopped, her attention on the ceiling. "This is a granite cavern. Austin, I thought you said it was limestone."

Austin started to reply, but Jason was determined to have *his* chance to impress her. "Where the cave paintings are is limestone. This valley is what a few scientists and geologists call a freak of nature. It was always explained to me that millions of years ago the layers were disturbed by a massive shift in the earth's surface. The granite, limestone and chalk layers erupted, splintered and split. Now the valley basically consists of three layers—clay-caulky, a granite dome, then limestone. The natural movement of the ancient rivers and lakes carved out the cavern and caves before they seeped down into the underground aquifers.''

She was impressed. He wasn't just a great body and a pretty face, after all. But she wasn't about to let him know. ''How do we get to the caves?''

Jason pointed to the inky blackness at the back of the cavern. ''Through there. Listen, Matt's right about this being dangerous. I know you don't like to take orders from men, but you should make an exception this time.''

''I have no problem taking intelligent instructions from men.''

''Right.''

Austin looked from one adult to the other, feeling the tension and puzzled by it. This was the most exciting thing that had happened to him in months, and he didn't want it ruined. ''He's right, Laura. You have to follow Jason and be very careful.''

''Thank you, Buddha,'' said his uncle.

Laura laughed. ''Buddha?''

''Sure, the bearer of enlightenment and wisdom, all knowing, all seeing, wise beyond time. That's my nephew, don't you think?''

''Yes, it fits him to a tee. He's an amazing young man.'' They actually smiled at each other.

''I'm glad you two agree on something,'' Austin said impatiently, ''but can we go?''

"Okay. Now you're both to do exactly as I say." Jason didn't wait for a response but flicked on the flashlight he'd picked up from the supply by the wine-cellar door.

Laura motioned for Austin to go between them, then set out, her own light penetrating the darkness around her. The smooth granite walls quickly narrowed, then the granite abruptly ended. The walls and ceiling were rough limestone with jagged, protruding edges. They walked on for some time until they came to a fork in the formation and Jason veered right. Suddenly the tunnel narrowed even further and the ceiling lowered, and he had to hunch his six-foot frame.

Laura was so busy trying to take everything in, to make a mental map of the place, that she wasn't watching her footing and stumbled over a scattering of rocks on the floor. Jason's light swung around and she waved him on. "I'm fine."

"I'm okay, too, Uncle Jason. Keep going."

After a while longer Jason stopped, swung the beam of his flashlight around and noted the deterioration of the wall since he'd last seen it. There was more rubble on the sandy floor. "Watch your step here and don't touch the walls."

Laura and Austin followed Jason for what seemed a mile. The tunnel became so narrow and low at times that she and Jason had to almost bend double, then at other times the ceiling rose majestically, giving them all the room in the world.

Jason stopped, waiting for Austin and Laura to catch up with him. When they were beside him, he directed the beam of his flashlight down another narrow tunnel. "We'll have to move through this sideways."

Austin grabbed Laura's arm. "We're almost there. The tunnel curves, then opens into the cave at the other end."

"God," she whispered, "this place is fascinating." She followed Jason's lead, turning her body sideways and edging through the tunnel. Just when she thought they'd never reach the end, they stepped into a huge chamber.

She played her beam over the walls and ceiling, and marveled at the sight. The limestone was a brilliant white, and their flashlight beams made yellowish pools on the surface. The cavern ceiling, she estimated, was as high as a two-story building, and the rough walls were deeply gouged in places. The floor was soft and sandy with a scattering of rocks and boulders. At last her light settled on the first of the cave paintings, and she was pulled to the wall as if by an unseen hand on her shoulder. This was far beyond her dreams.

Jason almost laughed and remarked about the spectacle of Laura nose to nose with the wall, but something held his amusement in check. Maybe it was the way Austin looked at Laura, with a mixture of excitement and hero worship, that kept him silent. Maybe it was the tension that vibrated between the two. Then Laura backed away a few steps, and her gaze swung from Austin to him. He saw the shimmer of tears mixed with awe and wonder.

He couldn't move.

There was so much naked emotion in those hazel eyes his breath caught in his throat. The feeling was almost sensual, electric. He realized for the first time how important this find was for her. It was her life's work come true. Her dream. Whatever comment was on the tip of his tongue quickly died. He could never intrude, make fun of or belittle this moment. It was a good thing she wasn't his type, he thought, because if she had been, he would have fallen in love with that face.

CHAPTER THREE

LAURA WAS LOST in another world. Dreaming of long ago, back in a time where people gathered in caves, some squatting around a small fire with their family, as others, the shaman and hunters, told tales of their day and painted pictures on the walls of their life or a successful hunt. She could hear the low murmur of the women doing what women through the ages have done: cooked, cleaned, discussed their children and men.

If she tried really hard she could see one of the men, hear his voice as he told of his bravery on the hunt. He was tall, muscular, his loincloth-clad body glistening in the firelight. His long, blond hair flowed around his shoulders, and his blue eyes flashed and glittered as he told his tale.

Blond hair? Blue eyes? No, no, no! Laura jerked out of her dream, her day-mare. She couldn't believe what she'd been doing, and until she managed to regain control of her wildly careering imagination, she refused to look Jason's way. Instead, she focused her attention on Austin. "This painting is more than I, we, hoped for. If it's all I think it is, do you know what you've got here?"

Austin couldn't contain his excitement. He let out a whoop and danced a little jig of happiness, causing a white cloud of dust to rise. When he calmed down and waved his way through the dusty curtain, he resembled a ghost, a fitting image in the caves. He was too thrilled to mind

Laura and his uncle's laughter. "The caves weren't used just for shelter and daily living, were they?" He tried to be adult about the find and control his enthusiasm, but he couldn't hold back the huge grin when she shook her head. "They were used for rituals, religious ceremonies, right? And there's a progression of age in the drawings? They go back a lot further than I thought?"

"That I don't know by one quick glance, but it wouldn't surprise me."

"You're going to stay and thoroughly document everything, aren't you?"

"I hope so, but that's up to your father, isn't it."

"And Uncle Jason."

They both turned, stared at the object of their discussion, then fell silent.

Finally, he thought, he not only had her full attention but the upper hand. He shined his light around, spotted a large flat boulder, went over to it and sat down. He'd supported Laura and Austin just to needle Matt, but his brother had neatly turned the tables on him. He analyzed the situation, decided if he had to play baby-sitter, then he was damn well going to have some fun while he was at it. "Matt did say no Jason, no lookie, didn't he?"

"Don't tease Laura, Uncle Jason, it's not fair. Besides, if we're going to get Dad to go along with us, we have to have a solid plan to put before him."

Jason looked at Laura. "Can't take a little ribbing?"

She couldn't afford to be unpleasant or sarcastic with him, not now. Yet, the thought of having to be in his company all the time gave her a sinking feeling in the pit of her stomach. He didn't know who she was, but proximity just might make him remember, and she'd just die if he did. "I like a good joke as much as the next person. But this—" she waved her light around the cave "—is serious."

Jason nodded. "You're right." He shifted his position on the boulder, brought his knees up and folded his arms around them. "You have to understand that I have obligations and work to do. How many hours a day do you estimate it'll take to complete the job?"

He was being reasonable. She decided she needed to be the same. "I don't know yet. Let me take a better look around, then I'll be able to give you some sort of timetable."

"Fair enough." Jason handed his flashlight to Austin for extra light, then watched as they walked around the cave, talking in low tones, shining lights up, down and around the walls. As he sat thoughtfully following their every move, he suddenly had a nebulous, nibbling feeling that he'd seen or met Laura before, but he couldn't recall where or when. Maybe he'd caught sight of her on campus when he'd gone to pick Austin up for the weekend. That had to be it, he concluded.

Gradually he became aware that the darkness around him had increased, and he could no longer hear their voices, only an eerie, quiet rumble—like a ghost. He couldn't see any lights moving around, either.

Jason jumped to his feet in fear, realizing they were somewhere in the back of the cave. "Laura, Austin. Don't go any farther. That's where the cave-in started." He relaxed slightly when Austin called out they were coming back, but he wasn't at ease completely until he saw lights working their way toward him. If he was going to be responsible for taking care of Laura and Austin, he'd better be more observant. His failure this time made him angry and he took it out on them. "Dammit, don't just slip off like that!"

Austin was surprised at his uncle's tone but recognized where it was coming from. "Sorry. We got sidetracked." He shivered and wrapped his arms around his chest. "Uncle Jason, Laura thinks there's another cave that's blocked by part of the cave-in."

"Well, I wouldn't say anything about that to your father. If he thinks either of you are likely to go crawling around back there, he'll pull the plug on his approval altogether." He paused. "And I damn well agree with him."

His gaze bounced from Austin to Laura and back again. "You know," he said, "you both look like ghosts."

They'd stirred up the floor as they'd moved around the cave and were covered from head to toe in white limestone dust. "You should see yourself," Laura said as she attempted to shake the dust out of her hair. "Maybe we should rename you Casper."

Jason looked down at himself, realizing he was in pretty much the same condition as Austin and Laura. He was about to comment when he saw Austin shiver, and he realized how cold it was in the cave. "We need to get out of here before we freeze. Do you have a better idea now how long it will take you to complete your work down here?"

Laura found it easier to talk to him when she couldn't see him clearly. "A couple of weeks, three at the most. Is that a problem for you?"

"Nah, Uncle Jason's—"

"Austin!" He used the same warning tone Matt would have used and was surprised to see it actually work. Then Austin shivered again, hard this time, and he felt like a heel. "Let's get out of here and warm up." He rubbed his hands together. "Then we'll talk about working something out."

Wanting to stay longer, Laura would have argued, come to terms with the damn man right then and there. She was used to the harsh conditions on archaeology digs and adapted to them easily. But she could see Austin was more than uncomfortably cold. His teeth were beginning to sound like castanets.

She followed them out, teasing Austin all the way to keep his mind off how cold he was by singing a Spanish song, using his chattering teeth as an embellishment. By the time they reached the wine cellar, Jason had added his deep voice to the singing and Austin was laughing more than he was shivering.

As they stepped through the wide double doors, the heat hit, sucking Laura's breath away as effectively as a hand at her throat. She was blinded by the brilliance of the sun. Reflex made her squeeze her eyes shut, but she kept walking and collided with Jason. Off balance, she grabbed hold of him, and because he'd half turned to steady her, his footing wasn't secure and they both tumbled to the ground.

She tried to ask if he was all right, but her concern was choked off by a fit of the giggles. "Oh, my. We've done this before, haven't we." She wasn't normally a clumsy person and couldn't understand why she kept falling all over this man.

Jason tried to sit up, glanced at Laura, grinned, then fell back to the ground and put his arms behind his head. "You untangle yourself this time. Just watch where you put your hands."

Laura was on her knees when she noticed an old man standing only a few feet away, watching them with interest. His Stetson was pulled low on his forehead, shadowing his face, but she sensed he was frowning. She scrambled to her feet and began beating at her clothes and brushing herself off.

Jason was quick to notice Laura's shift of attention and glanced around. "Hey, Jericho. What's happening?" He didn't understand the old man's silence, especially when a pretty woman was around. "Laura, this is Jericho Jones. He's been around forever and does just about everything."

"You all been down in them Indian caves?" Jericho yanked his hat off, nodded politely at Laura and scowled.

Laura noted on closer inspection that the man was a lot older than she'd first thought. When he saw her staring, he turned his back, fumbled in his pocket, then twisted around again. He smiled, this time showing a mouthful of gleaming white teeth.

Jericho directed his attention at Austin. "I thought your pa told you to stay away from them caves, boy."

Austin ignored the censorious tone. "Jericho, this is my friend from college, Laura. She's an archaeologist and she's going to investigate and document the cave paintings."

Jericho settled his hat back into position and shook his head. "What's come over Matt?" he said irritably to no one in particular. "It's too dangerous down there." He nodded again to Laura and said, "Ma'am," then wheeled around and headed for the main house, mumbling to himself.

Austin and Jason shared knowing looks while dusting themselves off, then saw Laura's confused expression. Jason felt compelled to explain, "Jericho's never one to mince words, and he's a little overprotective of Austin and Ginny."

Laura thought "overprotective" was too weak a word to explain the fierce anger in the old man's expression. But maybe she'd misread his reaction. As they approached the house, she could hear men's raised voices, and as they got closer the screen door flew open and Jericho marched out, passed them without a look or a word and continued toward the barn.

She swung her pack off and said, "I think I'll put this stuff back in the van."

Jason grasped her arm as she started to walk away. "No, you don't. We all have to face the music sometime. Besides, my brother's bark is worse than his bite." He opened the door wide, told a bristling Dog to behave himself and gave Laura a friendly nudge.

Matt glance up from his protective, hovering position over Ginny. "Dammit to hell, Jericho..." Then he saw who it was and continued pushing the pillow behind Ginny's back. Next he lifted her feet up on a nearby chair.

Austin flashed by everyone and was at Ginny's side. "Are you hurt? Is something wrong with the baby?"

Ginny hugged the worried boy and swallowed hard around the lump in her throat. It had only been a little over a year since his mother had died, and though he tried not to show it, he was scared something would happen to her, too. "I'm fine. The baby's fine. Everything's fine, except Jericho's upset about you or anyone else being in the caves." She smiled at Jason to reassure him.

Austin still wasn't totally convinced she was all right. "What's Dad doing with the pillows? Why aren't you lying down, taking a nap or something?"

Matt pulled out a chair and sat down with a sigh. "Because she's mule-headed, that's why. She's afraid if she's upstairs resting like she should, she'll miss something down here."

Ginny gave them all a superior look. "That's not it at all. I'm more comfortable sitting up right now."

"Sure you are," Jason said, patting Ginny's shoulder as he passed her. "And pigs fly. You and Austin are the two nosiest people I know." He pulled down three tall glasses, fetched the pitcher of iced tea from the refrigerator, filled the glasses and handed one to Austin and Laura.

Laura watched Jason's every move. This teasing and sparring with his family was a side of him she'd never considered before. She'd always thought of him as kind of one-dimensional. That he actually cared about someone other than himself was a real eye-opener, and it shot some of her preconceived notions about him all to hell.

She jumped when she felt Austin pulling on her arm. She realized they were watching her and that someone had asked her a question. Her cheeks suddenly burned when her gaze collided with Matt's. She had a feeling he knew she'd been thinking about Jason. "Sorry," she said as she sat down, "but my mind was on the caves."

Jason sat beside Laura, watching her closely over the rim of his glass. "Depending on your decision, brother, Laura and I are about to work out a deal."

Laura knew he was gazing at her, taking in every detail of her disheveled appearance. She asked herself how he would've looked at her if he'd remembered who she was and what she'd done. She knew the answer and steeled herself to totally ignore him.

"Mr. Bolt—Matt," Laura said, "I won't try to convince you that the caves are exactly safe. I don't know when you were last down there, nor do I know the extent of the damage, but there's evidence of deterioration. I'd say it looks recent enough to have happened in the past year or so. But with care—and let me remind you I'm always careful—I can date and document the cave paintings."

"You think what's down there is worth the risk?" Matt asked.

"God, yes. It's fantastic. There're some truly ancient paintings down there and also some unusual man-made rock formations." She couldn't stand his noncommittal expression. "I'd be honored if you'd let me do the research."

Matt glanced at Ginny, and when she nodded, he said, "Okay, but on one condition. You don't take chances or do anything to endanger your life."

Laura held up her right hand. "I promise." She was so excited she could barely contain herself.

"How long?" Matt asked.

His question brought her back to earth. "A couple of weeks. Three, maybe." She noticed Matt again look at Ginny, and she stepped into the breach. "If it's all right with you, I can pull my van under a tree and camp out there. I've done it before for weeks on end." She didn't miss their shocked expressions, and she laughed. "I'm used to camping out, and the van's very well equipped."

"I won't hear of it," Ginny said. "You'll stay in the guest room."

"Oh, no. I couldn't. A couple of weeks is a long time. Really, the van's no problem."

"Can you cook?" Jason asked. "Clean up? Things like that?"

"Woman things?" she asked tartly.

Jason smiled. "Hey, I do those *woman things* around here." He looked pointedly at Ginny. "We all pitch in."

Well, Laura thought, she'd stepped in it again. She'd let him get to her and in the process he'd made her look foolish. Laura ignored him and addressed Ginny. "I love to cook and clean, and I'd help any way I could."

"Liar." Ginny laughed. "No woman with any intelligence loves to do dog work."

At the mention of his name, Dog stuck his head out from under the table beside Ginny's chair and showed his teeth.

Laura scooted back at the show of those sharp teeth, which were entirely too close to her leg. She shuddered and wondered why the vicious animal was allowed in the house. He was a big, ugly mixed breed—more wolf than dog, she thought. His longish hair was a patchwork of brown and black, making his light blue eyes even more menacing.

No one missed Laura's reaction to Dog. Jason sympathized with her, having been on the losing end of the animal's teeth himself at times. "Dog—and, yes, his name really is Dog—can be damn scary, but he's Ginny and Austin's dog, mostly Ginny's, and he protects her—kind of like Matt does. So don't be put off by his show of loyalty."

"I swear, Jason…" Ginny said, striving to sound stern, but her eyes sparkled. She caressed Dog's ears and the show of teeth widened. "Don't scare her. Laura, Dog isn't snarling at you, he's smiling. He's a love, an old softy, really."

Matt coughed, trying to keep from making any comment about Dog's disposition. He couldn't even make the animal sleep outside anymore.

The thought of Dog being an old softy made Austin giggle.

Jason shook his head at the notion. He could show them the teeth marks and scars on his expensive Italian shoes. "Ginny, you'd better introduce them."

Laura wasn't sure she wanted to make Dog's acquaintance. But she did as she was told, if reluctantly, holding out her hand for Dog to sniff. "I need my fingers, please, Dog," she said, earning a chuckle from everyone.

But Dog, it seemed, found her quite acceptable. He licked her fingers and smiled at her. Laura smiled back and patted him on the head.

"Great," Ginny said. "Dog thinks you're okay, so everything's settled."

Jason rocked back in his chair. "Not everything."

Laura had a feeling he wasn't going to give in or up so easily, and she jerked around to demand to know what he wanted. Her foot caught one of the legs of his chair, knocking it just enough to unbalance it. As Jason crashed to the floor she covered her face, refusing to look at him, afraid she'd laugh and everyone would think she was insensitive or, worse, crazy.

Jason saw Matt start to rise and he waved him off. Austin, he noticed, was watching Laura, and he turned his attention to his tormentor. "You did that on purpose."

Laura shook her head, unable to speak.

"You must have done it on purpose. No one can be that clumsy."

"Maybe you're just accident prone," she said through her fingers.

"No. Let me put it this way," he said as he got to his feet, uprighted the chair, then sat down gingerly. "I've been on my butt more since you showed up than I have in years."

Once again under control, Laura lowered her hands. Still refusing to look at Jason, she turned to Ginny. "Is there anything I can do now?"

"No." It was Jason who answered. "We have a problem to settle."

Laura looked at him. "Problem?"

"Yes. Like a little negotiation for my time." He gave her his most charming smile. "You do remember Matt saying that for you to go into the caves, I'd have to be there. Well,

I'm a busy man." He shot his amused family a quelling glance. "I have work to do. A ranch to run. A barn to remodel. Lots of manual labor."

"And don't forget the girls, Uncle Jason."

"Right. There're my girls to take care of." He started to lean back in the chair again then, quickly brought it forward on all four legs. "How many hours a day do you think you'll need in the caves?"

She didn't like the way he was grinning at her, nor the way his eyes gleamed brighter. "A couple of hours at the most."

"Then it shouldn't be too much to ask that you help me out at my place for a couple of hours."

"Uncle Jason! She's my friend."

"Jason!" Ginny snapped. "Laura's our guest. You can't ask her..." Her objection dwindled away when she saw the way Matt was looking at Jason and Laura.

Jason scowled at everyone. "For heaven's sake, it's only a fair exchange I'm asking for, not slave labor. A few hours' trade won't hurt."

"Okay." Laura surprised them all with her quick capitulation. He knew damn well she'd do just about anything to document the caves. If she continued to argue and negotiate, she'd be playing into his hands and affording him too much enjoyment of his victory. This was going to be *her* triumph.

"Let me see your hands," Jason requested.

She didn't want him to touch her and tried to move away, but Jason was too quick and captured her hands.

He liked her hands. They were long and slender, but strong, not pampered like the sort he was used to; her nails were short and unpolished. She clearly wasn't one to shy away from hard work. "These will do," he said. "Have you ever used a hammer?"

"Yes." She knew everyone was watching them and didn't dare not look at him. She had to keep her expression neutral, as bland as possible, as if his touch, the way he rubbed his thumb across her palms and over her wrists, didn't make her shiver.

"Think you can drive a nail straight?"

"As an arrow." She remembered how she'd touched *him* once before. Could even now almost feel the way her fingers had trailed— She had to stop thinking about that night.

"Hmm. Well, it's a deal, then. I accompany you to the caves in exchange for some manual labor." He continued to hold her hands a second longer than necessary.

When he finally let go, her breath came a little easier.

"Laura, did you by chance pack a bathing suit?"

Ginny's question broke the spell Laura seemed to be under and forced her to pay attention. "Austin told me to bring one."

Ginny smiled. "Good, because we usually go swimming down at the river after dinner." Her smile widened when Laura glanced at the big mound of her stomach. "I get to wade and watch. But it's a good way to end a hot evening."

Laura could feel Jason's gaze on her, but refused to return it, wishing he'd leave so she could get to know Austin's parents better. When Matt asked how old she was and if her family was from Texas, it was Austin who saved her.

"She's like me, Dad."

Matt chuckled. "I don't think so, son. I thought I talked to you about the birds and bees."

Austin flushed bright red to the tips of his ears. "Da-a-d!" He scowled at Ginny as if it was her fault his father had embarrassed him. But he couldn't be angry at Ginny, not when she loved him so much. "She's like me, Dad, because she started college when she was young, too. She was a child genius—*is* a genius." He rubbed his head in frustration. "Tell them how old you were when you started college, Laura."

"I wasn't ten like Austin but fifteen, though I should've been in college way before that." She had to be very careful what she said about herself with Jason around. The slightest slip, and he might catch on and remember. "I think Austin's the youngest the University of Texas has ever accepted."

"Why did you wait until you were fifteen?" Jason asked, not in the least intimidated by the fact that she was a genius like his nephew. After all, brains had nothing to do with being feminine or desirable.

"At the time, my parents didn't think a thirteen-year-old girl was emotionally equipped to handle college." She shrugged. "I thought they were wrong, but I had little say-so."

Jason stood. "I could sit here all morning and chitchat, but I have to see about the girls." As he passed behind Laura, he placed his hands on her shoulders and leaned over a little. "Don't move or you might knock me down again."

She kept still as he moved toward the door. She wondered who "the girls" were and how many he had. A mental image of a harem of women just waiting for him popped into her mind. It wouldn't have surprised her.

"Don't let Jason get to you," Ginny said as the door slammed shut. "He likes to tease."

"To the point where he can drive you stark raving mad," Matt added as he headed for the door, too. "I've got work to do in the cellar." He paused at the door. "Austin, didn't you tell Ginny you'd weed her herb garden?" When his son looked determined to stay put, he made a sharp motion with his hand toward the door, then watched as Austin stomped reluctantly out.

"I don't remember saying I'd weed today, Dad."

"No? Well, I say today. Besides, give Ginny and Laura time to get acquainted."

Ginny and Laura, privy to the whole conversation outside the screen door, smiled at each other. "Now," Ginny said, "you want to tell me why you dislike Jason so much?"

"I...I don't dislike him. I just know enough about him not to trust him."

Ginny threw back her head and laughed. "Oh, smart girl." She sobered, then said, "Okay, let's have the truth. You know Jason a lot better than that."

Laura couldn't figure it out. With anyone else she would have been offended, even angry, but there was something about Ginny Bolt, the way her eyes twinkled and the way she smiled. Though with that red hair, Ginny probably didn't take much nonsense from anyone, including Jason.

She liked Ginny immediately, yet she wasn't ready to trust her feelings or share her humiliation about what she'd done with anyone. "Come on, there's not a female between eighteen and fifty in Austin who doesn't know Jason Van der Bollen, even if it's only from the gossip and society pages of the newspaper."

"True," Ginny agreed. "But he hasn't been in Austin lately. He's been living here."

Laura glanced around, feeling suddenly sick at the thought of being under the same roof with him. Some of her apprehension must have shown in her eyes.

"Jason doesn't live in this house—though sometimes it seems like he does, he's here so much. He has a place across the highway."

"I heard his house in Austin had been sold, but I just assumed he was buying something else in the city." She couldn't believe Jason was willing to tuck himself away in the country. "But here?" Embarrassment at her unkind slip made her cheeks turn bright red.

"Boggles the mind, doesn't it?"

Ginny drained her iced tea and started to rise, but Laura stopped her and fetched the pitcher from the refrigerator. "Is he helping Matt or something?" She refilled both glasses.

"No, it's the other way around. Fill up Dog's bowl, will you?"

"With iced tea?"

"Yeah. He loves it."

She spotted a couple of bowls in the far corner of the kitchen, and under the watchful eyes of Dog, she filled one. When Dog gave her a sharp-toothed smile, she ventured a pat on his head, received a lick on the hand and immediately moved aside so he could enjoy his drink. "Do you mean Matt's helping Jason?"

"I guess Austin didn't tell you. Jason decided he wanted to move back to Two Rivers and try his hand at ranching. He sold everything he owns and took up the land across the highway that his father left him. Now he's in the process of remodeling an old barn to live in. I must admit I'm impressed by his knowledge and willingness to work."

"Jason. Manual labor."

Ginny laughed. "I know it's shocking. I thought he was just a pretty face and glib tongue when I first met him, too." Ginny didn't want to give too much away. It was better if this young woman saw for herself and made up her own mind. But she liked Laura. There was something childlike in her clear hazel eyes that reminded her of Austin. She didn't want to see her hurt and would have warned her, yet something inside, a feeling that Laura Ghant could take care of herself, kept her silent.

"Somehow, I just don't think of Jason when I think of labor." It was a spiteful thing to say, and she wished she could have taken the words back the minute they were out of her mouth.

Ginny laughed. "I see you know Jason better than you've letting on." She waved her hand when Laura opened her mouth to protest. "No. Don't say anything. Maybe one day you'll tell me. Just do me a favor. Be careful where Jason is concerned. He loves women, maybe too much, and he tires of them easily. Don't let yourself be added to his list."

"I'm always careful, Ginny." Always, except for eight years ago, she thought, and that was best forgotten.

CHAPTER FOUR

LAURA WATCHED the sunrise from her bed. When the light made its first peek through the sheer lace curtain, she decided it was a reasonable hour to be up. Several times she thought she smelled coffee, but when she looked at the clock beside the bed, she realized it was just wishful thinking.

It was hell to be an early riser and one of those people who needed only five or six hours' sleep. But she was a guest and didn't want to make anyone feel obligated, out of good manners, to take care of her. Ginny had made it clear she also liked the mornings, but she didn't say how early, and Laura suspected a woman eight months' pregnant needed all the rest she could get.

Enough was enough. She threw back the covers and shivered. Someone had turned the air conditioner so high that the room felt like a meat locker. Once she was up and busy thinking about what she needed to do to set up her work, she rushed through her shower. After slapping on a minuscule amount of makeup, she quickly dressed.

As she left her room, she paused and stared at the closed door across the hall. She eased the door open and peeked inside. Austin lay curled into a tight ball, his covers twisted around the foot of the bed. She tiptoed to his side, brushed the hair off his forehead and pulled the covers back over him. He looked so young and helpless, she thought, then shook her head. Austin Bolt was anything but helpless. He was a master manipulator. Still, at that moment, she felt sorry for him.

It hadn't taken long after dinner last night for everyone to realize that Austin had caught a cold from being in the caves then weeding Ginny's garden in the hot sun afterward. They all decided since he wasn't well, they'd pass on the evening swim. He'd protested, but Laura could tell he was delighted to be told that the evening just wouldn't be any fun without him. Considering Ginny's protectiveness, one thing was for sure—Austin wouldn't be venturing into the caves anytime soon.

In a way she was glad the swim was called off. She'd already had to face Jason across the dinner table, endure his teasing and Matt and Austin's comments about her cooking. Forewarned by Ginny, she took the ribbing and was pleased to see they cleaned their plates. Her spaghetti sauce and meatballs, Caesar salad and garlic bread were old standbys that never failed. Though she'd told Ginny her repertoire was limited to only four or five meals, she was willing to cook anything Ginny had a recipe for.

As she headed for the stairs, she thought how this family seemed to have so many secrets, a sharing of looks that everyone understood. It left her feeling a little disconcerted. Her own family was about as dysfunctional as they came, and she wasn't used to close family ties. Nevertheless, she envied them.

Laura sniffed the air as she descended the stairs. It *was* coffee she smelled! She followed the heavenly aroma into the kitchen. Spotting the big pot on the stove, she poured herself a mug, then wandered over to the door and stepped outside.

She strolled out into the yard, stopping every so often to listen to the birds chirping and the oak leaves rustling in the breeze. This was her favorite time of the day; the serenity seemed to seep into her bones. On every dig she was always the first up. She could watch the dawn and experience the renewed feeling it gave her.

Laura walked over to the low stone wall and jumped atop it. She hugged her knees to her chest, took a couple of sips of the strong coffee and closed her eyes. She started planning her strategy for the day when voices and a barking dog surprised her out of her peaceful contemplation.

She was just about to hop off the wall when she spotted Ginny, Dog bouncing happily along beside her, coming up the long drive. Ginny waved, and as she drew closer Laura could see she was dressed in a pair of denim cutoffs and a man's shirt, obviously Matt's. "I didn't think anyone was up until I smelled the coffee."

Ginny leaned against the wall to catch her breath while Dog wandered off to lap from a bowl of water by the porch door. After a moment, Ginny said, "I told you I get up early. In fact, everyone here is pretty much an early riser. Have you seen Matt yet?"

Laura shook her head. "You walk every morning?"

"Four miles. Two down to the gate and two back." She looked down at her stomach and rubbed it affectionately. "Dog and I used to run it, but I've had to slow down a bit."

"You and Dog?"

"Sure, he's my running buddy. If he wasn't with me, there'd be no way Matt would let me take off in the dark." Dog returned to her side and she reached down to rub his ears. "There was a time when he scared the hell out of me. As a matter of fact, he's responsible for Matt and I meeting in the first place." She glanced at Laura. "Austin didn't tell you anything about me, about my past, did he?"

Laura shook her head and sipped her coffee, then set it down on the stone. She was curious and wasn't about to do or say anything to discourage Ginny from talking.

"Over a year ago I was in the FBI's Witness Protection Program." She laughed at Laura's shock.

"The FBI?" Laura said.

"Yep. It wasn't anything I did, you understand, but what I knew and had testified to." She hiked herself, with a little help from Laura, up onto the stone wall. "I was an attorney practicing in Boston with a husband and a daughter when I found out my stepfather was laundering dirty money through the family bank.

"To make a long story short, after I'd discovered what he was up to and had the proof, I approached the FBI. They in turn needed me to testify against my stepfather, which I was willing to do. But I started getting threats, and the government was supposed to protect me and my family. They failed. My husband and daughter were killed in a car bombing."

Laura gasped. "How dreadful!"

"Yeah, it was," said Ginny, then she picked up Laura's coffee and took a sip, savoring the taste. "Sorry, but Matt doesn't allow me coffee very often. Anyway," she went on, "my stepfather thought he'd stopped me, but he was wrong. I testified, anyway, and he went to prison. The FBI put me into the program, and after four years of being moved around to different states, different jobs, I'd had enough. I was being delivered to Austin, Texas, when the agents I was riding with had a car accident. I lived, they didn't and I ran.

"I finally stopped running here. Actually—" she pointed off into the distance "—it was down by the river that Dog found me. I'd slipped and fallen, knocked myself out cold. Dog brought Austin and Matt, and they carted me back to the house and here I am.''

"Oh, no, you can't stop there, Ginny. Not fair," Laura protested. "What happened after that?"

"I fell madly in love and held her prisoner here until she agreed to marry me."

Neither of them had heard Matt slip up behind them, and they screamed when he spoke.

"Damn you, Matthew Bolt." Ginny tried to sound stern but failed miserably as he wrapped an arm around her shoulders and kissed her on the cheek. "You finish the story," she said, and leaned back against him, letting him rock her.

"Well, Austin and I decided we wanted to keep her. I put her to work cooking for the men and Austin worked his magic on her so she couldn't leave. But there was the FBI, who wanted her back, and her stepbrother who wanted her dead. We dealt with them all, and just as an added precaution the town set up an elaborate alarm system for when any car came through town. Usually the unfortunates are met by the sheriff and told if they don't have business here to move on. I'm surprised the sheriff didn't meet you or warn us you were coming out here.''

Laura laughed. "I think I understand. After I'd parked the van, and before I even had time to reach for the door, Jason was there, standing in my way. I think he was going to give me the same advice as your sheriff does, but things got kind of tangled up." She laughed again, and when she saw them staring at her, she said, "I didn't get a good look at him and just thought he was some local yokel trying to pick me up, when he only wanted to find out who I was."

Matt explained, "You must have told Jason your name, and it clicked with what Austin had told us earlier. So Jason cleared you with the town, then raced back here as fast as he could, knowing you'd be a shock to us."

"A shock?" Laura was puzzled.

Ginny picked up the story. "Austin had told us earlier that morning he'd invited a friend from school. We were expecting . . . someone more his own age."

They all had a good laugh, then Matt sobered. "Tell me something, Laura. How well do you know Austin? Does he talk to you? Does he have many friends? How's he managing? Oh, I know his work is exceptional, but I mean, personally, how's he doing? He's always reassuring us he's okay, but . . ."

Laura swallowed hard around the lump in her throat. She wished her family had cared that much about her. "He's the most well-adjusted boy I've ever met. I've been where he is, and I know how lonely it can be, but Austin's not like that. He makes friends. Did you know he's even tutoring one of the football players in chemistry?"

Ginny look both pleased and confused. "Why would he do that? It's not like he needs the money." She glanced at Matt. "You did increase his allowance, didn't you?"

"Of course. But, sweetheart, you forget Austin's taste for expensive gadgets and software for his computer. Maybe he wanted something and didn't like to ask for more money."

Laura wasn't about to tell them that one of the reasons Austin was tutoring was hidden under a tarp in her van. He'd worked and saved to buy Ginny and the baby a child's car seat. Not just any child's car seat, but the one his extensive research showed was the best.

"How did you meet Austin?" Ginny asked.

"Wait'll I come back before you answer that," Matt said, picking up Laura's coffee mug and heading for the kitchen. When he returned, the mug was refilled and he handed Ginny a big glass of juice.

Ginny wrinkled her nose. "I hate cranberry juice."

"Drink up," Matt said. "It's good for you and the baby." He turned to Laura. "Now, tell us how you met my son." But he didn't get his answer. Spotting Jason walking up the drive, Ginny waved and called to him.

Oh, no. Not so early! Laura thought. Then she scolded herself. She was going to have to get used to being in his company. There were sacrifices to be made for anything worth having, and she intended to work the caves. As he drew closer she noticed he was dressed, like herself, in jeans and a long-sleeved cotton shirt. He'd even thought to bring a lightweight jacket to ward off the cold in the caves.

"Good morning, Professor," Jason called, not stopping but continuing on to the house. In a moment he came out carrying an oversize cup, more like a soup bowl with a handle, and positioned himself beside Matt, leaning against the stone wall. "What's everyone doing out here? I'm starving."

"Is there any time you're not starving?" Matt grumbled.

"Some—" his eyebrows wiggled wickedly "—but you forget, I'm a hardworking man. I need nourishment. Matt, do you know Bill Lake?" His brother shook his head. "Well, he's got a small farm, about ten acres of peach trees. Anyway, you know those twenty-five acres I own on the other side of town? Bill's place is across the highway, and he called me last night to tell me some men were out there looking around. Have you heard of anyone wanting to buy that property?"

"No."

Jason could tell no one was interested in his story, then realized he'd interrupted them. "Were you having a private conversation?" He grinned. "Should I leave?"

"It's about Austin," Ginny said. "Go on, Laura. You were going to tell us how you met Austin."

Laura smiled. "He showed up in the archaeology department about four months ago. He went around introducing himself to everyone—students, staff, assistants and the professors. We were all aware of him. The college had been abuzz with the news of a child genius from the beginning. There'd been a story about Austin in the staff bulletin and the school newspaper.

"Normally we wouldn't have put up with his hanging around and all his questions, but he was so sincere and frighteningly knowledgeable. The thing is, you can't *not* like and be impressed with Austin. It wasn't until later that I realized he'd actually been interviewing each of us, assessing his best chances to get someone to help him with his project."

Matt shook his head. "The caves. He's been after me from the first moment he saw the cave paintings to do something about them."

Jason was watching Laura closely. "Why'd he pick you?"

"Jason!" Ginny said, obviously horrified at his rudeness.

"No, that's all right," Laura said. "Austin chose me because he realized I was the most likely to come here, the most needy. There are a few of us on staff who are working on our doctorates. Academia is a dog-eat-dog world. I needed a dig, a find, of my own. I need to be published, to research, date and document my findings. Austin figured all this out, made his choice and came to me about three months ago."

"Three months ago?" Matt was puzzled. "He's kept this to himself all that time?"

"Actually, he did it for me. I didn't want anyone finding out."

Jason laughed. "You mean you didn't want a superior or someone else horning in on your project, taking over and getting all the credit?"

"That's right," she replied curtly. "Austin and I made a deal. He'd keep his knowledge to himself and I'd share, let him do some grunt work for me, like cataloging—things like that."

She waited in the ensuing silence with a sinking feeling. Using an eleven-year-old, no matter how intelligent or grown-up, was despicable.

"Good for you," Matt said. "You'll never get anywhere in life if you don't go for it."

"I guess I sort of manipulated Austin, though. I'm sorry."

Ginny patted her hand and chuckled. "Are you kidding? That kid got exactly what he wanted. If there was any manipulating done it was on his part." With Matt's help she eased off the wall and headed for the house. "We're going to have to keep a closer eye on him this summer, Matthew. He could get out of hand."

"What have I been trying to tell you?"

Laura and Jason watched them go, then Laura felt Jason staring at her. "You think I was wrong?"

"Hey, like Matt says, you only get what you go for." He could see she was in a mood to argue, and knowing women and that look well enough, he knew that no matter what side he took or how logical he was, it was a no-win situation. "Come on, let's go in. I'm starving to death."

The wind had been expertly taken out of her sails, and she didn't like it one bit. She was smarter than he was and better educated. Then why, she wondered, did he make her feel so...ignorant and lacking?

She pondered the question all through breakfast and while she helped Jason clean up. Later, when she left to gather her equipment, she was still puzzling out her problem.

As he followed her out of the kitchen, Jason tried to figure her out. There was a stiffness about her when he was around. A coldness he couldn't fathom. "Have I done something to make you angry with me?" he asked when they reached the van.

Laura opened the rear doors and was just about to crawl in when his question made her pause. "Why, no. Nothing you could say would bother me."

Jason's eyes narrowed a fraction. She'd answered him with a sweet-enough tone and a smile, but there was a sting to her words. He would have questioned her again, but she started handing him things to carry. After juggling a few, he said, "I'm not your personal pack animal."

Laura didn't respond to that, just crawled out from the depths of the van and started taking the objects from him one by one, rechecking to make sure she had everything. He was so damn sexy it was hard sometimes just to look at him. She wondered how many women he'd had, and resented her sudden jealousy. What happened eight years ago wasn't relevant, she reminded herself. She was a different person, older, wiser, and she'd never fall into the trap of gazing in those damn blue eyes again.

Jason watched her the way a cat watches a bird as she continued to inventory her gear. She didn't like him. The thought shocked him. She really didn't like him. He followed her mutely all the way to the wine cellar, then just as quietly took the lead. She didn't like him. It was unthinkable. What had he ever done to her? Hell, he hardly knew her.

Just as they were about to enter the cave, Jason abruptly came to a halt, a dozen questions on the tip of his tongue, but then he shrugged and headed on in. This wasn't the time, not when all she could think about was the cave paintings. When they'd reached the cavern and were standing in the exact spot as the last time, he asked, "Where do you want this stuff?"

Laura was almost surprised to hear his voice. They'd been so quiet all the way down, and she'd been so lost in her plans, that she'd nearly forgotten he was there. But it wasn't possible to forget now. They were alone in the dark together, and she could sense him looking at her.

"You don't have to help, you know," she said.

"I can't sit around and twiddle my thumbs."

She directed the beam of her flashlight to a dark corner. "Okay, you can set up the tripods, one on each end of that wall, and tighten down the lights."

She helped him, holding her flashlight so he could see what he was doing. As much as she tried to keep her attention only on the job he was doing, she couldn't seem to drag her gaze from the way he moved, leaned over, squatted down or stretched. The light and shadow played over him, accentuating the way his shirt pulled tight over his shoulders. Then the light illuminated his blond hair, making it shine like gold. At times the light created deep shadows, hollowing his cheekbones, giving him an almost sinister look.

When the portable lights were set up, her hands trembled as she inserted the batteries. The cave came to life and the faded paintings on the wall seemed to jump out at them. It was a magical moment, and she knew by the way Jason froze for an instant and caught his breath that he felt it, too. She smiled, the first sincere smile she'd allowed herself in his presence.

"Did I imagine that . . . ?" He couldn't think how to explain the moment. His heart still pounded in excitement, and without thought, with nothing other than an automatic reflex, he put his arm around Laura's shoulders. "It's sort of how you feel when you're alone in a dark room, then turn on the lights and catch movement in your peripheral vision. You feel scared and foolish at the same time."

She couldn't have explained it better herself, and she eased out from under his arm, slowly, reluctantly, immediately ashamed of the soft glow she felt from such a casual touch. To cover her ragged emotions she set to work, moving around quickly, adjusting the way the light fell across the wall and every so often stopping to motion Jason out of her way until he finally gave up, sat down and just watched.

Then with her camera at the ready, she rechecked the film speed, the light meter and took aim. She tried working at different angles, but she finally had to admit to herself she couldn't do it alone. She lowered her camera and twisted around. He had such a smug look she could have sworn he'd read her mind and knew what was coming. He wasn't going to make this easy, she thought.

"The lighting's not right," she said. "Too many shadows. I can't get any clear shots." He sat there staring at her, smiling that beautiful, infuriating smile of his. She swallowed her pride. "Would you help me?"

"Sure." Jason thought he'd figured her out. She was proud and prickly and thought she could do everything on her own. It hurt her to ask for help. He wondered what had happened to her to make her so distrustful. "Tell me what you need me to do."

She couldn't believe he'd agreed so readily and waited a moment for him to make some wry comment. When he only moved over to one of the lights and glanced at her for instructions, she dropped her gaze and pretended to make an adjustment to her camera. What was going on? she wondered. He wasn't anything like she'd expected.

She brought the camera up to her eye and took aim at the wall. "Move the light to the left. Now to the right, no, to the left just a couple of inches. No, that's still not working."

"What if I take the light off the stand and you tell me where you need it?"

When he eased the beam of light across the area she wanted, she exclaimed, "There! Right there. Yes, yes, that's better. Hold it steady now."

For more than an hour they worked as a team. After a while, as if they'd been doing this together for years, she didn't even have to tell Jason where to direct the light. He seemed to know precisely how the shadows collected around a protruding formation in the wall and was able to highlight them perfectly. She hadn't even realized she'd been giving Jason a running commentary on what she thought or hoped the paintings were until she stopped to reload the camera and he asked her questions about what she'd told him.

The harmony between them unnerved her to the point that she lost her concentration. She promptly finished the roll of film, walked over to the flat boulder in the middle of the cavern and sat down. When Jason joined her, she ducked her head and began reloading the camera. She was afraid to look at him, afraid the confusion she was feeling would show on her face.

Jason stuck the nubby steel arm of the portable light in the sandy floor so the beam was aimed at the ceiling and a pale circle of light surrounded them. Contrary to what everyone thought, and he was well aware of his reputation, he loved intelligent women. They were a wonderful source of endless entertainment, and he didn't mean that contemptuously or the least bit unflatteringly. He never had any trouble getting along with them, was never at a loss for words—until now. Laura Ghant was a mystery. That she didn't care for him was obvious, yet why did he have the feeling she was acting? No, that wasn't right, he thought, more like she was hiding something.

As Laura had lain awake that morning, waiting for the sun, she'd tried to plan out her options for working with Jason. With all her planning she'd decided inactivity was going to be her biggest hurdle to overcome. There were times when she would have to stop for a rest. She dreaded the idleness, knowing if she didn't want to appear an idiot, she was going to have to converse with him.

In the natural scheme of things, two people who carry on a conversation share information about themselves. Her dilemma was she couldn't afford to divulge anything to Jason, not if she wanted to stay and do her work, and she wasn't about to risk losing her chance to document the cave.

After all the worrying she'd done in the predawn, Laura finally decided her course of action. If she didn't want to draw attention to herself, she had to act natural. Jason had quite a reputation as a ladies' man. But in the few hours she'd been in his company and seeing him with his family, she'd recognized he wasn't a pushover.

She'd realized long ago that a man was like a dog with a bone. The harder you tried to take it away from him, the more he'd fight to hold on. If she kept ignoring Jason and acting strangely, he'd only become more interested. Somehow, though, she was going to have to dodge any area of conversation that pertained to her family, her background or where she was from.

She shivered, rudely reminded that her inaction had allowed the cold of the cave to steal into her bones. She carefully set the camera in her lap, dug a cardigan sweater from her backpack, slipped it on, then looked at the luminous dial of her watch. They'd been in the cave almost two hours. "Have you had enough or can we work longer?"

"I'm game for staying if you are." Jason put his jacket on and sat quietly. Then he leaned back on his elbows so he could watch her. "What's next, Professor?"

Laura shot him an annoyed glance, then smiled. She was going to have to learn not to let him get under her skin, but it wasn't going to be easy. "I'd like to take some shots of the back of the cave."

Jason sat up and dusted off his hands. "That's not a smart move, Laura. It's—"

"I know, dangerous. But if we're very careful... Listen, Jason—" she gave him a pleading look "—I saw something back there that I believe to be the oldest in this cave. I have to get some shots." She waited, and when he didn't immediately give in, she smiled and added, "Please."

He stood and held out his hand. She hesitated but finally grasped it and allowed him to pull her upright. "Smile at me like that more often," he said, "and I'll do anything for you."

Laura laughed and shook her head as she swung the camera strap over her shoulder. "It must be very hard on you." She waved him in front of her since he had the lights.

"What do you mean? What's hard?"

"Being so handsome, glib and wonderful must be a real burden."

"Why would you think that?"

"Because no one takes you seriously." She followed him around a rocky outcropping. "I mean, women must use you like a piece of meat." She gingerly stepped over a knee-high pile of rocks. "No respect must play havoc with your ego. Know what I mean?"

"Piece of meat! Me? Dammit to hell, I've never—" Jason stopped abruptly and spun around fast. Laura was too close, and in a grunting tangle, they grabbed each other and stumbled around a few steps as if in some primitive dance while the light bounced and jerked around the walls. A huge cloud of white dust engulfed them as they slammed to the floor and the room went inky dark.

Trying to save her camera, Laura rolled with the motion. She coughed and waved her hand to clear the dust, but her camera was in her hand and it made solid contact with something, eliciting a moan of pain. She flinched and said, "I'm sorry."

This time Jason thought he had the advantage by being on top. But when she clobbered the side of his head with the camera he simply rested his forehead on her chest and started to laugh. "Professor, you're a walking disaster."

How could she not have watched where she was going? How could she be so damn clumsy? "Are you okay?" she muttered.

"No. I'm going to have the devil of a headache, thanks to you."

"It wasn't my fault. You stopped too quickly."

"Well, hell and damnation, Professor. If you'd stop walking on my heels ..." He let the sentence trail away. "Don't move."

"Why."

"Because I've lost the light."

"Wonderful," she snapped.

"And don't get snippy with me because of something *you* did." He stretched out his arm and blindly began to search around them. "Aha. Here it is." Jason found the switch and flicked it on. Nothing happened. He didn't want to think of the trouble they were in if they'd lost their only source of light.

"Did you find it?" She didn't dare move an inch.

"Yes."

"Then turn it on, for heaven's sake."

Jason gave the switch a couple of off and on clicks, shook it, then sighed when the cave came to life. He looked at Laura beneath him and laughed. "If you could see your face." She looked like someone had dusted her with flour, and with the dark areas around her eyes, she resembled a ghost—or a clown someone had forgotten to paint a smile on. He stuck his finger in his mouth, then pulled it out and carefully drew an ear-to-ear smile on her face.

Laura could feel his laughter against her long before she heard it. She would have made a snide remark, but she was stunned and mesmerized by what he was doing. His comical face mirrored hers, and though she wanted to laugh, she seemed to have lost her voice. She could only gaze at him in silence, stare into his eyes and watch as he did the same.

When his lips lightly touched hers, she started to protest. She swore later that she'd tried, but couldn't force herself to form the rejection. When the pressure of his mouth increased, and she dropped her precious camera in the dust and threaded her fingers through his hair, she told herself that she wasn't going to open her lips. She wasn't going to allow him to kiss her deeply and passionately. This wasn't eight years ago, and she wouldn't allow herself to be hurt.

She refused to fall in love with Jason again.

CHAPTER FIVE

SHE'D MADE PROMISES to herself long ago, promises that if she ever saw Jason Van der Bollen again, she would never let him find that hurt place inside her where she'd so carefully packed her memories away.

Everything—every thought, every promise she'd ever made to herself—floated away on his lips. The kiss was nothing like she remembered. As it deepened with a mutual hunger and an electric sensuality, she told herself she couldn't even blame Jason for what was happening. How could she accuse him of taking advantage of her when she was a more-than-willing participant?

She was the first to break away and lay limp, gazing at him. He looked as confused as she felt. It came to her suddenly that for eight years she'd held him responsible for what had happened. But now she knew differently. She'd needed a scapegoat for her own shame and humiliation, and who better to hold accountable than Jason? The realization that she'd been her own worst enemy was a stunning blow.

As he caught his breath and regained his equilibrium, Jason tried to figure out what she was thinking. How angry was she going to be? The kiss had just happened. One of those delicious, unpredictable, rather magical moments. He damn well wasn't going to apologize, either. "Maybe the next time you follow me, we should call out soundings before we make any sudden moves."

"Soundings?"

"Sure. A measurement. I'll ask for a sounding, how far you are from my back, and you tell me in feet or inches whether or not I can turn around without knocking you over."

"Sounds logical and workable to me." She was thankful he hadn't said anything or teased her about the kiss.

"Thought so." He started to get up, then spotted her camera. "Oh, hell, I'm sorry."

She followed his gaze and sighed. Her expensive camera was half-buried in the sandy floor where she'd dropped it. She couldn't even work up a good head of steam of anger or regret. The kiss had been well worth it. "I've brought others."

Jason helped her to stand, then scooped up the camera, shaking and blowing on it to clean off some of the dust. "It's a good thing you hadn't taken any shots with it— they'd be ruined." He leaned over and picked up the light. "I guess that's it for today."

She glanced around, disappointment etched in her grimace. "I guess."

Jason started to take down the light tripods, then paused. "Why don't we leave these where they are?" Here he was, Mr. Glib, Mr. Smooth, suddenly at a loss for some clever remark. "What's on the agenda for tomorrow? More photos?"

"Some," she mumbled absently and kept studying the walls. That damn kiss, she thought. Now she felt strange, stupid. Almost shy. Her, shy! It was laughable.

It didn't sit right, Jason thought as he picked up the backpack. After that fabulous, intriguing kiss, she was more interested in the old cave paintings than him. His mood immediately brightened. He was going to be with her, alone, for two or three hours every morning. Then he'd have her at his place for a while, too. Things could get interesting. As if she'd read his thoughts, Laura glared at him.

That sexy smile again, she thought. It was designed to make females, her in particular, weak in the knees. Trouble was, it worked, but she would never let him see that. She plucked her backpack from his hand, slipped the strap over one shoulder, flicked on her flashlight, turned off the floodlight and motioned for him to lead the way.

Damn woman. Jason headed out of the cave. As they neared the wine cellar, he slowed down and called over his shoulder, "Sounding."

"Three feet behind you," Laura said with a laugh.

"See? Told you it would work."

The fragrance of the cellar was the first thing she noticed, followed by the rise in temperature, then the gradual increase of light. When Jason pushed open the outer doors, she remembered the painful first glare of the sunlight and turned her head a fraction.

The blast of heat made her gasp. The sharp shaft of sunlight stabbed at her eyes like a thousand needles. The picture of yesterday's fiasco was too clear in her mind. This time, to be on the safe side, she grabbed hold of the back of Jason's jeans to keep from walking into him. When he stopped, she blinked away the pain and finally opened her eyes fully.

They had an audience of at least five men she'd never seen before. Plus, there were Ginny, Matt and that old man, Jericho. It was Ginny's laughter that kicked everyone off. In a second they were all laughing. Laura glanced at Jason, then down at herself. Except for the darkness around their eyes and mouths, they looked like something out of a horror movie—pale, hollow-eyed zombies.

"What," Matt asked, "did you two do? Roll around on the floor?"

"She tripped me," Jason said, grinning.

"Me? Matt, you need to take Jason to a doctor. He has this balance problem."

Matt glanced from one to the other. "If Laura tripped you, then how come she's in the same condition?"

"Fate," Jason grumbled, and grabbed Laura's hand. "Come on, we need to get cleaned up and head over to my place. The girls are going to be frantic with worry." They strolled away, and every step brought a puff of dust, as if they were walking on the moon.

GINNY SOBERED as she watched them leave, then poked Matt in the ribs. "Did you get a good look at their faces?"

His laughter faded away as he saw how serious Ginny had become. "What's wrong?"

"The dust was worn off in almost identical circles around their mouths."

"So?" He jumped when she poked him again.

"I'd swear they've been kissing. Matt, you have to have a talk with Jason. Just because he's bored, I won't have him seducing and hurting Laura. You know that's what's going to happen. You know how he is with women. I won't have it, Matthew."

"They're adults, Red."

She glared at him and walked, or rather, waddled, away. Matt watched affectionately and sighed deeply. She could work up a good head of steam before she blew. Dammit, he knew Jason was going to pull something. His brother had been entirely too quiet, dependable and amenable lately. Things were bound to get complicated.

LAURA TRIED to get most of the dust off her clothing before she entered the house. Jason was doing the same, and glancing over her shoulder in time to see him beat at his chest, she chuckled. "I'm going to take a shower and change clothes. Do you want me to meet you at your place?"

"No, I'll wait for you." He opened the back door into the kitchen and was greeted by a snarling Dog and his red-nosed nephew. When Laura would have stopped to talk to Austin, Jason gave her a gentle push. "Go on. I'll tell him everything—well, not everything."

She was trying to discourage any conversation concerning the kiss by pretending it never happened. He wasn't going to allow that, so she smiled wanly and continued on up the stairs.

Austin glared at his uncle, plucked another tissue from the box and blew his nose loudly. "What did you do?"

Jason held up his hand and said, "Nothing. I swear." When Austin continued to stare, he realized that his nephew was asking about the work they'd done, that was all. "How you feeling, Einstein?"

"Awful." He sniffed miserably. "Why'd I have to get a cold? Why couldn't you have caught it? Have you seen Ginny? She was going to make me some chicken noodle soup."

Jason bit his lip. "Thanks for wishing me sick."

Austin waved his tissue and sneezed. "Tell me what you did."

"Laura photographed the wall."

"Uncle Jason—" Austin gave a dramatic sigh of disgust "—I know that. Tell me what you saw. What she thinks. What you think. Did anything exciting happen?"

"Austin, archaeology is not my field. I saw what you've seen. A bunch of faded paintings on a cave wall. But from the way Laura was talking and acting, I'd say she was excited." He gave a quick conspiratorial glance around. "We were going to photograph the back of the cave, but I dropped the light and it went out."

Austin absently swiped the tissue across his nose. "Man-oh-man, I bet that scared the piss out of you."

"Watch your mouth."

"There's no one around but us."

"Yeah," Jason said, "but it becomes a habit, and the first time you slip up and say things like that in front of Ginny or Laura, your Dad and I will whip your scrawny butt."

"Sorry," Austin mumbled, then he perked up. "When's Laura going to develop the pictures?"

"I have no idea. We're going to head over to my place for the rest of the afternoon."

Austin cocked his head and gave his uncle a jaundiced look. "You're not going to monopolize *all* her time while she's here, are you, Uncle Jason?"

"Of course not. But a promise is a promise, and Laura did promise to help me out if I went with her to the caves. Remember, this was all your doing in the first place."

Austin immediately changed the subject. "How's she going to develop the pictures and do her other work if she's helping you in the afternoons?"

His nephew's questions were going to get very precise and to the point in a moment. He was going to try to pin him down on Laura's time with him, and Jason wasn't ready for that to happen just yet. "If she does her own developing, then she can do it either here or at my place. Maybe my place would be better. Since there's nothing there, she won't have to worry about making a mess."

Austin didn't like it, but it made sense. Reluctantly he nodded. "Sounds okay. But you'll bring them right away so I can look at them?"

"Bring what?" Ginny asked as she entered the kitchen and rubbed Dog's ears.

"The cave pictures. Soup, Ginny. Please. I feel awful," Austin croaked.

Jason hid his grin. It didn't surprise him that his nephew suddenly sounded like he was on his deathbed. He'd have done the same. He heard Laura coming down the stairs and glanced up when she came through the doorway—then swallowed. Hard. His smile faded. She was wearing a pair of white shorts, pristine white tennis shoes and a black-and-white-striped tank top. There was a lot of tanned skin showing that held his interest longer than was polite. It was time for a break from the ranch, work and Two Rivers.

"You might want to rethink those clothes." His eyes lingered on her long, bare legs. "I mean, they're nice. Great, really." Damn, he was beginning to sound more and more like Austin. "When I say nice, I mean fine for strolling around or sitting by a pool—but not for working." He stood up. "Never mind, I have some old paint stained shirts you can wear. Come on."

He was out the door before she could open her mouth. Shrugging, Laura glanced at Ginny, then at Austin. "If you're up to it tonight, I'll tell you everything I saw." Then she raced out the door. "Jason, wait."

He let her catch up, then they set off down the drive. Laura's gaze took in the vast fields of vines. "You're not in the wine business with Matt?"

"No. I just take a share of the profits." He glanced at her, saw her frown and decided to explain the flip answer.

"According to my father's will, the firstborn son would inherit the business, the wine, the land, the vines and all that goes with it. I get a portion of the profits." He knew by her expression what she was thinking. "You're wrong."

"What?"

"That I should have gotten half. I never was and never would be a vintner. It's a part of Matt, who he is, in his blood."

"But he was a cop living in Houston."

Jason opened the gate, waited until she was through, then closed and locked it. "Matt and my father hated each other with about the same passion they felt for the vineyard. Even after my father's death, Matt might never have come home if he hadn't been shot and forced to retire from the force."

"You don't resent your brother getting the vineyard?"

"Hell, no. Too damn much work." He thought about what he'd been doing, the backbreaking manual labor, and laughed. Jason touched her arm to slow her pace as they came to the edge of the two-lane highway.

Laura couldn't explain the deep disappointment she felt at his explanation. But after all, she reminded herself, Jason was nothing but a playboy and used to the easy life. She headed out across the highway, two steps ahead of him. Eight years ago Jason was a hedonistic young man pursuing debauchery with zeal. Maybe age had slowed him down, mellowed him a little, but she figured nothing much else had changed. But then, who was she to judge? She had her own crosses to bear, and as much as she might want to blame others, Jason in particular, she was the only one accountable for her actions.

She tried to keep the specter of the past from rising up again and sapping her emotionally. As they walked up the long gravel lane, she made herself take notice of her surroundings, which were extremely different from the vineyards. Her first impression was of wild, untended land.

The fence line by the highway was nothing but shrub oaks and cedar. As she walked farther, the wildness was tamed. No one could live in the Hill Country without recognizing peach orchards.

Jason's land was only dotted with peach trees, and instead of being carefully pruned, they'd been allowed to grow naturally. The trees partially shaded the blanket of grass that rolled and dipped with the terrain. Wide, unshaded areas were thick with a rainbow of wildflowers.

She stopped a moment and gazed around in delighted wonder. "This is beautiful, Jason."

He experienced the strangest feeling of contentment as he surveyed the land. "It is, isn't it?"

"There's something enchanting, even magical, about a field of wildflowers." As they moved on up the road, the sun glinted and seemed to sparkle off a gray slate roof. As they followed the curve of the road, she suddenly got a full view of a massive stone barn.

"Home sweet home," Jason said. "Or it will be soon."

"You're living there?"

"If you call it living. I sleep there and now I can bathe there, but it's far from being in a livable condition." He touched her arm and motioned her to follow him around the side of the building. "I want to show you something back here. Introduce you to my girls."

She couldn't take her eyes off the barn as she passed beside it. Its walls were of native stone that soared at least two stories high. There were a few wide windows along the side, but they were boarded up from the inside. Then suddenly Jason's last words penetrated, and she lost all interest in the barn. "Your girls?" she asked. "What girls?" She certainly didn't want to meet any of Jason's women.

Laura spotted a sweeping area of rolling land fenced off with a high-post, four-bar cedar fence. As she drew closer, she could see that at the back of the area was a long, low stone building that appeared to be stables. Jason whistled a couple of times, leaned against the fence and waited. The whistling set off a noisy racket.

Above the clamor, Laura could hear the sound of feet, lots of feet, pounding the ground, and she backed away cautiously. Suddenly she stopped. Then she laughed. A small herd of big birds came running, heading directly for Jason. As they drew closer she could see their beige-and-brown shaggy-looking feathers, their long necks. A moment later she could clearly see their short beaks and big, round eyes with long lashes. "Oh," she cooed, "what darlings! Ostriches?"

"Emus." Jason opened the gate, drew Laura in behind him and relocked the gate. "Stay back until I introduce you." The emus were almost upon them. Jason stepped away from Laura and held out his arms. "My babies. Come to Papa."

She watched in total disbelief. Six of the ten birds surrounded him and he oohed and aahed over them, petting and hugging each one, talking to them in the most ridiculous baby talk. Up close she could see that the emus were smaller than she'd first thought. They ranged between four and five feet tall and probably weighed anywhere between eighty and 140 pounds.

The birds rubbed their heads against Jason's shoulders and chest, pecked lightly at his hair and face and were in general affectionate, almost loving. These of course, were his girls. How could they be anything *but* females? They only had eyes for Jason, and were typical of their sex; they couldn't keep their hands—or beaks—off him. Damn, but she had to admit they were adorable.

"Laura, come here." Jason gently pushed one of the birds aside and grabbed her hand. "I want to introduce you to my girls. This is Cleo, Helen and Bessie.'' He scratched one on the head and stroked another. ''This is Mary and Eleanor. Come here, sweetheart. And this is Marie.''

He touched each one as if he expected Laura to shake their hands—feet—or maybe a wing. She grinned, desperately struggling to keep from laughing. He was so serious and sincere, all she could do was stare at each one. She could have sworn that as each bird's name was called it seemed to glance her way with an alert interest in its dark eyes.

''These,'' Jason said as he motioned to two of the birds that were hanging back a little, ''are Joan and Ginny.'' Then he pointed to another two birds standing by the fence, eyeing them suspiciously. ''Those are the two males, Attila and Elvis.''

''Attila and Elvis.'' She bit her lip hard to keep from laughing. However, her amusement was evident to the emus, who suddenly surrounded her for a closer inspection. As she stroked their soft feathers and solid bodies, she chanced a glance at Jason, relieved to see that he hadn't noticed her stifled mirth. ''I take it you named one after Ginny. Do I dare ask who the rest are named after?''

Jason waded into the flock of emus to rescue Laura. ''Only if you promise me you won't laugh. You could hurt their feelings—and mine.'' He waited, and when she held up three fingers like a good Girl Scout, he nodded. ''Cleo's short for Cleopatra—she's coy and can't make up her mind whether she wants Attila or Elvis. Helen is Helen of Troy, of course, and she's pushy. Bessie is Queen Elizabeth I— she's standoffish and arrogant. Mary is Mary, Queen Of Scots, and she's just plain dumb. Joan, Joan of Arc—she's the smallest and shy. Then there's Eleanor—that's Eleanor of Aquitaine—and she's bold and adventurous. And there's Marie, for Marie Antoinette—she loves anything that glitters, and sweets, too. She's a bit of a glutton."

Laura couldn't keep a straight face any longer. Spinning around, ignoring the startled birds, she headed for the gate.

"No, you don't." Jason followed her. "You promised you wouldn't laugh. Girl Scout's honor, remember?" He locked the gate, caught up with her and grasped her shoulder.

Laura looked at him, and as seriously as she could said, "I lied. I was never a Girl Scout." She started laughing again and was happy to see Jason laugh with her and at himself. He knew all too well how silly the names were, but then that was part of his charm. His sense of humor, his ability to tease, to handle being teased himself and openly laugh at himself.

She wasn't paying attention to where they were going and realized he'd steered her down the path leading to the barn. "The emus are adorable, Jason, but what are they good for?"

"Making money. Their beeflike meat is low in fat and low in cholesterol. Plus, emu oil is expensive—it's being used in skin-care products and sports-related treatments. Also as a penetrating oil to treat stiffness, bruises and strains. It's anti-inflammatory, antimicrobial and anti-bacterial. Emus are tolerant of heat and cold, eat inexpensive food and are gentle and easy to raise. They have a sweet disposition, easygoing and inquisitive, not like ostriches, which can kick a hole in a chain-link fence. Emus don't need pampering."

But Jason pampered his emus. She was confused. A person raising stock for profit didn't usually care for his revenue producers with so much affection. You'd slaughter them for money, a few pieces of silver?"

"Good heavens, no!" Jason was appalled at the thought. "No, you don't understand. I'm raising them to sell stock, either young hatchlings or the eggs. What an awful thing to think, that I'd kill my girls."

She couldn't tell whether he was teasing or serious, then decided he was horrified at the thought of his emus going to the slaughterhouse. But then, what about the hatchlings or the eggs? They'd grow up to be adorable, too. She was about to put the question to him, then thought better of it.

Jason started to open the door to the barn, but then he paused, feeling it necessary to explain what she was about to witness. "The place isn't near finished, but it's going to be a showplace when I'm through." He twisted the knob and stopped again. "Don't expect too much, and don't freak out on me."

He had only asked her if she could hammer a nail straight. So why did she suddenly have the feeling he had something totally different in mind? Her doubts were answered as soon as the front door swung open. She almost strangled from shock and would have backed out, except Jason was blocking her exit.

Jason's dream home, his palace, was dreadful, a horror of an abode. Utter chaos met her everywhere she looked. There were new plumbing pipes traveling against the stone walls from floor to ceiling in geometric designs. Then there were all the new electrical wires, weaving and clinging like ivy gone wild. The wires clung to the beams, boards and anything else they happened to touch. Some even hung from the most obscure places and had big light bulbs stuck in their sockets.

She couldn't understand why the huge barn was so cold. The stone walls were about three feet thick. But there was a cold breeze blowing across her body. Then she realized after some careful thought that the round silver tubes that snaked across the roof's ceiling and the bottom of the second floor were air-conditioning ducts. She had a feeling Jason was waiting for her to comment, but she was at a loss for words.

"Give it time," Jason whispered in her ear, "and you'll begin to see some order."

"And method to your madness?" she whispered. "Jason, surely you're not really living here? It's...it's..."

"Going to be beautiful." He gave her a gentle push to move her a little farther into what would eventually be the living room—though there were no walls or ceiling, and only the subflooring to walk on.

Once the initial shock was over, she began to look around. He was obviously seeing something she couldn't. There were very few walls, only beams and studs, wires and pipes, where the walls were supposed to be. Then she looked up through the beams and studs of the second floor to the ceiling. She was astounded and delighted. Across the ceiling were four enormous skylights. "Now those have potential."

"I'm going to have a cathedral ceiling over the living room that will take in two of the skylights. Then one light will fall over the gallery and the last over my bedroom—right over my bed. So I can see the sunrise each day."

She spotted the roughed-in stairway toward the back of the barn and let her gaze follow the stairs up to the only floored part of the second story. "Your room?"

"Come on, I'll show you, then I'm going to shower off the dust from the cave, change and we'll get to work."

As he led her up the stairs, Laura looked around, speechless and at a loss as to what work she could possibly do here. When she reached the landing, she waited until he waved her through an imaginary doorway. Part of the bathroom had been partitioned off, and the lavatory, toilet and a tub were in place. In the mirror over the lavatory she could see the frosted glass door of the shower. Jason sat down on the edge of a neatly made double bed and began pulling off his boots and socks. "Since there're no doors, maybe you'd like to go downstairs, for modesty's sake." He stood up and placed his hands on the front of his jeans. "Unless you want to watch me shower." His eyes ran over her suggestively. "Or you could join me."

She steeled herself to control the shiver of pleasure that moved up her spine like lightning. "In your dreams," she said, and couldn't stop the snap of irritation in her voice. *The guy's a pro,* she thought, and shot him a disdainful look before she calmly and slowly made her way down the stairs.

As she waited for Jason's return, she wandered around. It was amazing really, but she was actually beginning to see a plan in the jumbled mess. She could tell where the kitchen sink and cabinets would go. Off of the kitchen she easily visualized a sizable breakfast room utilizing one of the huge windows. Then she saw where a bathroom and extra bedroom would be situated. Both areas were stacked high with slabs of Sheetrock.

"Have you figured it all out?" Jason had stopped halfway down the stairs, watching and enjoying the sight of Laura's changing facial expressions as she inspected everything and tried to decide what was what.

She turned and with one hand caught the shirt flying at her. "What's this for?"

"To protect your clothes."

Laura pulled on the shirt—the tail reached her knees— and rolled up the sleeves. Then Jason motioned for her to follow him.

"This is where I want to start," he said. He glanced around the kitchen, then looked up through what was to be the ceiling. Laura did likewise, noting the sawhorses and the wide boards placed across them.

It was crazy, Jason thought, but his shirt looked damn sexy on her. "You can help me stack some of the Sheetrock up in here first."

She could do that—if she could keep her attention away from his bare chest and tight-fitting jeans. After making about twenty trips, she was breathing hard. He'd said this was what they'd do first. What came next? she wondered. She watched Jason strap on a leather utility belt, a deep pocket of which was filled with screws and a cordless screwdriver.

"Where's my hammer, or do I get a screwdriver, too?" she asked, distrusting his smile and the twinkle in his bright blue eyes.

"Have you ever hung Sheetrock on a ceiling?"

"No." She started unbuttoning his shirt. "And I don't care to learn, thank you very much."

"Come on, Laura. Please." He swatted her hands away, grabbed the front of the shirt, pulled her toward him and immediately started to rebutton it. "All you have to do is help me get the Sheetrock boards up on the braces." His voice was soft, persuasive, his hands slow at their task. "Then you can help me line them up and hold them still while I secure them with the screws."

He was too close. There was too much bare skin. His fingers kept brushing against her breasts as he buttoned the shirt, and every time they did, she felt her heart slam wildly against her rib cage. Damn con artist, she thought. Yet, as hard as she tried, she couldn't muster up any anger. He was too much of an expert at what he was doing and she was too near to think straight. It galled her to realize she was just as susceptible to his charm as the rest of the females who came in contact with him. She was also weak-kneed with the memory of the kiss in the cave.

Laura kept her gaze on his hands, watching until he had finished buttoning the shirt. When he placed his hands on her shoulders, she angrily shrugged them off. "You're smooth. I'll have to hand you that, but I didn't agree to be slave labor in exchange for a few hours of your time. I have work to do of my own."

"Smooth? No, no, no. You've misunderstood."

"I don't think so. You said hammer a few nails. You've already conned me into hauling heavy slabs of Sheetrock. Now you want me to stand with my arms above my head for God only knows how long while you set the Sheetrock screws." She didn't take her eyes off his, noting the way his look of outraged indignation faded to frustration. Her uneasiness grew when he suddenly smiled, flashing an excessive amount of teeth.

"Tell you what. You can set up your film-developing lab in the laundry room for a renegotiation of your job description."

Oh, he was clever. She wondered how he'd found out about her developing her own film. His nephew, of course. Austin was the only one who knew. She pondered the offer. It would, after all, save her endless trips to the city.

As she examined her options, she glanced around. She was suddenly a little baffled. "You're a rich man, Jason. Why don't you hire some men to help you?"

Jason sighed and sat down on the end of the sawhorse. "Do you have any idea how much emus cost?" He didn't wait for her to finish. "A bundle, let me tell you. Then there's their feed, and I had to renovate the stable. It needed a new roof, and I wanted it to match the barn. Slate's expensive. Then I had to keep the birds cool, so the stable had to be equipped with fans, also a heating unit for the winter.''

He gave a mock shudder and studied the tips of his boots. ''I don't even like to remember what the state-of-the-art hatchery cost. Of course, before I could actually start remodeling the barn, I had to have the place wired and the plumbing installed. I went a little overboard with the air-conditioning, but I couldn't stand the thought of working in here in this heat.'' He looked up. ''Fact is, I've overextended myself.''

''You're broke?''

Jason sighed, nodded and smiled sadly. ''Pretty much. I can afford the supplies, but not labor costs. That's why I could use your help.''

How could she refuse?

CHAPTER SIX

DAWN WAS SPECTACULAR. The sun was rapidly pushing at the edges of night, blending the dark into ribbons of color, striping the sky in graduating shades of red, orange and finally pink. There had been a light rain during the night, and the air smelled clean and fresh, newly washed. Moisture beaded the grass and clung to the trees. Every so often a delicate breeze ruffled the leaves, sending down a misty spray through the shadows and over the ground.

Laura sat crossed-legged atop the stone fence waiting for Ginny and Dog's return from their morning walk. She shivered in the moist air and sipped her coffee. The movement made her hiss with pain. Her shoulders and arms were sore and stiff, and as she rolled her shoulders and worked her head in circles, she silently cursed her own stupidity.

Once she'd made her pact with the devil, she'd been determined to show him she was no sissy. She could pull her own weight. When they'd finished putting the drywall on the kitchen ceiling, she and Jason had stood back and admired their work. She'd actually felt a sense of accomplishment, one she hadn't felt about anything in a long time.

For his part, Jason truly enjoyed the work. She'd asked him how he'd found time between chasing women to learn about construction, and he'd laughingly told her he'd taken shop when he was in high school, but in fact didn't know the first thing about what he was doing. He'd pointed out the stack of how-to books and videotapes. He'd taken on the task of teaching himself about building and construction. From what she could see and what little she knew, he'd been doing a fine job.

When she thought he was ready to quit for the day, he'd amazed her by offering to help set up her lab so she could develop her photographs. While she'd retrieved her van and carried in what equipment she needed, he'd been working fast to finish the last wall in the laundry room so she could have her darkroom. He'd helped her set up, and when she'd been ready to go to work, he'd stacked a couple of sheets of plywood across the door opening, so she could have the total darkness she needed. He'd even strung a light bulb over her work space.

As she sat on the stone wall, she smiled just thinking about yesterday. There was no telling how long she'd worked; she hadn't marked time. Reality had returned when she'd finished the last roll of film. Then she'd pushed aside one of the boards, ready to call for Jason to come see the pictures, but just managed to stop from calling out his name. He'd made himself comfortable on the floor, with his back against a stack of boxes, and was deeply engrossed in another how-to book on flooring and insulation.

"You're pretty deep in thought for so early in the morning." Ginny laughed when Laura almost fell off the wall. "Careful."

"How was your walk?"

Ginny rubbed Dog's ears, then hauled herself atop the wall beside Laura. She picked up her plastic bottle of water and gulped down about half before she answered. "Wonderful." She placed her hands on her stomach. "You know, I believe she's going to be a runner, too. Every morning while I'm walking she likes to roll and jerk around. Not uncomfortably, just like she's moving with me." Ginny threw the empty bottle as far as she could, and they watched Dog chase it, pounce on it with a vicious growl and proceed to rip it apart. "He's not much on fetch, is he."

Laura laughed, then said, "Can I ask you something?"

"Sure."

"As protective as Matt is about you and the baby, how could he let you go off by yourself in the dark for a four-mile walk?"

Ginny's brown eyes twinkled. "Protective, huh? He's worse than a warden. But Dog's always with me, and Matt trusts that animal with my life." She chuckled at Laura's doubtful glance. "Dog actually did save my life a couple of times. Jason and Austin love to tell the stories—ask them sometime. As for Matt, don't think for a minute he totally depends on Dog for my safety. From one of our bedroom windows, we get a full view of the drive. Matt doesn't know I know, but he sits by the window and watches me until I'm on the return trip and about halfway back before he goes to take his shower.

"By the way," Ginny said, "thanks for bringing the photos of the cave to Austin. Needless to say he's not a very good patient, but they kept him occupied for a while. I swear if I hear him whine, 'I'm bored,' or 'I don't feel good,' one more time, I'll scream."

"He's going to have a zillion questions for me this morning." Laura couldn't contain her curiosity any longer. "Have you been over to Jason's and seen what he's done?"

"Mind-boggling, isn't it?"

Laura only nodded in answer.

"He worked you to death, didn't he."

"Let's just say hammering a few nails was a loose description for what Jason had in mind. But after a little negotiating we came to a compromise. He set up the laundry room as a film-developing lab."

"He's a charming devil and has his own style of getting his way—and not only with women. He'll get Matt to help him, at first, for something small, then talk him into giving him a hand with a host of other things."

"I guess what shocked me is Jason doing the work himself."

Ginny chuckled. "Shocked the pants off me, too. But Matt says Jason has a good foundation, knows the basics, and the rest can be learned. Matt's impressed—we both are. Jason's proved to be surprisingly capable, willing to research anything he's not sure of. But I must tell you, we're both skeptical as to how long he'll stick with this wild scheme of his. I take it he introduced you to his girls?"

"Yes, and they're wonderful, aren't they?"

"Expensive beasts, but his venture's sound, and if he sticks with it, it'll work. He stands a chance to make a lot of money."

The back screen door slammed shut and they both turned to see Matt carrying a tray with a big glass of Ginny's morning cranberry juice and two coffee mugs. Before he reached them, Ginny said quickly, "Be careful with Jason, Laura. He's—"

"A charming heartbreaker with about as much staying power in a relationship as a rabbit."

Ginny burst out laughing.

Matt was close enough to hear the last line, and his laughter joined theirs. "I don't even have to guess who you're talking about. Has my brother been making passes at you?"

Embarrassed, Laura took a sip of the hot coffee he'd brought before she answered. "No, not really. Actually he's been nice. I think his manner of teasing comes so naturally to him that he doesn't even realize how it's taken. Most of the time I try to ignore him." She was pleased to see that Ginny nodded in full agreement, but she caught Matt staring at her and immediately turned her attention to the drive. Then she could have bitten her tongue for saying, "Jason's late this morning."

"He told me last night, while you were going over the pictures of the cave with Austin, that you worked the hell out of him yesterday. I'm sure he's nursing some sore muscles this morning and moving slower than usual."

Matt got a real kick out of watching Laura. She had such a sweet, innocent face, except for her eyes. They were pellucid, intelligent, and seemed to possess an old wisdom. The look reminded him of his son, and maybe it should be attributed to geniuses; they were wise beyond their years. He was very sure his brother had never come in contact with a woman like Laura, and it would be interesting to see what happened.

Dog announced Jason's arrival. They had a good laugh watching the way he danced around Jason's feet, pouncing, snapping and tugging at the shoelaces of his running shoes.

Ginny sighed. "That's become a real game with them, and it's always a toss-up as to who'll win."

It looked to Laura as if Jason was the victor this time. As he approached them, his shoe laces were intact, though Dog was still making halfhearted attempts to change that.

"Morning, all. Is there coffee?"

Matt grinned. "Always is. How come you're late? Have a little trouble moving this morning?"

"A little." Jason glanced at Laura. "How about you?"

"I'm fine," she lied.

"Sure you are." Jason started off toward the house and the others followed. "I'm starving."

Ginny grimaced. "That's all I hear lately."

Just as they neared the house, Dog alerted them to the fact that Jericho was approaching. Ginny told Dog to be quiet. "Good morning," Jericho.

The old man pulled off his Stetson, and he smiled his toothy smile. "Mornin', ma'am." Then he nodded his greetings to the others.

"We're about to cook breakfast," Ginny said. "You're welcome to join us."

"Already ate, but thank you." He paused a moment and straightened his shoulders. "Matt, those caves are too dangerous for people to be crawling around in. You shouldn't ought to let the boy or anyone else go down there."

Laura glanced from Ginny to Matt and felt a sinking feeling in the pit of her stomach. They obviously respected the old man and his opinions and cared a great deal for him, but she was ready to strangle him for interfering again.

"We're very careful, Jericho, really we are," Jason said.

A muscle twitched under the leathery skin of Jericho's jaw. "Careful's fine, Jason, but that won't stop a cave-in."

"Jericho," Matt said, "Laura and Jason are adults. They know the dangers and are willing to take their chances. As for Austin— I can promise you he won't step another foot down there. Now, how are you doing on the rest of the riddling frames you're making? If you need any help, get the Gillespie boys to give you a hand."

Laura watched the old man stomp off, knowing he wasn't happy with Matt's answer, but there was no bucking the boss when he'd made up his mind. She followed the others into the house, more than a little relieved with her reprieve and the fact that Matt offered to cook breakfast.

As Laura worked her way through hot biscuits, scrambled eggs and a mountain of spicy breakfast sausage, she wondered if she'd ever get any work done that morning. She helped Ginny clean the kitchen, worrying that Austin was going to show up and start a question marathon. Then she felt guilty for her thoughts. She adored Austin, but she was anxious to get to the caves. Finally the kitchen work was completed and she hurried out to the van, where Jason was already waiting.

After cleaning up at Jason's last evening, they'd brought her van back and parked it at the rear of the house under the shade of an oak tree. As she started to dig the keys out of her pocket, she remembered Jason had made fun of her security, telling her no one on the vineyard would dare touch a thing of hers. She opened the cargo doors and crawled in, picking up equipment and handing it to Jason as she moved around.

"Bring some extra batteries," Jason said, remembering the horrible feeling of being thrown into pitch darkness. He touched his jeans pocket, reassuring himself that the penlight was there. Under normal circumstances the tiny light was about as useless as teats on a boar hog, but in a situation like yesterday it could be a lifesaver.

As he stuffed the items she was handing him into the backpack, noting each one, his concern grew. "What are all these plastic Ziploc bags for, and the sketch pad and pencils?" He'd thought they were only going to take a few more photographs, then head for his place. He was so pleased with the way they'd worked together and the progress they'd made, he was eager to get back at it. "What are you planning to do this morning?"

From the corner of her eye, Laura had watched his curiosity being slowly replaced with frustration. She didn't bother to try to alleviate it. He'd find out soon enough.

THE CAVE SEEMED colder, darker and almost foreboding as they made their way to the rock they'd used as a bench and a place for her equipment. Laura held the flashlights while Jason checked the lights of the tripods they'd left set up. She shivered, acutely aware of the cold and the deep shadows at the edge of the light.

"Damn," Jason swore as he rubbed his hands together. "Is it colder in here or is it just my imagination?"

"Feels colder to me." Laura was relieved Jason had noticed, too. She picked up her cardigan and put it on, then pulled out the sketch pad, a couple of pencils and a sharpener.

Jason watched, amused and curious at her seriousness. She was all business today, he thought. "Do you need me to move the lights or hold them?"

Laura folded one of the square rubber pads she'd thought to bring along, placed it on the boulder and sat down. She stared at the wall for a moment before answering. "The lights are fine the way they are, but if you'll get the other light and sit down, I'll tell you where I need it." She watched as he copied her technique of folding the rubber pad before sitting down on it.

Jason sighed. "You've done this before, haven't you."

"Absolutely. You learn very quickly when you're out in the field to improvise and make yourself as cozy as possible. Believe me, spending hours sitting or kneeling on the ground can kill you and your enthusiasm. It helps to be prepared." She set a plastic cup with a top beside her.

His curiosity got the better of him. "What's the cup for?"

"For the pencil shavings. Now, find a comfortable position holding the light and point it on the right half of the wall." She waited while he did so, propping his arms on his legs as he held the light. "That's good. Hold it there and don't move."

When he tried to see what she was doing, it caused him to move, and she snapped, "Keep still." Then she relented. "Move closer to me if you have to watch." She waited until once again he'd settled and the light was right. "The sketch pad is drawn off in grids, and I've divided it into four equal parts. What I'm going to do is locate each picture, each symbol and marking, in their proper place in the section and on the grid. Later I'll take measurements of the wall, then by the photographs, the sketches and the measurements, I'll redraw the entire wall and have an accurate reproduction."

None of it sounded particularly difficult. Jason looked over her shoulder and kept track of her progress; he became as engrossed in watching as she was in working. While she drew, he frequently rechecked the wall and marveled at her eye for detail and her talent. She was a gifted artist, and he wondered what else she was good at.

"You don't think of me as just a pretty face, do you?"

She'd been so engrossed in her work that Jason's voice made her jump and almost ruin her drawing. She glanced at him, then wished she hadn't. He was too close, his gaze too compelling, and she refocused on her work. "You can read—that was a surprise—and you can follow directions and hammer nails." She laughed at the strangled sound he made. "I'd have thought you'd have a gaggle of women happily doing all your work for you like some rich potentate."

"That's unfair. You don't even know me."

She was treading on dangerous ground and decided to lighten up, but her mouth, as usual, overcame her good sense. "True, but I know your kind."

"What kind?"

"Come on, Jason. Don't sound so outraged. You know very well what I'm talking about. I've lived in Austin awhile. I've read the papers. I've heard talk."

"Surely you don't believe everything you read or the gossip you hear, do you?"

She glanced at him, her expression serious but her hazel eyes dancing with laughter. "Yes." Then she calmly returned her attention to her drawing.

She'd left him speechless and with his mouth hanging open, and not for the first time. He stared at her profile and something inside him clicked, a feeling of déjà vu. But that couldn't be. Yet why did the odd feeling persist? "Have we met before?" When she didn't answer and refused to even look at him, he said, "We have, haven't we? When? Where?"

Her heart had stopped beating and she couldn't breathe, as if she'd just been punched in the stomach. She couldn't move, and it was a good thing or she would have given herself away. When her heart finally kicked in again she was sure he could hear it banging against her chest.

Act natural, she warned herself. Over the years, she'd become convinced that Jason was just another one of those handsome, charming men who preyed on women for physical gratification. She'd been fooling herself as a way to protect her self-esteem. Jason was as sharp as a razor's edge, and if she was to keep her secret, she was going to have to stop playing games with him. "We've never met before you tripped me the other morning."

"Maybe I saw you with my nephew. Were you around when I picked him up or something?"

It was an out and she jumped at it. "That could be. I'm good friends with the dean and his family, and I've been there a lot lately since I've met Austin. Would you move your light over to the left a fraction?"

He could tell by the way she pointedly went back to work that his questions weren't going to be received with any sort of civility. He had to be satisfied with what he had, but there was still a kernel of doubt that planted itself in the back of his mind. He knew it would worry him like a pebble in a shoe.

She could feel his gaze on her. He was so close her arm grazed his, and sometimes, when he was hovering over her shoulder, his breath tickled her ear. Her heart was beating fast again, and it had nothing to do with fear of exposure. This closeness was harder than she'd thought it would be. If she inhaled deeply, she could catch the faint scent of his after-shave. His body seemed to radiate heat, and she felt that heat against her side.

As hard as she tried to fight it, she had to admit she wanted him—bad—and if she didn't put some distance between them, she wasn't going to be able to hide her feelings. Her treacherous thoughts caused her fingers to tremble, making the pencil wobble noticeably. She set aside the sketch pad, stood and stretched. "Hand me my pack, will you? I'm going to take some scrapings."

"Can the paintings be dated by the paints?"

"Yes. But it'll be difficult. There are paintings over paintings. This cave has been used by different tribes over a long period of time."

"What tribes?"

"With some of these drawings, I'd say Kiowa, Comanche, maybe Cheyenne and perhaps even very early Apache."

"Those are plains Indians. Nomads."

He surprised her, and she paused. "Right, but if this cave has been here as long as I think it has, it must have become a sort of religious shrine to them. Their medicine men would have brought offerings."

"Sacrificed virgins? Or cut out hearts?"

"No." She laughed. "That was the Mayans and Aztecs."

Jason followed her like a faithful puppy, helping where he could, balancing the light and a box of small Ziploc bags. He liked to watch her work, the way her long fingers caressed the limestone wall without really touching it. The graceful way she handled the scalpel and tweezers, meticulously took each scraping or specimen, placed it in a bag and labeled it. His vivid imagination was working overtime; he could almost feel her hands on him.

"Jason."

He started as if she'd read his mind. "What?" He was still by the wall, frozen in place by his thoughts, when he realized Laura had already moved back to where her gear was. She was replacing the sketch pad and supplies. "Are we through?" he asked.

"No. But I'm tired and cold and need to move around." She'd sensed a subtle shift in the atmosphere while Jason had been staring at her. She might want him, but wanting and dreaming were a far cry from actually doing anything about it. She couldn't afford to get involved with Jason, not again.

Laura kept her gaze on what she was doing and dug out a camera. "I want to get those pictures of the back of the cave."

He wasn't eager to have a repeat of yesterday and touched his pocket, making sure the penlight hadn't worked its way out. "Let me go first." He used the spotlight, illuminating a path, then, just before he stopped, he asked, "Sounding?"

"A foot behind you. Why are you stopping?" They were just about beyond the lights that shone on the wall paintings, and the shadows were beginning to close in on them, the inky darkness threatening.

"Look up," Jason said.

She followed his gaze and gasped. Her pulse raced. The ceiling of the cave made a dramatic incline and the light barely illuminated the top. What shocked her was that, there, the limestone was black, not the white she'd expected. "Watch where you put your big feet," she said.

Jason spun around. "Why? What are you talking about?"

"The ceiling, Jason. It's stained with soot from years of smoke and fires."

"Is that good or bad?"

She would have expressed impatience, but told herself he wasn't an archaeologist and had no idea of the significance. "It's good. Interesting. The area was probably used as either a meeting place or to hold religious ceremonies. So, just watch where you put your feet, because there might be remnants of the fires around."

Jason adjusted the light so he could get a wider area of illumination. Suddenly, echoing from the dimness behind them came a noise like a gunshot. They both jumped and Laura screamed. Jason grabbed her arm. "Be still."

"What was that?" Laura looked behind her and the noise came again. Now their only light was the one Jason was holding. "What happened, Jason?"

"I'd say your spotlights overheated and blew." But he had a feeling he was wrong.

"That's not possible." She edged closer to Jason's side. "Those are special lights, Jason. They don't overheat."

"Okay, they shorted out, then."

"They're not supposed to do that, either." When he grumbled in disbelief, she said, "They were designed for NASA and space travel. They do what they're supposed to—millions of dollars were spent on their development. They—"

"Why are you so nervous?" It puzzled him because he didn't think she was the type to scare easily.

"I am, aren't I." She was as surprised as he was. "I don't know. Maybe the excessive cold this morning."

Jason started off toward the back again, dodging the fallen rocks from previous cave-ins. "That's explainable—I think. These caves have been carved out above an aquifer. That water is frigid, and after it rains the level of the aquifer rises, bringing the cold water up toward the cave floor." He was about to halt his steps, then remembered and said, "Give me a sounding?"

"About two inches off your heels, so don't make any fast moves."

"I'm stopping." He waited a second, then turned. She was very close, and he was touched by the trust she put in him—or maybe it was just that she didn't want to be too far from the source of the only light in the cave. "Once when I was a kid and explored these caves, I found a small waterfall and deep pool way toward the back."

"Can we get there?" She was excited. Where there was water, such as a pool, there would be bones, maybe of just small rodents but possibly larger animals, even human remains.

"No. Jericho told me that portion of the cave was destroyed years ago."

"He's been down here?"

"Sure. He's probably the only person on the place besides Matt who knows these caves."

"But he doesn't want me down here?"

"He doesn't want *anyone* down here, Laura. They're—"

"I know, dangerous." She could see she wasn't going to win any arguments here and decided she needed to make friends with the old man and pick his brain about what he'd seen over the years. Suddenly she shivered. "Let's not stand around. At least when I'm moving I'm not so cold."

Jason started off again, keeping most of the wide beam of light trained on the area in front of them. He figured they had to be close to the back wall— Suddenly he stopped, as if his feet had frozen to the ground.

He stumbled when she shoved him in the center of the back. "Don't do that, Jason!"

The noise came again and he cocked his head, trying to figure out what direction it came from.

"Dammit, don't pull your perverse sense of humor in here," she said. When he didn't answer, she noticed how stiffly he held himself, and her next words clogged her throat. She listened to the sound as it came again. A low moan almost like a whisper echoed softly around the cave. An icy chill slithered over every inch of her skin, making her scalp tighten and tingle. Her sudden fear almost choked her. It had to be her imagination, but she could have sworn over the moaning she heard rhythmic thumps, like the pounding of drums.

"Jason, you hear it, too, don't you?" She knew very well he did by the way his arm muscle she was squeezing for dear life tightened to rock hardness.

Jason swallowed. "Yeah. I hear. What the hell is it?"

"Has it gotten colder, too?"

He nodded, then motioned her to be quiet so he could hear better. He didn't believe in ghosts and things that go bump in the night. There had to be an explanation. Suddenly he relaxed.

"I think we ought to leave, Jason. There are some things you just can't explain. I've come across them before on digs."

"Remember it rained last night," he said. "It has to be water moving through the ground that's making the moaning sounds."

"Fine. What about the drums?"

Jason laughed, wrapped his arm around her shoulders and hugged her close to his side. "Probably a cave-in deep underground. The sounds echo upward. You don't want to give up documenting the cave just because of a few weird noises, do you?"

"Of course not. But sometimes it's best to back off for a while." She sensed he was fighting to keep from smiling. "I'm not an alarmist and I don't jump at my own shadow. But I've seen and heard things before at some of the old pueblos in New Mexico and at the Anasazi cliff dwellings in Arizona. Believe me, it's best just to let things settle down a bit."

"Fine, we'll get your things together and leave." He glanced at his watch. "And if we hurry we can just make it in time for lunch." He immediately brightened. "Then we can get an early start at my place."

As they headed back to the front of the cave, Laura knew Jason thought she was being silly. She couldn't explain her feelings, but there was something in the cave that wasn't right. The tranquillity she'd felt earlier had been disturbed by some force, and it wasn't them. She was trying to figure out why nothing had happened to alert them to a presence the day before when it suddenly hit her what he'd just said about getting an early start.

"I'm not your personal fetch and carry. Don't get used to taking up all my time." They'd reached the rock where her equipment was. "You hear me, Jason? I have lots of work to do outside the cave visits."

"I understand perfectly. Tell me something, Laura. Have you told anyone at the university of your find here?"

"No."

"Do you plan to?"

"Maybe." The bastard. He was going to try to blackmail her. She released the lights from the tripods—and realized they *had* blown out—then stuffed them into her backpack and snatched the third light from Jason's hand. "Professor Williams is out of the country, and the rest of the staff is scattered around digs in Montana."

"You could send a telegram. I have to go into town sometime today. Would you like me to do it for you?" Before he could finish the sentence he found himself alone in the dark. She'd already started to head out of the cave. He should have known better, he grumbled to himself as he pulled the penlight from his pocket. He stumbled a couple of times and almost fell. He missed the opening of the cave entrance and was searching along one wall when a light almost blinded him. "You play hardball, Laura."

"I'm sorry. I didn't mean to leave you in the dark."

"Sure you did." He lightly brushed an errant curl from her forehead.

"Stay out of my business, Jason." Her tone was pleasant, but there was an edge to it that made his eyebrows arch. "Listen. No matter how liberal the university is, archaeology is still basically a man's field. At least, men feel superior. You really know nothing about me or what I've had to endure to get where I am."

"Has the 'old boy' network been giving you trouble?"

Laura smiled. "You know, I thought cracking that boy's club was tough, but coming up against your Southern good old boys has been the most difficult, most maddening thing I've ever encountered before."

He knew exactly what she was talking about; he'd seen it too many times, even in this so-called enlightened age of equality. "I'm sorry I gave you a hard time, but I was just teasing."

"And pigs fly. You were going to try to negotiate a few new chores to our deal."

Jason took the light from her hand and led the way out of the cave. They were halfway to the wine cellar when something she'd said came back to him. He abruptly stopped—but forgot to call for a sounding. Reflex made him brace himself, then he grunted when she slammed into his back.

"Jason."

"I know. Jeez, I'm not going to have any heels left if I keep this up." He carefully turned around and shone the light so he could see her face. "Where are you from originally?"

There was no way she could lie her way out of this one, but the half-truth would do. "From Maine."

Jason wondered why she was playing games and shook his head. "Maybe you were born there, but it's been a long time since you've lived there." He was delighted by her scowl and the fact that she obviously wasn't going to give him any more answers. Hell, he dearly loved a mystery and decided to let the questioning go. For now.

CHAPTER SEVEN

THE SKY WAS CLOUDLESS and the sun hot, making the air intensely fragrant with the sweetness of honeysuckle and jasmine. Laura and Jason immediately began pulling off their outer clothing and dusting themselves off. They quickly headed for her van to deposit her equipment.

Jason again marveled at the interior of the old camper van, where every piece of equipment seemed to have a special place of its own. "Who fixed this up for you?"

"I designed and did it myself."

He should have known without asking. It had her talent for detail. When he spotted several sizes of fan belts hanging from a hook, he said, "Are you a mechanic, too?"

Laura was in the process of crawling out, but she paused, expecting the usual male-style ridicule. A sarcastic remark was on the tip of her tongue when she glanced at him and realized he was not only sincere, but genuinely impressed and interested. She sat down and crossed her legs while he leaned against one of the doors. "These old vehicles are a lot easier to take care of than the newer ones. No computers or high-tech thingamajigs that only a rocket scientist or a high-priced auto mechanic can fix. I can take this engine apart and put it back together again myself." She waited for a contemptuous remark or a disdainful look, and when there was none, she reminded herself that

Jason wasn't like most men. Though that realization didn't help her any, it made her heart beat faster.

"I see. Easy repair and upkeep lets you go just about anywhere worry free."

She caught his amused smile and knew she'd been staring, admiring his good looks. She quickly climbed out, shut the doors and sniffed the air. "Do I smell food?"

"You bet, and if we don't hurry, there won't be any left. Those guys are like a bunch of animals around the feed trough."

They headed for the long building with the screened-in area she'd noticed before. As they drew closer she could hear men's voices, and the smell of food was much stronger. Her stomach growled loudly as she dusted herself off more thoroughly this time before she climbed the stone steps.

Jason laughed and grabbed her arm. She was like Dog following the scent of food. "Let's wash up," he said, and pointed to the outdoor sinks.

When they entered the cook house, her concentration was more on the food piled on the table than on the occupants of the room. She was only vaguely aware of Jason making introductions, the sounds of chairs scraping backward as the men stood politely. She acknowledged the three men, Roberto, Dan and Gomez, plus Jericho who was at one end of the table, opposite Matt. Then she smiled at the two Gillespie boys, who refused to look up, and again at the others as they quickly gave nods of greeting. Laura motioned for them to sit down and continue eating just as Austin came barreling out of the kitchen with a cart loaded with more food.

Austin skidded to a stop and grinned. "Hey, Laura. Hungry?"

Jason answered for her. "I tell you, Einstein, she got one whiff of that food and I thought I was going to have to hogtie her to make her wash her face and hands first."

Ginny stuck her head through the swinging doors and called to Laura, "Why don't you come join me?"

Laura wasn't easily intimidated by men, but all those male eyes and hungry expressions courteously waiting for her to make up her mind so they could get back to their food sent her scurrying for the kitchen. When the doors swung shut behind her, she sighed loudly. She was surprised at the utilitarian, stainless-steel kitchen, more like a commercial kitchen than what she'd expected. Ginny was standing barefoot in front of a big stove, stirring a steaming pot. Laura stared at her. "I thought Matt said you were supposed to rest in the afternoons."

Ginny laughed, replaced the lid on the pot, then struggled into her shoes before she sat down at the table. "You're kidding. I rest after the noon meal's on the table." She motioned the small Mexican woman over. "Lupe is Roberto's wife. She's deaf and doesn't speak, but she reads lips, and with Austin teaching me to sign a little we get by." She signed what she'd said and introduced Lupe to Laura.

Lupe offered Laura an empty plate, smiled and waved her hand around the kitchen.

Laura didn't have to be asked twice, and she filled her plate with crispy fried chicken, hot biscuits, mashed potatoes and green beans. She balanced her green salad on top of her glass of iced tea and returned to the table. Ginny laughed when she saw Laura's plate.

"Well, I'm hungry," Laura said. "I think it's the cold in the caves that saps the energy. I noticed Jason eyeing the food like a hungry dog, too."

Austin lunged through the doors, stopping long enough to blow his nose and pitch the tissue in the trash before he picked up an empty plate. "Since Laura's here to keep you company, Ginny, I'm going to eat with the men. That okay?"

Ginny looked crestfallen. "You mean I'm to be denied your bitching and griping for a while?"

"Oh, Ginny, I'm sorry. Have I been that bad?"

"Like a bear with a sore foot. No, go on. Go bother someone else. I'll just sit here and eat surrounded by women for a change. Go on. Leave the one who takes care of you and makes you chicken noodle soup when you're sick."

Austin's dark eyes narrowed, making him look so much like Matt when he was trying to figure her out that a lump came to Ginny's throat.

"You're overacting again, Ginny," said Austin. "I keep telling you, don't pile it on too thick at one time. Spread it around. Make it last."

Laura burst out laughing when Austin disappeared. "He's something, isn't he?"

"Yeah. It's scary how quickly the young bounce back. Last night he thought he was dying. Today he just has a runny nose and an appetite to equal those men out there." Ginny glanced at Laura. "How was the trip to the caves? We haven't had much time to talk about them. Or you."

Laura was savoring the chicken and could only nod.

"Don't bother," Ginny said. "I'm used to coming in second to food."

Laura swallowed and took a sip of her iced tea. "This chicken is so good. I've never been able to get mine to come out so crispy. I guess it's a family secret."

"A deep, dark one," Ginny teased. "What are your plans for tomorrow?"

Laura shrugged. "The same as today. Why?"

"I'm not supposed to drive anymore and I have something I want to do. Would you like to go to Fredericksburg with me and do a little shopping? I'll treat you to lunch at a wonderful German restaurant."

Laura savored the bite of hot biscuit she'd just taken, letting it melt in her mouth. "I'd love to go. But I'll tell you, I don't think any restaurant could outdo you in the cooking department."

"I agree," Matt said from the doorway.

He had such a quiet way about him, it unnerved her. Laura watched as he placed his plate on the counter and pulled a chair out, turning it around and sitting down with his arms crossed over the back. His dark eyes were directed at her, and she met his gaze.

"Jason behaving himself?" He surprised himself by asking, but there was something so young about Laura and the fact that Ginny was worried.

Laura kept a straight face and said, "Depends on what you consider behaving in Jason's case."

Matt chuckled and nodded. Unlike Ginny, he didn't think Laura was a pushover. She probably gave as good as she got. Jason might be in for a surprise. Matt stood up, replaced the chair and kissed Ginny on the cheek. "Go rest. Lupe will take care of everything." He was about to leave when he paused and asked Laura, "Are you taking Ginny shopping tomorrow?"

Laura smiled and said, "You bet."

"Thanks. If you hadn't agreed, I'd have had to go." Matt recognized the gleam in Laura's eyes. His wife's eyes looked the same way at the mere mention of shopping. He groaned. "Don't tell me. You love to shop, too?"

"Yes." She watched the way Ginny and Matt traded glances, the way they smiled and how their eyes seemed to devour each other. They had their own special language, one for which no words were needed.

"I hope you're prepared. My wife can walk the skin off Dog's paws on one of her sprees."

As soon as he left, Laura and Ginny grinned at each other, pleased to discover they had something in common. "Do you like antiques?" Ginny asked hopefully.

"Absolutely. I heard Fredericksburg has a couple of places that sell antique Indian jewelry."

"I know the exact shops." Ginny shivered in anticipation, then rubbed her hands together. "We'll go as soon as you get through in the caves."

Laura explained about her spotlights. "Until I get bulb replacements we can't work. But if you don't mind leaving early we can drive into Austin. I'll pick up some extras, then by the time we get to Fredericksburg the stores will be just opening."

"Yes, yes, yes!" Ginny almost did a dance of joy, then stopped. "You won't mind Dog coming along, will you? I can't leave him behind."

Dog heard his name from the back-porch step and raised his ugly head.

Laura thought that he knew what was being arranged and was suddenly on his best behavior. His tail thumped loudly against the cement, his ears stood up at attention, and his usual toothy grin was wider than usual. She'd have sworn there was almost a pleading look in those spooky light blue eyes.

Ginny sensed Laura's uncertainty. "He's really well behaved."

Still staring at the animal, Laura said, "Sure, but don't you think he needs a bath?"

"Austin!" Ginny yelled, then laughed as Dog snarled, slunk down the porch steps and disappeared.

JASON WAS EAGER to finish putting up the Sheetrock in the kitchen and drove Laura with the efficiency of a slave driver with a whip in hand. Except Jason's way was more persuasive. He used charm. He made her laugh. Most of all it was his teasing and his enthusiasm for what he was doing that kept her following his every request.

As she moved around the walls with him, helping either to hold up or hammer in the drywall slabs, he explained in detail his ideas for finishing the kitchen. He even asked for her opinions and seemed pleased with some of her suggestions.

It was all wonderful and fun, but she had to get away from Jason or go crazy. For heaven's sake, she told herself, she was only human, and what was happening to her was as natural as breathing. She just wished she could breathe normally and not heat up the Sheetrock to the melting point.

To make things worse, she had a feeling Jason was beginning to feel the strain, too. She could tell by the way he started to move just a little too slowly and the way he lingered a little too close. Of course, the position she was in, had been in for the past thirty minutes, wasn't helping, either. She stood with her legs wide apart, her arms spread-eagled and her nose almost touching the wall as she held another panel of Sheetrock in place.

Jason was positioned directly behind her, his body touching hers, sometimes pressing against hers as he put the screws in the panel she was holding. She felt vulnerable, exposed. It was so bad at times when he touched her, she imagined herself naked, not in the cropped T-shirt and cutoffs; then she would imagine Jason naked, too. Fantasies were dangerous things. She closed her eyes as he strained against her once more so he could line up the nails along the top edge.

His bare chest covered her back, then as he stretched upward his entire body seemed to engulf hers, making her head reel with the most intimate thoughts. Her breath caught in her throat. She closed her eyes, rested her forehead against the wall and counted the seconds until he was finished. But he wasn't moving very fast, seemed to be taking an ungodly amount of time. It was a physical effort to keep from sighing out loud when she thought he was about to move.

She expected him to step away, prayed he would do it quickly, and almost jumped out of her skin when his hands grasped her shoulders. Slowly he turned her around. She wanted to avoid his gaze, afraid of what he might see, afraid she couldn't hide her feelings any longer. She was embarrassed, knowing her emotions were as exposed as her raw nerves. But as she twisted her head away, Jason touched her chin, tipped her head up and stared at her. His words surprised her.

"You're driving me crazy and I can't stand it any longer." He lowered his head and whispered against her mouth. "I'm going to kiss you, Laura. No matter what you want, I've got to kiss you, so don't hit me until afterward, all right?"

His eyes were dark, full of passion, and she wouldn't have stopped him for all the money in the world. She watched, tantalized, wanting, as his mouth lowered slowly, as if he was testing the waters first. When his lips touched hers, she opened to him, sensing the controlled gentleness behind his kiss.

"Dammit, Laura," Jason murmured against her mouth, "why do you have to be so sweet?"

A gulp was the only answer she could manage before his mouth claimed hers once more. The gentleness was gone, and passion stirred too strongly between them to be ignored. Laura slid her hands up along the smooth, warm skin of his arms, grasped his shoulders and pulled his body as close as she could. But it wasn't close enough and he must have felt the same.

Jason untangled his fingers from Laura's hair, ran his hands up and down her arms before breaking her hold on him. Then he intertwined their fingers, spread her arms against the wall high above her head and pressed his body into hers, gently moving his hips against hers. She was all soft flesh, yielding and wanting. His lips wandered down her neck and he could feel the way her heart was racing.

There wasn't a doubt in his mind that he could take her right then and there, but Laura wasn't his usual type of woman and he couldn't treat her like one. He realized the more he kept telling himself she wasn't his type, the more he wanted her. The more he wanted her, the crazier she made him.

Her passion was like a heat wave rolling through her, taking her on a staggering ride of sensations. When Jason shifted his weight and lowered their arms, she thought he was going to pull away completely. He surprised her by swinging her up into his arms and beginning to walk toward the stairs. She rested her head against his shoulder, thinking she should stop him. Stop herself before it all got out of hand.

There was an urgency in him, pushing him, making him forget any attempt at logical reasoning. He didn't even pause at the bottom of the stairs. He wasn't about to give her a second to think of anything but him, and least of all, time to consider stopping.

He had to pause at the top of the stairs to catch his breath, which gave him a moment to glance around. His rapidly beating heart sunk to his toes. The place was a disaster area. Besides all the unfinished surfaces, the exposed wiring, plumbing and air-conditioning tubing there were clothes slung over every available space and a couple of towels scattered across the floor. The bed was unmade, and though he was thankful for the clean sheets, the bedspread lay crumpled on the floor at the foot. It was a monumental mess and Laura deserved better.

He glanced down at her in his arms and caught her smile. "You deserve satin sheets..."

"You'd bump into me and we'd slide off." She couldn't believe it. He was having second thoughts. Dear God, she wondered if this was going to be a repeat of that night eight years ago. Or would he remember and be totally disgusted?

He loved her sharp tongue and kissed her deeply in appreciation, then lowered her feet to the floor. But he didn't let go, just held her closer and walked her backward until he could lower her onto his bed. Then his hand, which had slipped under her T-shirt, cupped her breast.

She watched him, the way he slowly pulled her top up over her breasts, the way his gaze lingered on her before he lowered his head, taking first one nipple, then the other in his mouth. She couldn't stop her guttural moan or the way her back arched. And when he yanked the top over her head, she wrapped her arms around him, loving the warmth of his skin touching her.

This time it was Jason who moaned as she rubbed her breast against his chest like a lazy cat. But there was nothing lazy about the sensation of nipples rubbing against nipples; more like a surge of electricity rushing through him, and it was his turn to catch his breath. Then her lips were moving on him, along his neck, down across his chest, lingering on each hardened nipple. She was a strange mixture of shyness and boldness, and as her hand moved below his waist and grasped him firmly through his jeans, he was shocked to realize that he'd almost lost control.

His kisses deepened, becoming more passionate, and she savored every touch, every sensation. He lifted her up on her knees, facing him. His arms went around her and his hands began to caress her back, then slid slowly downward, slipped under the waistband of her cutoffs and under her panties as he cupped her hips and pulled her against him, making her aware of the hardness between them.

He'd always given his women a way out. Plenty of time to change their minds—after all, that was their prerogative, their right. But not this time. He wanted Laura so much he could barely think straight. He kissed her again to keep her from saying anything.

Laura thought she was going crazy. If he didn't stop touching her and kissing her, if he didn't enter her soon, she was going to scream in frustration. Still facing each other on their knees, she slid her hand between them and unfastened the top button of his jeans, then slowly, carefully, drew the zipper down.

Jason chuckled against her mouth and whispered, "Thank you." What he would have said next was cut off as her fingers wrapped around him. His weight shifted and they fell sideways on the bed. He yanked at the zipper of her cutoffs and slipped his hand between her legs.

"Stop. Jason, stop. You're driving me nuts." He kept pushing at her loosened cutoffs with his free hand, and when they were finally down around her knees, she managed to kick them across the room.

"Good," he said. "That's what I'm supposed to do."

She sucked in a deep breath and tensed, feeling a flush of heat travel all over her. When she could breathe again, she started trying to strip off his jeans, but they resisted her efforts. "Dammit, you wear them too tight. Help me."

He loved it. She was so hot for him he couldn't get his clothes off fast enough, and when he finally slung them away and reached for her, she slipped into his arms. She felt good there, like she belonged.

Jason rolled Laura over on her back, gazed into her eyes, kissed her eyelids, her cheeks, then nibbled at her earlobes. "Laura," he whispered, "are you on any type of birth control?" He didn't give the question time to shock her out of her sexual contentment but kept working slowly downward, feasting on the softness of her neck and shoulders before his mouth moved on to savor a rosy nipple.

It took a second for her to realize that he'd asked her a question and a moment more to figure out what it was. As his mouth moved from one breast to the other, she said no on a sigh of pleasure.

Jason worked back up the other side of her neck and nibbled at the other earlobe. "Don't worry, I'll take care of everything."

The sensual fog lifted for a moment, and she would have questioned him further, but soon Jason was kissing her again and she felt drugged with the very scent and feel of him. There was an urgency in her hands as she touched him, moving closer to him as if she wanted to get inside his skin. When he spread her legs and entered her slowly, she threaded her fingers through his hair and gazed up at him. His face was a study of control, his eyes dark, the lids narrowed.

She tried to master her own hunger, but for eight years she'd dreamed of this moment, and the realization that it was really happening tipped her over the edge. She thrust her hips forward, taking him deep inside her. They both froze a second as if each was afraid to move.

"Devil." Jason chuckled on a resonant growl, then he smiled and began to move inside her, watching the way her face softened and her eyes melted closed. He quickened the pace, catching the sudden tension in her peaceful expression. His thrust became deeper, longer, slower, then he sped up the pace. Just before he thought her fingernails would break the skin on his back, he gave one strong thrust and felt her body shudder beneath him. He was surprised and moved to hear her call his name. Then all thought fled and the only thing he was aware of was the urgency and need for release within his own body.

Laura aroused herself from the lingering remnant of pleasure long enough to hold Jason tightly and move her hips to the rhythm he set. Then, as he found his release and collapsed in her arms, she was shocked to feel the heat of her own climax. It crashed within her like a tidal wave until she felt as if she were shattering into a million pieces.

He would have said something—teased her, made her laugh—so there wouldn't be any awkwardness. It was part of his usual routine with women; make them comfortable, at ease, and they'd come back for more. But he could barely breathe much less talk or be a comedian when his mind was a blank. Then he realized what his problem was. There was nothing amusing about what had just happened.

His heart started hammering wildly and he rolled off Laura, taking her with him in his arms. He was stunned in more ways than one and needed time to think. Burying his face in the curve of her neck, he wriggled closer, shaping his body to hers as he held her, then as added security he cupped one breast.

He knew he couldn't let the silence go on between them. It was like a death sentence, like building a wall. He racked his brain for something special to say. But nothing came. When Laura started to move as if to slip out of his hold, he refused to let her go and tightened his hold. "Please don't leave me yet."

"Jason."

"Shh," he whispered in her ear. "Don't say anything. Just let me hold you for a while." He felt her relax and snuggle closer. He needed time to clear his thoughts. Make a plan. Figure out what was going on in his head. He only knew he didn't want to let go of her yet.

Reality was a cruel wake-up call, like a dash of cold water in the face, and Laura was fully awake. Well, she thought, forcing herself to go limp in his arms, she'd really done it this time. Her dreams had come true. Now all she had to do was get up and walk away. She'd always thought that if she ever had a chance to make her fantasies real, if she ever actually made love to Jason, then the shame and humiliation of eight years ago would vanish. Obviously it didn't work that way.

Now there was a brand-new hatchet hanging over her head. She couldn't stand it if, after actually making love, Jason remembered who she was. The image of what he would say or the look of distaste he'd direct at her—worse still, his weird sense of humor and his amusement—would kill her. After a moment she tried to bolster her flagging thoughts. If after all the time she'd spent with Jason, and now in his bed, he hadn't had the least twinge of a memory, what were the chances of that long-ago night coming back to him?

The question was in itself a conclusion, one she clung to. She'd done some stupid things in her life, but staying in Two Rivers the minute she saw Jason was the most foolish. Then she remembered just why she'd come. No one was going to stand in her way over the cave paintings. They meant too much to her. But the milk, so to speak, was spilled, and she'd better make the best of her situation.

Laura became aware of her position, the warm, naked body cuddled behind her and the hand firmly holding one of her breasts as if it might fly away. She'd certainly made the best of this situation, she thought, then tried not to laugh. Damn, but his reputation did precede him. He was good. An expert, a clever and thrilling lover. She couldn't remember ever feeling quite the way he'd made her feel.

"Are you asleep?" Jason whispered.

"No. I thought you were."

"Never. I was thinking about how beautiful and incredible you are." He felt the sudden tension in her.

Laura rolled over to face him, then propped herself up on her elbow. "You don't have to flatter me or make pretty speeches like you probably do with your other women." She sat up, unconcerned about the way his eyes roamed over her body. When he started to say something, she placed her hand over his mouth. "You don't have to make me feel comfortable with what happened. Hey!" she said with a chuckle. "I'm a grown woman. These things just happen sometimes, don't they?" She removed her hand and quickly slipped out of bed. "You're very good at what you do, Jason."

"Do. Do?" Jason couldn't figure out what was going on. He felt used. Taken advantage of. "Dammit, I don't do this as a profession, you know."

She searched for each item of clothing and hurriedly began to dress. "Well, if you ever need money, maybe you should consider it."

"What the hell's going on here?" He jumped out of bed and tried to catch her arm as she moved around the room. "Laura, I was not treating you like my women. It's not like that. I didn't ... I mean—"

They were both surprised into silence when the telephone rang.

"You better answer that," she said as she tied her running shoes.

"Screw the phone."

There was a loud click as the answering machine picked up, and when a throaty female voice called Jason's name, all he could do was close his eyes and wonder what else could go wrong.

Laura listened and watched him. If he only knew how tempting he was, standing in front of her, naked, the most surprised and guilty expression on his face. She bit her lip to keep from laughing.

"Jason, sweetheart. This is Pat. The photo session has been called off, so I can meet you earlier than we planned. Say around seven? If you can't make that, give me a call. See you then. Bye."

It looked bad. He could tell by the way Laura was gazing at him.

"I won't hold it against you for being the way you are, Jason. What happened here was great. It was spontaneous and sexy and I hope it happens again sometime." She was on her way down the stairs when she paused and glanced over her shoulder, getting another eyeful of him. "I'm going to go spend some time with Austin." She gave him a wave. "See you later." And was gone. She couldn't refrain from slamming the front door as hard as she could.

Jason stood at the top of the stairs, watching as sawdust and dust fell like a light snow from the rafters. He smiled. He knew women all right, and a slammed door was a pretty good barometer of their mood. She wasn't quite as composed and unfeeling as she wanted him to believe. His smile grew and his eyes began to sparkle.

CHAPTER EIGHT

THE LONG WALK back to the vineyard gave her time to think and compose herself. In all her efforts to be clever and act nonchalant about what had happened, she'd forgotten one thing. The totally unreasonable hurt she'd felt when he'd made love to her knowing he was seeing another woman in a few hours.

Laura swallowed around the baseball-size lump in her throat and squared her shoulders. She had enough problems without adding jealousy to the list, but she couldn't help wondering what Pat looked like, nor could she stop the thought that he might make love to her, too.

This wasn't getting her anywhere, she decided, and stomped up the vineyard's long drive. She was so deeply mired in her own thoughts that she didn't see Dog coming at her until he was almost upon her. When she did spot him, she halted. Instead of the black-and-brown shaggy coat, he was sporting swirls of fluffy white suds. A particularly large dollop sat between his ears like a crown. He looked so comical she started to laugh.

Dog obviously didn't see the humor in his appearance, and before she knew it he bounded up to her and began to shake vigorously. Laura covered her face, laughing harder, trying to make him quit. "Stop it, you mutt. No!" He either didn't know what the word *no* meant or was the most ornery animal she'd ever met. By the time he did stop she was thoroughly soaked. She looked at herself, then gazed at Dog and found him smiling his weird smile, but this time it seemed wider than usual and his tail cut the air like an out-of-control windshield wiper.

"You think that's funny, don't you."

Dog barked and took off running in the direction he'd come from. She followed him around the side of the cook house and halted. Ginny and Austin were both in the same condition. Fluffy globs of soap were stuck to their bodies, and their clothes were soaked. Dog sat between them, his tongue hanging out the side of his mouth, his tail pounding the ground.

Ginny glanced up, spotted Laura and the suds running down her legs and arms. She struggled to keep from laughing.

Austin followed his stepmother's gaze. He wasn't as polite. "Got you, too, huh?" He glared at Dog. "You are a bad dog." Dog threw back his head and howled as if at a full moon. Then he walked over to Austin, who was holding the hose, and sat like a well-trained pet to be rinsed off. Austin didn't take any chances and quickly finished his chore.

"As soon as he's finished," Ginny said, "we can wash off." She pointed to a couple of lawn chairs under the oak tree. "Come on. I've chased that mutt enough." Then she gave Dog an affectionate glance and shook her head. "Believe it or not, he actually likes baths. He just has to be macho, like the rest of the males on this place. Isn't that right, Jericho?"

"He's a real devil, Miss Ginny."

Laura hadn't seen the old man, and she watched with amusement as he stood and helped Ginny to sit down, then pulled out the footrest of the lawn chair.

"How you coming along in the caves, Miss Laura?"

"Slow." She knew that Jason hadn't told them about this morning's adventure, and she wasn't sure she wanted anyone to know, especially Austin. "The lighting and the cold are problems."

Jericho adjusted his Stetson a little lower on his forehead and settled back in his chair. "It's a dangerous place. Shouldn't be in there, no matter how important. Those old paintings don't mean nothing against a person's life and limb."

"Jericho," Austin said as he worked at rinsing Dog, "the paintings are history, a legacy of a people long dead. They might tell us something about those people."

"Ain't nothing to tell. They lived hard and died hard, like the rest of us. Maybe they didn't have all the conveniences we have, but for their time they had all they needed—food, shelter, fire, family and friends. Don't make no sense to endanger lives over those folks gone to their maker." He stood up in slow degrees and glanced at Ginny. "You going to come talk to Ernestine and Ernie?"

"In a minute." They watched Jericho leave, and when he was out of earshot, Ginny said, "Don't pay any attention to what he says."

"Well, he's right about endangering lives for the sake of learning about the dead. But I'm very careful down there. And—"

"You know what you're doing," Ginny finished for her. "I believe it. What's more, so does Matt, or you'd be out of there before you could blink."

Laura didn't want to linger on the subject of the cave and possibly have to end up answering questions or, worse, lying. "Who's Ernestine?" She thought she'd met everyone at the vineyard.

"A beautiful quarter horse that use to jog with me and Dog in the mornings."

Laura knew that Ginny and her animals seemed to have a kind of unearthly bond. "And Ernie?" she asked.

"He's her colt. Matt and I watched him being born."

"I see," Laura said.

Ginny's expression turned dreamy for a second, then she shivered, smiled and said, "Jason never stops this early. How'd you get out of working for the day?"

Laura wanted desperately to share her problems with Ginny but thought better of it. For too many years she'd kept to herself about her family and her feelings, and she didn't have the courage to open up now. "I told him I wanted to spend some time with Austin."

"Take cover," Austin yelled, and turned his back as Dog started shaking the water off his coat. They watched for a while, amused as Dog ran around them in circles, stopping every now and then by one of them to shake again. When he was dry, they all headed for the house to clean up.

LAURA WAS SURPRISED at how fast the afternoon passed—and with very few thoughts of Jason. Austin kept her busy as they spent most of the time on the floor of the spacious family room working on her photographs of the cave. Ginny rested on the sofa, her feet propped up, reading through a stack of legal papers from her Two Rivers clients.

"Do you have a law office in town, Ginny?"

Ginny looked at Laura over the tops of her granny glasses. "I took over Parnel Hoffmann-Bonn's law practice about six months ago."

"Parnel was the town drunk," Austin said. At Ginny's censorious frown, he added, "Well, he was, but he couldn't help it and everyone liked him. Hey, we need to take Laura to town and introduce her to Charlie. He makes kaleidoscopes, and his brother, Byron, makes dulcimers. They're neat. Byron taught me to play the dulcimer.'' He caught Ginny's eye again, laughed and amended his statement. ''He's *trying* to teach me. I'm not very good yet. Dad says my talent wavers between a squealing pig and a dying chicken. But man, can he and Uncle Jason play! You should hear them together. Byron taught them when they were kids, not kids together, you understand, but separately.''

''Austin—'' Ginny reached down, touched his forehead and tipped his head up so she could see his eyes ''—did you measure out your medicine or just drink it from the bottle again? You're hyper and talking a mile a minute.''

Austin sighed. He might have Ginny wrapped around his finger, but he couldn't put anything over on her, and he knew better than to ever lie to her. ''The bottle.''

''You overdosed. Don't do it again. Use the spoon.''

''Yes, ma'am. Are we going swimming after dinner?'' There was a pleading note in his voice, and he watched her waver. ''I'm not really sick, you know, just a stupid head cold, and the medicine takes care of that. Please.''

''Only if you go lie down for a while,'' Ginny said.

''A nap!'' He was outraged and his voice rose a couple of octaves. ''You want me, a college man, to take a nap?''

''I want an eleven-year-old boy who's had a fever to rest. I didn't say anything about a nap. Just lie down. Read awhile but no computer. That's if you want to go to the river.''

He was being manipulated and he knew it, but couldn't think of an argument that would work. He narrowed his dark eyes at Laura, wondering if it was worth the effort to bring her into the fray. Then he sighed and stood up. ''Laura, can we work on the photographs tonight?''

"Absolutely. I like what you've done so far."

Ginny waited until she heard his footsteps upstairs, then asked, "Are you sure he hasn't destroyed your work? I almost died when I saw he was cutting all the photographs up."

Laura shook her head in wonder. "Actually, he's doing something I never thought of doing, and I can print more pictures from the negatives when I need them." Austin had laid out all the photographs she'd taken of the cave wall and placed them in order. After he'd studied the way she'd deliberately overlapped each section, he'd cut off the overlaps and glued them down like a jigsaw puzzle on a poster board. It was a perfect reproduction, and after she finished her detail drawings, she would use Austin's creation as a reference.

Later that afternoon found her back on the floor of the family room, working with Austin again on his arrangement, listening to Ginny and Matt discuss their day and talk about the baby.

There were moments she had to bite her lip to keep from laughing out loud over Matt's concern about the new arrival. He was scared of being a father again, but what weighed uppermost on his mind was the actual birth and the fact that Ginny not only wanted to do it at home, but wanted him present and participating.

For a time Laura imagined herself as part of the family, but knew it was only because she'd had no real family life of her own and envied them their closeness and love. If occasionally she checked the grandfather clock and wondered where Jason was, she felt sure it was only because of the family environment.

Since they'd all eaten a heavy lunch, she and Ginny fixed a light dinner of pasta salad and fruit. Then while Matt and Austin cleared the table and cleaned the kitchen, she changed into her swimsuit, a black one-piece with high-cut legs.

Austin and Dog ran ahead of them—one reckless with youth, the other surefooted and alert to any dangers that might crop up. Laura, Ginny and Matt followed more slowly, walking around the back of the vineyard and down the steep slope to the Perdernales River. The path was shaded with oak trees, and the air was heavily scented with mimosa. The onset of the evening had stirred up a breeze.

Matt, at the rear of the single-file line, warned Ginny—as he did every evening they made the trip—to watch her step while they maneuvered the narrow path beside the river and limestone cliffs. Once they were around the wide curve of a chiseled outcropping of rock, they came out on a rock shelf that extended over the river.

"Hey, Laura, look." Austin pointed upward.

She followed his finger. High on the cliff behind them was a majestic old oak tree, some of its roots exposed and growing all the way down to the water's edge. But it was the long rope with the tire attached to a massive overhanging branch that made her smile.

With Matt's help, Ginny made herself comfortable at the edge of the flat rock and dangled her feet in the water. Matt whipped off his shirt, hung it over Ginny's head and dove in. Austin took a running start from his position, and just as he was in midair, Dog was suddenly beside him and the two hit the water at the same time.

"How deep is it here?" Laura asked. The Perdernales was a clear, spring-fed river, so clear in the shallows you could count the pebbles on the bottom. But she was looking at a wide area where the water was dark green and the bottom invisible.

Ginny yanked Matt's shirt off her head. "I'm not sure how deep it is, but Matt will only dive from this rock. Are you scared of deep water? Do you swim?'' She laughed and pitched Matt's shirt at Laura. "Hey, stop drooling over my husband.''

Laura knew she was teasing, and she came over and sat down. "Well, he is drop-dead gorgeous, you know.''

"Yes, indeed I do,'' Ginny said. "And he fills out that swimsuit very nicely, too, doesn't he?''

"I couldn't say.'' Laura struggled to keep the laughter out of her voice.

"Talk about gorgeous,'' Ginny went on, "you should see Jason. He has this sexy black Speedo...'' She gave a low whistle, enjoying the way Laura's cheeks bloomed with color.

Austin and Dog swam toward them. Dog, with Ginny's help, struggled up onto the rock platform and took off down a path only stopping long enough to shake. Austin treaded water in front of them. "Come on, Laura, it feels great. Dad and I promise you we won't try and dunk you.''

"You're a bad liar, Austin. And you've got this glint in your eyes I don't trust.''

Austin laughed wildly and swam a little farther away, only to bump into Matt and be pushed under the water. When he came up, he was laughing and suddenly all over Matt.

"Go on in,'' Ginny said. "You don't have to sit here and keep me company.''

Laura looked at Ginny's oversize shirt and cotton shorts. "You're not going in?''

"Doctor doesn't think it's a good idea. But really, Laura, I like to watch, and later Matt and I always go for a walk. We wade a little and hunt for arrowheads along the river banks. There's an abundance of them around here and we enjoy finding them.'' She watched Matt and Austin in their water-splashing contest. "Go on. Have some fun."

Laura kicked off her tennis shoes and dove in. The water was colder than where she'd been dangling her feet, and she came up gasping for air. But she didn't get much of it before she was immediately pounced on by Austin and Matt. They'd found someone new to torment, but she gave back as good as she got. When they ganged up on her, she prepared herself with a big gulp of air.

After an hour of hard play, she was exhausted, but she was having too much fun to give up. They'd swung off the rope into the water so many times she didn't think she had the strength to haul herself out. Then she saw her chance to get even with Austin.

She slipped underwater, going quite deep so she could come up behind the boy and surprise him. It happened when she was on her way up. A strong male arm suddenly snaked around her waist. She was shocked at the way Matt held her against him, the way his body molded to her. A thousand questions flipped through her mind, but one thing was uppermost—she didn't like the way he was touching her and tried to push away. As she rose nearer to the surface, she attempted a backward kick, but they were too close together. Then as her head broke the surface, she gasped for air and twisted around.

"Jason?"

"Just who the hell did you think it was," he whispered for her ear only, "holding you like that?"

She quickly calculated the time and realized it must be only around eight o'clock. "What are you doing here?"

Jason shrugged and grinned, placed his hand on top of her head and pushed her under. Damn, but she looked good to him. He wasn't about to tell her or anyone that after a couple of minutes with Pat he'd become bored, or that his mind kept straying to Laura. So he'd made some excuses—he didn't even remember what—and left Pat's apartment.

Laura came up spitting water, and she faked a coughing fit. When he became concerned, she returned the favor and dunked him, managing to get well away before he came up. She swam hard for Ginny, only to have her ankle caught and her head pulled under again. This time when she came up for air, her arms were pinned straight against her sides. She tried to kick backward and met empty space. Like an otter, Jason was beside her, splashed her in the face, and then suddenly he was out of the water and sitting beside Ginny.

Laura wiped her face and drew back her arm, ready to slap water at him, but he shook his finger at her.

"Don't do it. You'll get Ginny all wet."

He was too smug. "Shame on you, hiding behind a woman's skirts."

"She's not wearing a skirt, so how—"

Laura caught Ginny's wink. She grabbed Jason's feet and yanked as Ginny gave him a hard push. By the time Jason's head surfaced she was sitting beside Ginny and smiling. Visible only from the nose up, Jason glided toward her, his hair slicked back, his electric blue eyes alive with laughter—and something else. She couldn't move as she watched the way his gaze ran over her, observing how her suit clung to her, outlining every goose bump.

Ginny sensed immediate danger, and she quickly got up and moved aside. Then she stopped and glared at Jason. She recognized that predatory assessing look. The way his eyes seem to eat Laura up, unable to get enough of her. "Matt," she yelled, then jumped, unaware that he was right beside her watching, too. "Matt, stop him," she hissed.

Matt took hold of Ginny's arm and began to lead her to the edge of the river. "Austin's waiting up ahead. Let's go look for arrowheads."

"Matt," Ginny pleaded. "I want you to stop him. I know that look."

"Oh. Does my brother look at you like that?"

"Of course not, but you do, and I damn well know what happens when you do." She tried to pull her arm free, but couldn't. When she wanted to look over her shoulder, he just kept walking. "Do something, Matt."

"I am. We are. We're leaving."

"But, Matt—"

"Hush, love, and leave things alone."

"He'll hurt her. You know he will."

"We'll see." Matt helped her over a large rock and glanced back before the bend in the river obscured his view. He smiled and whispered almost to himself, "I wish you luck, brother. You're going to need it."

"What did you say?" Ginny managed to get a quick backward glance over her shoulder and saw Jason kissing Laura. She sighed and glared at Matt. "This is all your fault." She shook off his hand and moved away to catch up with Austin and Dog.

Matt nodded, agreeing, taking all the blame for everything that happened and anything that could happen in the future. It was the easiest way. He'd quickly learned you didn't argue with a pregnant woman, at least not a pregnant Ginny.

JASON HAD COME out of the water fast, knowing just where to place his feet so he could stand. He'd grasped Laura by the shoulders and kissed her long and hard. When he let go they were both breathless. "You looked so adorable I couldn't resist."

"Try, will you?" She scrambled to her feet and glanced around for the others only to find they'd deserted her. She felt naked under his gaze. "Stop looking at me like that."

"Like what? Like I'd like to strip that suit off you? By the way, for a swimsuit that covers so much..." He smiled and shook his head. "Do you know how sexy that thing is? Well, it is. But you're so much more appealing without it."

"Stop it, Jason. Everything doesn't revolve around sex."

"Maybe it should."

She'd imagined from Ginny's description that Jason wore one of those men's bikinis that she thought vulgar. Instead, his swimsuit had legs to midthigh and fit like skin, and he wasn't in the least embarrassed by the fact that his desire for her was visible.

What was it about a swimsuit that was so different? She'd seen him in shorts, cutoffs, jeans, even naked. Yet she hadn't been as aware of his body as she was now. Maybe she'd been too busy fighting her emotions to really notice his sculptured physique, or the way his stomach had that washboard effect and how his smooth skin was nicely tanned. She was considering jumping back in the river to cool her disconcerting thoughts when Jason scooped her up in his arms and held her over the water.

"If you keep looking at me like that, I won't be responsible for what happens." He grinned at her scowl. "Don't deny it, either." On the last word he dropped her in the water and quickly followed.

Laura came up sputtering, only to see Jason's laughing face close to hers.

He tread water and held up his hands in surrender. "Let's swim to the other side and see if we can find more arrowheads than the rest of them."

As she swam beside him, matching his long, smooth strokes across the river, she had to admit she was a little disappointed. But only, she told herself, because she didn't have the upper hand in the situation. She didn't like Jason calling the shots.

When they reached the opposite side of the river and pulled themselves out onto a flat rock, Jason threw his arm around her shoulders and grinned. "Now listen carefully. This is important."

Laura stood stiffly, waiting for him to start his line of teasing again. This time he wouldn't catch her off guard.

"We can't let the others outdo us. I know a place upriver that's a treasure trove of arrowheads, but I don't want Austin or Matt to find it. If I show you where it is, you have to promise me to keep it secret."

Laura agreed but couldn't help remarking, "Is everything a game with you, and do you always have to win?"

"Sure. That's part of life." He took the lead, but realizing she wasn't following him, paused and glanced over his shoulder. "Dammit, Laura, lighten up. Life should always be a challenge and fun, for heaven's sake."

Maybe she was too serious. She had been a brain in school, but she'd never had much luck with personal relationships. They were usually serious, and painful when they ended. Laura knew Jason was waiting for an answer. "I'll keep your secret." She motioned for him to go ahead and she'd follow.

After carefully maneuvering around rocks and boulders, they spotted Austin, Ginny and Matt on the other side of the river and far ahead of them. When Matt waved, Jason waved back, then motioned for her to slow down.

"We'll let them get far enough around the next bend and out of sight, then I'll show you something interesting."

Laura hadn't realized how high the limestone cliffs rose around them. She studied the opposite bank, following the sheer line across the cliff, and gasped. The scene reminded her of something out of a fairy tale. Sitting precariously close to the edge of the cliff was a stone cottage. The gray-and-white stones were partially covered with ivy, and the windows facing the river had shutters that were open and somehow inviting. Two big oaks sheltered the cottage from the sun.

"That's were Jericho lives."

"It's very old, isn't it?"

"Yes, but no one's sure just how old. Jericho says it was the original Van der Bollen homestead built back in 1836, but that hasn't been proved."

Laura continued to gaze across the river. "I think he may be right. I bet it had a great view of the surrounding land, a good vantage point. A place to make a stand against an Indian attack."

"Speaking of which," Jason said, "how do you feel about a little rock-climbing?"

That got her attention, but she looked down at her bathing suit. "Well, I'm not actually dressed for rock-climbing, but I'm a pretty fair hand at it."

Jason smiled. She was probably a damn expert. He put his arm over her shoulders and pulled her around, pointing to an area above them, about ten feet straight up. "There's a small cavern up there. I found it when I was a kid. Actually, when I got into trouble with my dad, it used to be my sanctuary. Of course, I never realized that Jericho always knew where I was." His gaze followed the approximate location of the cavern to the cottage across the river.

"I don't see any signs of a cavern." She could only make out the rocky cliff studded with tree roots and small outcroppings of bushes, vines and vegetation.

Jason chuckled. "Watch where I put my feet." He started up the side of the cliff, pausing every so often to make sure she was right behind him. When he was about ten feet up, he found the ledge and pulled himself up by tree roots. Standing, he turned and grabbed Laura's arm and pulled her up beside him.

Laura noted that the evening sun was lower, a ball of orange fire in the sky making the shadows longer and darker. The air was cooling, and she shivered in her wet bathing suit. Off in the distance, she could see the others, walking along the river's edge. Jericho's cottage seemed closer, and she could have sworn she saw movement in one of the windows. Suddenly, for the first time, she felt an inner peace and comfort in Jason's presence.

"This is beautiful," she said, but when she turned around he'd disappeared. She was about to call his name when a hand snaked out from behind a bushy cedar tree that clung to the side of the cliff.

"Hurry up," Jason said. "In a moment the sun's going to set and there won't be any more light in here. Watch your head."

She ducked inside, half-bent over as she crab-walked inside. It took a moment for her eyes to adjust to the light, and when they did, she saw him sitting beside a pile of arrowheads. "Where did they all come from?"

"These have been here for years. From back when I was a kid. After years of hunting, I'd bring my treasures here for safekeeping. Dad thought the past was a waste of time and energy and would've thrown them out."

She squatted down beside him, her gaze bouncing from the horde of arrowheads to the walls. "Jason, there are some incised and pecked petroglyphs in here."

"Pecked?"

She reached out and touched one, tracing it with her finger, trying to identify the figure. But time had almost obscured the indentations. "Sure, look." She took his hand and placed it over the engraved figure. "They took tools and pecked out a design or drawing, instead of painting. Some of it is actually incised and stippled. They're old, though. I wish I had more light."

The small, confined space was getting darker, making the walls seem as if they were closing in around them. She was fascinated and lost to everything around her. Jason could have sat there and watched her all night, but this wasn't a place he'd like to be caught in after dark with no flashlight. "Here." He placed a few arrowheads in her hand and took some himself. "We need to get down, Laura."

She understood the reason for the urgency in his voice and quickly turned toward the opening. They made their way down the side of the cliff and were in the water swimming toward the opposite side when they heard Dog and Austin. Just as they pulled themselves out of the water and laid their arrowheads on the rock, Austin hurried around the bend waving his arm at them.

"They always think what they've found will be better than what I've collected, that is, until they see what I have."

"You cheat."

"Of course. I spent my youth searching for—"

"Sex and women, most likely."

"—perfection, and I'm not about to let my efforts go to waste now over a little thing like ethics."

"He's a little boy and you take the fun out of the game."

"Einstein? Are we talking about the same Austin Bolt? Listen, he's an unscrupulous little weasel. Just look at that grin. He thinks he's outdone me this time."

Laura laughed. "Just like his uncle Jason." She felt the sharp edges of the three perfectly shaped arrowheads in her hand, and if she'd been anyone else, she would have pitched them into the river.

"Uncle Jason, look what Dad and I found." He opened his hand to show Laura the object. "It's a tool, isn't it, Laura?"

She rolled the ax-shaped rock, inspecting the chipped edges. "You're right. Probably used for making arrowheads. It's very old, Austin."

"I know." He looked at his uncle and grinned. "What did you find?" He gave the arrowheads a glance. "Aren't you depleting your stockpile from the cavern again?"

Jason let out a bark of laughter. "Who told you?"

"Dad."

Matt and Ginny strolled up, overhearing the last of the conversation.

"How did you know about the cavern?" Jason asked Matt.

"I'm older than you, and I used to hide things there when I was a kid. Hell, I used to hide there from Dad."

"I never found anything that showed you were there."

"That's because, before I ran away from home, I cleaned it out." Matt wrapped his arm around Ginny's shoulders. "It's getting late and Ginny's cold. Let's head home."

Laura and Ginny walked side by side, ahead of the men, each lost in their own thoughts. Then Ginny said, "It amazes me how different they are, yet how alike they are, too. I believe if Jason ever finds the right woman, ever falls deeply in love, he'll be a wonderful husband and father."

Laura laughed. "You've got to be kidding."

CHAPTER NINE

GINNY LAY AWAKE listening to the tick of the clock and thinking about Laura and Jason. There was something there, something between them. She felt it but couldn't think of a way to make them aware of it themselves. Matt was a man, so he wasn't going to be any help. She felt his body snuggled against her back, his hand spread on her stomach, and smiled. He loved to feel the baby move and kick. Placing her hand over his, she yawned, telling herself she should do as Matt advised and leave it alone. Still... She closed her eyes, only to have them immediately fly open again. "Matt," she whispered.

She pinched his hand. "Matt, wake up. I think there's someone in the house."

Matt sat upright. "Is it the baby?"

Ginny shushed him. "No. Listen."

"I don't hear anything."

"Dog barked, then I heard a thumping noise."

Matt tried to lie back down. "If Dog's not howling with rage, it's all right."

"No. I tell you, I heard something like a thump after Dog barked. He might be hurt. Go see, Matt."

Matt sighed. He was never going to be able to sleep again. Lately, every move she made woke him. Fear of the birth of his daughter rode his back like a demon. He slipped on his robe and opened the bedside-table drawer for his revolver. "Where's my gun?"

"I put it away. Why? You're not going down there armed, are you?"

He sighed again. "Well, it was a thought, Red. What if the intruder is armed? I'd stand a better chance." He felt her scowl more than saw it. "I was a cop, remember?"

"It's in the shoe box on the top shelf on your side of the closet. Hurry up, Matt. I hear noises again."

He had, too, so he retrieved his gun and was about to ease the bedroom door open when her voice stopped him.

"Be careful."

"Yes, dear," he said under his breath then as he left the room and eased his way down the stairs. When he got to the bottom, he paused and took a breath. Then he stepped through the doorway to the kitchen, crouched and, with his arm extended, pointed his gun toward the noise. He reached around the door frame and flicked on the overhead light.

"Hell and damnation," Jason said as he juggled a bottle of champagne and almost dropped it. "Are you trying to scare me to death?"

Matt lowered the gun, put the safety on and glared at his brother. "What are you doing here at—" he glanced at the clock "—at one o'clock in the morning?" He set the gun down on the table and snatched the bottle of Dom Pérignon from Jason's hand. "Stealing my most expensive stock?"

"I didn't have anything at my place."

"And you thought... Jason, what the hell are you doing drinking at this time of night?"

"Couldn't sleep." Jason snatched the bottle from his brother and began to open it. The cork popped loudly, and Matt flinched. You didn't treat champagne like that. When the golden liquid bubbled over the top, Matt snatched the bottle back, found a fluted glass, filled it up and held it out to Jason.

Jason took a sip and sat down at the kitchen table. He smiled at Dog. "He's been sleeping upstairs again," he said, and received a deep-throated growl from the mutt for telling tales. "He almost didn't hear me. I think he's been sacking out in Austin's room."

"Jason, what are you doing here? What's the matter?"

"I don't know." He emptied the glass and then filled it again. "Matt, I know women, don't I? I mean, you'd consider me pretty knowledgeable about them, wouldn't you?"

"Oh, hell." Matt rubbed his face and ran his fingers through his long hair. He resigned himself to a long night. Suddenly he thought of Ginny and how worried she'd be if she'd heard the champagne cork pop and he didn't immediately return. "I'm going to tell Ginny you're not a burglar. I'll be right back." Before he left, he handed Jason another glass. "Pour me some of that before you chugalug the rest."

"What do you mean, it's Jason," Ginny demanded. "Do you know what time it is? What's the matter? Is he sick?"

Matt pulled on a pair of jeans and a knit shirt, then paused a second. "Lovesick."

Ginny laughed and said, "What? Who?"

"Guess? But I don't think he knows what's hit him."

She pulled the sheet up to her mouth to muffle her laughter. Her eyes were dancing with mischief. "He's getting drunk? Why?"

"Because, Red, the poor soul hasn't a clue what's happening to him. All he knows is he feels like hell, kind of sick inside for no reason."

"Did you feel like that?"

"Worse."

"You don't think this is all an act because he got caught trying to sneak up to Laura's bedroom, do you?"

It was Matt's turn to laugh. "I don't think it's his devious mind or his overactive libido you have to worry about. Right now he's just damn confused. Start worrying when he realizes what's happening to him and tries to deny it. He'll make everyone within five miles of him utterly miserable."

"You didn't act like that." She delivered one of her sexiest, come hither looks, then grinned when he sat down on the side of the bed and kissed her long and deep. "You'd better be careful or I'll attack you," she whispered against his lips while caressing his cheek. "Damn. I hear those noises downstairs again. You better get down there before he decides to join us up here."

"He'd do it, too." Matt kissed her on the forehead, tucked the covers up around her shoulders and rubbed her stomach. "You two get some sleep."

He was at the door when he stopped and looked back. "By the way, is Dog sleeping upstairs?" Ginny snuggled down as if she hadn't heard. "Red? I was overruled about the mutt being in the house, but I absolutely put my foot down about his being allowed upstairs." It was like talking into the wind—he knew that—but it never hurt to try.

"I'll remind him. Don't stay up too late, and remember everything so you can tell me in the morning."

Jason was seated at the kitchen table with bottle and glass in front of him. He looked up. "I thought I was going to have to come get you. How's Ginny?"

"Very pregnant and uncomfortable."

"Amazing, isn't it, how they do that."

"Do what?"

"Have babies. It's always fascinated me."

Matt snorted. "Their ability to give birth is not what fascinates you about women, brother."

"No." Jason grinned, his eyes shining with alcohol and emotion. "I thought I understood them, Matt. I mean, really understood them. I always know what they want, but lately," he said, truly puzzled, "I don't know what's gone wrong. I'm slipping."

"What happened?" Matt eyed Jason over the rim of his glass, his amusement barely in check.

"Hey," Jason said, and sat up from his slumped position, "do you remember me telling you about Bill Lake and the men who were interested in my land that's across from his?"

"What does that have to do with women?" Matt was confused at the sudden change of subject and realized his brother had been drinking before he came over.

"Nothing. I just wanted to tell you before I forgot. I got a call this morning from a real-estate agent in Austin. He said he had a buyer for the twenty-five acres and offered me a terrific price for the land. Actually, the price was vastly overinflated, and when I asked who the buyer was, he hemmed and hawed, and in the end wouldn't tell me. You heard anything in the rumor mill about it?"

"Not a word. Are you going to sell?"

"Price is damn good. I could use the money, believe me, after everything I've spent, but I . . . I don't know. Matt, it doesn't feel right. I thought I'd do a little checking around first." He emptied his glass, immediately refilled it and sat in thoughtful silence for a moment. "Do you think I'm shallow or vain?"

That did it. Matt burst our laughing.

"Just another pretty face? Matthew—" Jason's voice rose in outrage "—she thinks of me like just a hunk of meat."

"Well, brother, you do have a reputation with the ladies."

"No! I've always been careful never to hurt anyone."

"Maybe it's your track record," Matt said, trying hard not to laugh again when he saw how serious Jason was.

"She doesn't think I have any substance." He tapped his head. "Nothing up here."

"Maybe that's because you can't keep your zipper up."

"What do brains have to do with my zipper? That's a damn cruel thing to say, Matt."

"You're right and I'm sorry."

Jason refilled their glasses. "I bet you didn't have to grease your zipper any to break it in."

"You're right." There was no use getting into an argument over that, Matt thought.

"I think she used me." Jason placed his elbows on the table and propped his chin on his fists. "Like a sex object. You know what I mean? It was great, thanks, babe, I'll call you soon. Or, see you around—that kind of thing."

"Who?" But Matt knew Jason wasn't about to put a name to his tormentor, at least not yet.

Jason shook his head. "I think they're the most wonderful creatures, Matt. I love to watch them, listen to them talk, even try to figure out how their minds work. You know they don't think like us?"

"That's been brought to my attention many times. More so, lately." Matt was beginning to feel just a little sorry for himself, too. "But let me give you a little brotherly advice—don't try to understand them. Can't be done."

Jason nodded, refilled their glasses and whispered, "You know they're smarter than we are, too? Cunning and tricky."

"I found that out," Matt said. "And I've got one on the way."

Jason didn't understand what his brother was moaning about. "What?"

"The baby. What am I going to do with a girl? I'm just getting used to being a father to an eleven-year-old boy. Girls are different. They have to be taught things."

Jason nodded sagely. "About men."

Matt thought about that and scowled. "Yeah," he growled. He propped his bare feet up on a chair and sipped his champagne. There were two empty bottles on the table now, and Jason was working at opening a third. "About men like you," Matt said after a long, thoughtful silence, "who lie to women to get into their pants."

Jason sat up. "I don't lie. I adore women."

Matt leaned forward and pointed his empty glass at Jason. "You use women. Charmingly, I'll give you that, but you're a user nonetheless."

"Hey, hey. I'm your brother—a friend—and don't tell me you've never lied or taken advantage of a woman?"

Matt nodded. "Guilty. That's why fate is giving me this little girl. I'll have to worry about her, protect her against men like you and me until the day they put me six feet under."

"I resent that." Jason filled their glasses. "Besides, I was always honest and up-front with the women I dated."

"What about Laura?" Matt's question brought on another long, thoughtful silence.

"She's different," Jason finally said. He pushed his half-empty champagne glass away and scrubbed at his face, then grinned at Matt. "I think I've had too much to drink, brother mine. A hike to my place isn't very appealing. Mind if I sack out on the couch in the family room?"

Matt eyed Jason suspiciously. "You wouldn't be thinking of tiptoeing up to Laura's room once I've gone to bed, would you?"

Jason came halfway out of his chair. "I'm cut to the quick." His head spun and he immediately sat back down.

"Be that as it may, answer my question."

"The truth, Matthew, is I couldn't get it up tonight if my life depended on it. So don't worry. Besides, I don't like to think what Ginny—" he shuddered violently "—would do to me."

Matt pushed back the chair and stood up, still unsure whether to trust Jason or not. "You better be more afraid of me than Ginny on this one."

Jason waved away the threat and weaved his way to the family room. The thought had crossed his mind that Laura was only a short walk away, but he'd kind of given his word. He fell on the couch and stared up at the ceiling. Her room was right above him. He fell asleep with a silly grin on his face, dreaming of tomorrow and his time with Laura.

She hadn't got the best of him yet.

LAURA WATCHED with mixed feelings as Ginny propped her feet up on the chair beside her and sighed loudly. "Are you sure you're all right?"

Ginny picked up the menu and looked at Laura over the top. "Just because Matt put the fear of God in you before we left doesn't mean you have to pay any attention to him. Stop worrying. I'm fine. It's my damn feet. They keep swelling." She glanced longingly at Laura's canvas espadrilles. She envied her tiny waist, too, which looked even tinier with the wide silver-and-turquoise concho belt.

Laura was simply dressed in a faded denim A-line skirt and plain white cotton shirt, neatly tucked in, the sleeves rolled up above the elbows. Laura was true to her trade, and Ginny was fascinated by the Native American jewelry she wore—wide, intricately engraved silver bracelets studded with turquoise and a single-strand necklace of small chunks of turquoise.

Ginny complimented her on her jewelry.

"You know, Laura," Ginny said, "I love your jewelry."

Laura rubbed one of her bracelets. "I've been collecting American Indian art and jewelry for years. This is a really old sand-cast bracelet." She noticed the way Ginny eyed it, and slipped it off. "Try it on. Go ahead. I bet you'll fall in love with it."

Ginny put the wide cuff bracelet on her arm and, like Laura, found herself rubbing the silver and stones, enjoying the warm, peaceful feeling it gave her. "Isn't that strange," she marveled. "Are they magic?"

"I think so sometimes. That one's the oldest piece, and I get the same feeling you're having. No. Don't take it off, wear it for a while."

Laura glanced around at the red Jeep Cherokee parked at the curb outside the restaurant. All the windows were down, the car was unlocked, and Dog sat with his head poking out of one of the open windows. "I don't think I've ever seen or heard of a dog who liked to shop."

"He's a fake. He actually loves people. It's that crazy grin of his that puts everyone off."

"Yes, indeed. And the fact that he likes to snarl."

"Only when someone looks like they're making a move on our shopping bags."

Laura had been amazed at first that Ginny would set her purchases outside the shop doors, leaving Dog to stand guard. But then when her own purchases grew, she added them to Ginny's, and her trust and amazement in Dog's loyalty grew. "He seems to have decided to like me."

"That's partly because you brought him water and bought him an ice cream cone," Ginny replied, "then had the nerve to hold it while he ate it."

"He looked so hot and thirsty."

"You've a soft heart under that shell of yours, Laura. What are you hiding from?"

"Myself mostly." The answer had slipped out unintentionally, and she felt her pulse begin to race. She liked Ginny and wanted to be friends, but she wasn't ready to share everything yet.

As if reading her mind, Ginny said, "You know, Laura, you don't talk about yourself, your past or your family." She held up her hand when she saw that the young woman wanted to deny what she'd just said. "I've been there, so don't say I'm imagining it. I lived for four years hiding from everything and became very good at it. And it taught me how to recognize when someone else is doing the same. If you're in some sort of trouble, I hope you'll tell me or Matt. We'd like to help you, Laura."

Laura struggled to keep the tears from her eyes. "Thank you, Ginny. But honestly, I'm not in any trouble other than that of my own making."

"And the reason for your troubles wouldn't be Jason-related, would it?"

Laura tried to laugh. "Partly. And they're partly related to a lie."

"But you don't want to tell me about it?"

Laura shook her head. "Not because I don't want to, but it's very...embarrassing."

"To you?"

"Oh, yes."

Ginny could see she was pushing too hard. Laura was getting uncomfortable. She decided to drop the subject, but not before she said, "Neither Matt or I are judgmental. If you need our help or just someone to talk to, we're here."

"Thanks. I'll remember that." Laura ducked her head, afraid she was going to cry. If only her own family had been like this, things might have been different.

They decided after lunch to do just an hour or so more of shopping before returning to Two Rivers. By the time they did return, they realized just how long their hour had stretched when they were met by a nervous Matt.

"I thought when you called you were only going to be a little longer. That was four hours ago."

"Don't fuss, Matt." Ginny kissed him on the cheek and strolled into the kitchen, only to be met by glares from Austin and Jason. "I can see he's made your day miserable, hasn't he?"

"Right," Austin groused.

Jason couldn't take his eyes off Laura. "You could've called and let us know. My brother was about to call the sheriff and have him look for you. Where were you two?" He spotted Dog, heading tiredly for his bed in the corner of the kitchen, and said, "Excuse me, the three of you."

"Someone told us about an old barn that had been turned into an antique shop," Laura said, watching as Matt stomped into the kitchen and Ginny grabbed his hands, placing them on her stomach. It amazed her how the very act seemed to calm him down.

"Where was this antique shop?" Jason asked. "San Antonio?"

Matt pulled out a chair for Ginny, and once she was seated he brought her a glass of iced tea. "Austin, Jason. Come help me unload the car."

When the men had left the kitchen, Ginny and Laura grinned at each other. Moments later, the men struggled in with the mountain of shopping bags, two antique chairs

Ginny wanted to refinish after the baby was born, and the two old crystal lamps she'd bought.

As Ginny and Laura sorted out their purchases, Laura handed Austin a bag. "I found something for you."

"Oh, wow," he said as he held up a thick book about Indian cave paintings of the Southwest. "Thanks, Laura."

Laura picked up her backpack-style purse, retrieved a smaller tissue-wrapped package and handed it to Jason. "This is for the house."

He was touched, and everyone watched as he carefully unwrapped the tissue. He had no idea what it was, but it was beautiful. He held the gift up by a long strip of leather and stared at it, trying to figure out its use. It was a circle of leather with fringe at the bottom, and inside the circle was a spiderweb of thin thread, with a turquoise bead in the center.

"It's called a dream catcher," Laura explained to a clearly mystified Jason. "Surprisingly, almost all of the American Indian tribes have them, in some form, in their culture. You hang one over your bed, and the web catches all your bad dreams. It only lets the good ones through, and the turquoise is for warding off evil, a kind of lucky piece to watch over you."

Jason surprised everyone by leaning over and kissing Laura. "Like Austin says—wow! I'll hang it right over my bed for luck." For her ear only, he whispered, "But luck is not what I've been thinking about." Then he sat back and smiled at the color in her cheeks and the way her eyes sparkled.

"You're bad, Jason," she said.

He grinned. "I know." Then he sobered. "I missed you at the house today."

Austin coughed loudly. "Don't fall for that, Laura. Dad said he and Uncle Jason had a champagne-tasting session last night and Uncle Jason spent the night on the couch. He stayed and bugged me half the day. Didn't go home to work till about three o'clock.''

Laura handed Austin another gift and watched as he tore at the tissue. "Neat. Oh, look." He held up a black T-shirt decorated with hand-painted Indian petroglyphs. The design was ghostly white, with touches of red and yellow. Austin lowered the shirt with a big smile. "You made this, didn't you."

Ginny pulled out an oversize T-shirt, much like Austin's, and held it up for everyone to see. "Laura makes and sells them at college. She gave me this one. Matt—" Ginny turned to him "—you should see Laura's apartment. She collects Indian pottery, blankets, art and antique American Indian jewelry. She's a really talented artist—you should see the ways she's painted and decorated antique furniture. I bet she could go into business."

Laura was embarrassed by all the attention and changed the subject. "Speaking of going into business, you better tell Matt about the items you bought that wouldn't fit in the car. He'll need a truck to pick them up."

Matt faked a scowl as he slipped off Ginny's running shoes and began to massage her feet. He didn't care if she bought out the damn city. "You were on your feet too long and you didn't rest."

"Don't you start," Ginny moaned as she wiggled her toes. "Laura made me lie down in the back seat on the way to the antique barn and all the way home. "I've had plenty of rest and I feel fine."

Everyone started talking at once. Talk about the baby and concern for Ginny made Laura feel uncomfortable with longing. So much family feeling, togetherness and love flying. She had to leave or burst into tears.

She dug through her bags, searching for the special light bulbs she'd carefully packed away. When she found them, she said, "I need to go check out some of my equipment." As she left, Ginny touched her shoulder as if to reassure her.

Ten minutes later she raced back to the kitchen. She stuck her head in the door and said, "Jason, could you come help me a moment?"

He knew Laura well enough by now to know something was wrong. When he caught up with her, he kept his questions to himself, waiting until she wanted to tell him. At the back of her van, he saw the lights that had burst in the caves lying side by side, the sockets empty of the ruined bulbs. Laura picked one up so he could look at it, but he didn't know what he was supposed to see. "What's wrong?"

"Jason..." she began, then fell silent for a moment. She didn't know a nice way to say what she had to say, and so she just blurted it out. "Someone sabotaged the lights, Jason. Whoever did it was very clever. He nipped only one of the connecting wires on each one so they would short out, but only after they'd been on awhile and warmed up."

"Are you sure?"

She sighed. Why had she thought he'd believe her? After all, the only people who had access to the unlocked van were those who worked on the vineyard. "Jason, these lights are very expensive. I take care of them, baby them. I also know how to take them apart and put them back together again if I have to clean them or if something goes wrong. That's never happened, though, until now." She held the light fixture so he could see where she'd taken part of the socket apart, and he could see the wires. "See the cut? The other one is exactly the same."

Jason pushed the light away. "I'm not doubting you, Laura. You're the only one who knows your equipment, and I believe you." He sat down on the ledge at the back of the van. "What I can't understand is why anyone, and it has to be someone at the vineyard, would do this. What reason could he have?"

"Did you tell anyone about what happened yesterday in the caves?" she asked.

"Not a soul. Did you?"

Laura shook her head. "I didn't want to take the chance that Matt might pull the plug on my going down to the cave." She paused. "God, Jason. What *about* the lights and the noises in the caves, and now this?" She lifted one of the lights, then said, "I think those noises were meant to scare me off. And the lights had to have been tampered with the night we left them there."

Jason touched her face comfortably, but she shook her head again and said, "You know, I don't feel threatened, but I'm sure I'm being warned. The question is, why?"

"I don't know, but we better find out." He was just as puzzled by the incidents as she was. But unlike him, she didn't see the danger, and he didn't like it one bit. If they hadn't had extra lights... it was unthinkable. The darkness in those caves was total. They could have had an accident bumbling around, could have caused a cave-in.

He watched as she packed away the lights in the specially made aluminum case with the thick foam liner, then tested each door as she locked up the van. He repeated Laura's question in his mind. Why? There had to be a reason. If someone didn't want them down there, that meant there was something in the caves someone didn't want them to see.

"We'll take a careful but good look around the caves tomorrow, Laura." He wasn't about to let anything happen to her, and he sure as hell wasn't about to let anyone scare her away.

CHAPTER TEN

THE CAVE WAS as dark and cold as before. Once the lights were attached to the tripod stands again and the wall was awash with illumination, Laura relaxed. Nothing had changed as far as she could see. There were no new footprints around the area; only her own, Jason's and a few of Austin's.

She followed the way the light arched to the ceiling, fading out in degrees before it actually reached the top. Turning around slowly in a circle, she saw how the light encased them and how the edges diminished like a hazy cloud. She stared at the way the same light ended in a dark curtain, no fading or dimming, just complete darkness beyond the wall with the paintings. The back of the cave was an uninviting black hole. She wasn't ready just yet to approach it, needing a little time to muster up her courage. Of course, she'd never in a million years let Jason know she was the least bit apprehensive.

Laura sat on the rock and gathered up her drawing materials. Jason relaxed beside her. They hadn't had much to say on the trip in, each lost in thought. As she started to sketch she asked, "How long have you known Jericho, Jason?"

"All my life." He studied her a moment, then said, "You don't think Jericho's the one trying to scare you, do you? He's been here for as long as I can remember, longer, really. He knew my grandfather."

"How old is he?"

"I haven't the foggiest, and I doubt if anyone does. He sure as hell won't tell." Jason sat up from his reclining position. "You really think he had something to do with it, don't you."

"He's the only one who blew a fuse about us going into the caves. He kept warning me off, telling me they were dangerous."

"And they are. Listen, Laura. Jericho all but raised me. I know him better than I did my father. Scaring a woman is not his style. He's always been honest and up-front with everyone. Hell, he was a Texas Ranger."

She would have asked what being a Texas Ranger had to do with anything, but realized it was some macho-man thing that she'd never understand no matter how he tried to explain. Being a Texas Ranger was obviously the next thing to being a saint. "Then who? Billy Bob and Wayne Gillespie? They're young. Could they be hiding something down here—drugs, maybe marijuana?"

Jason gave a snort of disbelief. "They're Sheriff Argus Gillespie's boys, and the strongest thing they'd dare smoke is a grapevine. Besides, they're good boys, honest and hardworking."

"Then that leaves who? Roberto and Lupe? Gomez and Dan?"

"They've all been here a long time. It's not anyone at the vineyard, I assure you."

She continued to work, sketching the figures on the wall. "Then maybe it's a restless spirit."

"Oh, no, you don't. I do not believe in ghosts and you're never going to convince me otherwise." He saw the way she was trying to keep from smiling. "You're not, Laura."

"Fine," she said, keeping her tone as serious as his but unable to stop the giggle that escaped.

"What?"

"You're scared."

"Damn straight, and I don't want to hear anything about that, either." To ensure she'd change the subject, he leaned his shoulder against hers, watched her struggling to keep from laughing and said, "Did you know you make this adorable little gasp, followed by something between a whimper and a laugh, when we make love?" That sobered her up quickly enough.

"I do not—did not." She scooted away from him. "And you're distracting me. I have to concentrate on my work."

He only moved closer and whispered, "It's very memorable and sexy as hell. But what sticks in my mind is the way you said my name right at the end."

That did it. She laid her sketch pad down, picked up her camera and stood. She wasn't about to sit there and be the brunt of his teasing, especially not about that, and not today. "If you'll get one of the lights, I'm going to the back of the cave."

Jason scrambled to his feet in time to catch her arm and stop her headlong rush. "Let's discuss this, Laura." She scowled and tried to twist her arm free, but he tightened his grip. "Be reasonable, dammit," he said.

The light caught the shine in her eyes and made them appear to glow. He couldn't tell whether she was amused or angry. "Laura, I'm not afraid of spirits, ghosts or things that go bump in the night. But think. Every time we've attempted to go back there, something has happened to stop us."

Laura nodded. It hurt to admit it, but damn, he was right.

"Let's just hang on a moment," he said, "and see if we can come up with a plan of action."

"What do you suggest?"

"First, check everything out. Lights. Flashlights. Your camera." He aimed the powerful handheld light toward the back of the cave, running it along the floor. "Make sure we pay close attention to where we put our feet. The area back there is a mine field of half-buried rocks. We don't need, either of us, to take a tumble and break any bones."

He was right again.

Laura checked her camera, then slipped the strap over her head. She pulled a flashlight from each deep pocket of her jacket and flicked them off and on. Then she glanced at Jason and found him grinning. "What?"

"You're not taking any chances of being left in the dark, are you."

"Absolutely not. Once was enough. What's your contribution?"

Jason pulled out an extra flashlight from one of his jacket pockets, then touched the other as if to check its contents.

"What have you got in there, Jason?"

He reached in and drew out a cellular phone. "I thought if all else failed, I could call for help. But it won't work in here—the rock's too thick."

Laura glanced at the ground, looked back up and pulled a cellular phone from one of her own cavernous pockets. "I'm glad you told me it wouldn't work." A vision of them being pitched into sudden darkness and both scrambling for their phones at the same time was an amusing picture. When Jason laughed, she realized he must have had the same idea. That they were in sync in any way scared the hell out of her.

"Shall we?" she murmured, and waved a hand for him to precede her.

As they passed out of the lighted area, Jason kept the strong beam aimed directly on the floor so only a few feet around them was visible. He warned Laura where to step and what to watch out for. Then he said, "Give me a sounding."

"Right on your heels. What's wrong?"

"Nothing, but I'm going to stop a moment."

Laura halted her steps and waited for him to say something. He directed the beam of light around the area, but the darkness was total, and they weren't close enough to see anything yet. "I don't think we're too far from the wall. But this damn dark..." He shook his head; he'd never experienced anything like it before.

"It has a strange thickness to it, doesn't it."

"Something. At least there's no moaning or drums today."

"I can't believe you've been in and out of these caves all your life and you've never come this far back."

Jason didn't want to admit that he wasn't exactly drawn to the caves and had only come here to defy his father or hide out. Jericho usually found him before he'd gone too far, anyway. He started walking forward again and Laura grabbed hold of his waistband. They'd covered only about twenty feet when Jason abruptly stopped.

"You didn't call for a sounding," she snapped. When Jason didn't answer, she said, "Jason, keep going." Still he didn't move, so she glanced around his shoulder. "Oh, my."

The light illuminated the back wall, and the sight absolutely took her breath away. Even Jason, who knew little about her work, was awed. Laura stepped to his side and stared. Now she could see that the cave where she'd been working was the largest area and the wall narrowed back to this small wall. The whole space was only about thirty feet wide by thirty feet high, but it was covered in petroglyphs.

Like a sleepwalker lost in another world, Laura started forward, only to stumble over a pile of rocks.

Jason grabbed her around the waist and helped her to stand. The damn woman was a walking disaster when she was involved in her work. She needed a keeper. "You okay now?" For answer she snatched the powerful light from his hand, shone it on the rocks she'd tripped over, then moved it back to the wall.

In her excitement, Laura whipped around. The edge of the light clipped Jason on the jaw, and he grunted in pain. "Jason, those rocks." She swung back around and shone the light on them.

Hell, he thought, she didn't need a keeper. *He* needed one to keep her from killing him. Pulling out one of his flashlights, he took a few steps away from her, rubbing his sore jaw at the same time. "What about the rocks?" But he was talking to thin air. Laura was on her knees, running her hands over the pile of stones.

"Look, every one of these are chipped along the edges." She thrust the light at him and he took it without a word. Then she sat back on her heels and began taking pictures. "If I'm right about the way this pile of rocks is centered, then it's a religious altar. Every rock has tool marks on it, and so does the wall. Oh, Jason! It looks like they're all incised, pecked and stippled."

"That means they're very old. Older than the cave paintings, right?"

Tears in her eyes, she answered, "Oh, yes. They're very old indeed."

"They look like something a three-year-old would do. They have no real human form, yet you can tell they're meant to be human."

"That's because they're anthropomorphic carvings." Wiping the tears away, she started taking pictures again. "I never thought, never dreamed I'd find something like this." As he'd done so many times before, he positioned the strong beam of light exactly where she needed it without her having to give him any direction.

Still on her knees in the white sandy floor, Laura looked up at him. Her tears of joy and excitement had left tracks down her cheeks, and her eyes were shining. There was a wildness in her, he thought, which she held in check. But it peeked out at the most wonderful times—when they were making love, and now as she knelt on the floor in front of that primitive pile of rocks.

Maybe it was the way she looked at him. Maybe it was the fact that she seemed so young with her short, curly hair highlighted by the harsh light. Maybe it was because he wanted to kiss her so badly he had to restrain himself. Whatever it was, his pulse was pounding and he could actually hear the beat of his heart.

Laura jumped to her feet and aimed her camera toward the wall. As Jason turned, too, she patted his shoulder. "How's your jaw?"

"I guess I ought to be thankful it wasn't my eye. I'd have a hard time explaining to Ginny and Matt why you clobbered me."

She focused, clicked and moved, then clicked and moved again, finally stopping to put in a new roll of film. "Ginny and Matt. What do they have to do with me giving you a black eye?" She lowered her camera and stared at him. "I didn't give you a black eye, did I?"

Only an idiot wouldn't have realized that Laura was somewhere over the moon and wasn't taking in anything but what she was capturing with her camera. He watched with amusement as she didn't wait for an answer but went back to work. "No, Professor, you didn't, and Ginny and Matt would skin me alive it they thought I'd in any way taken advantage of you."

"Why would they do that?" she murmured vaguely.

"Because they're crazy about you and have threatened my life if I so much as hurt your feelings."

Suddenly the scene beyond the viewfinder blurred. "Really?" She sniffed, but the rush of emotion didn't stop her from continuing to take her pictures. Again she stopped to reload, holding her camera outside the glare of the light, but in seconds was back to taking picture after picture.

Because her attention was so focused on the view of the wall through her lens, she wasn't watching where she walked. The toe of one shoe caught beneath a protruding rock and she stumbled, just managing to catch herself by dropping her camera and placing her hands on the wall. Suddenly she jerked and backed a couple of steps away.

"What's the matter?" Jason asked. She'd moved so fast he thought she might have been bitten.

Stunned, fascinated and curious all at once, Laura reached out and touched the wall again, this time with her fingertips, then she pulled away again. She captured Jason's hand and placed it on the wall. "Feel that?"

Jason closed his eyes. "Feels weird."

"Weird? It's wonderful."

"Feels like a slab of ice or cold steel. Or," he whispered, "a woman's heart."

She smiled. Leave it to Jason to think of the opposite sex.

Jason felt something fall against the back of his hand, something crawly, and he yanked his hand away. But the sensation didn't stop. He felt it on the top of his head and pushed at his hair. Unsure of what it was, he glanced at his hand and saw a light sprinkling of snow white sand.

He looked at the ceiling, then without a word of warning he grabbed Laura around the waist and dragged her backward. They'd no sooner left the spot where they'd been standing when a couple of rocks followed the shifting sand downward. A white cloud of dust erupted from the floor of the cave and floated in the air like a gauze curtain.

Jason was still moving fast when he tripped over a protruding obstacle. One arm was wrapped tightly around Laura, pulling her against his chest. His free hand, the one holding the light, windmilled crazily as he fought to reclaim his balance, but Laura's weight tipped the scales and they both went down with a grunt. The light flew out of his hand. There was a sharp pain in his head.

She didn't have time to protest or voice surprise. One moment she was being hauled backward, the next she was hitting the ground, her fall cushioned by Jason's body. They were plunged into darkness, and at the same time she felt Jason's arm go limp around her.

"Jason." She lay across him, her face close to his. "Jason, speak to me." Fear clutched at her throat as she became aware of the still-as-death quiet. "Jason, don't you dare do this to me." Grabbing a fistful of his jacket, she shook him, then stopped when she realized she was panicking. It took a second of talking to herself to make her locked fingers free the material. Then she dug into her pocket and pulled out a flashlight. She clicked it on and aimed it in Jason's face.

"I see a colorful rainbow and twinkling stars," he murmured.

"You can't. Your eyes are closed."

"Are they?" Jason opened them, winced, then said in a shaky voice, "What happened? Who are you? Where am I?"

"That's not funny, Jason." If he could joke, there was nothing wrong with him.

"Professor, have you ever thought that we're destined to fall all over each other?"

"No. More likely kill each other. What happened?"

"Don't know. The sky started falling?"

"Listen, Chicken Little, you've broken one of my lights and been knocked goofy, but the sky…" Her words trailed off when she felt his chest moving and realized he was laughing. For a moment she fought the urge to brain him with the flashlight, but she resisted. "Was the ceiling falling? And what do you suppose made the wall so cold?"

He had the beginnings of a bitch of a headache. "Yes. And I haven't the foggiest idea." He moved her arm so the light wasn't shining in his eyes. When Laura pushed off him and sat up, he grabbed hold of her hand. "Don't even think about it."

"I just want to feel the wall again."

Jason tightened his grip. "No."

She tried to twist her fingers free. "Just a little touch—"

"No. I mean it, Laura. You might think you're invincible, but I know damn well I'm not. We're not going to tempt fate any more today." He realized something new about her—she was bullheaded and mule-stubborn. But then, so was he.

They glared at each other for a long moment before Laura relaxed. "You win."

In slow, careful degrees Jason sat up, but he didn't let go of Laura's hand. "It's not a matter of winning, Professor. It has to do with common sense. Jericho was right—it's dangerous, at least back here. If you want to take any more pictures you'd best do it from here, because this is the last foray to this part of the cave."

"But..."

"There are no buts, Laura." He shook his head. "If you won't listen to me, I'll tell Matt and he'll stop the trips down here altogether. Do you want that?"

She'd forgotten that for all his charm, Jason was, after all, a man and he played dirty. "You know I don't. But, Jason, what a find! I can't walk away from it. Help me."

"Right know, be satisfied with your pictures." He couldn't stand to see the disappointment in her lovely eyes. "I promise I'll think about it, see what I can come up with. But, Laura, until I decide what to do, the back of the cave's off-limits." He pressed his point. "Agreed?"

"Yes," she said grudgingly. "How's your head?"

"Feels like it did the other morning—sore." He moaned and lay down, hoping for some sympathy and attention.

"Too bad." Laura stood up and began searching the floor of the cave for the light Jason had lost when he fell. "You better get up before more pebbles rain on us."

"Don't get nasty, Professor." Jason got to his feet. "And they were rocks. Sizable ones, too."

She noticed a shiny edge of aluminum sticking out of the sandy limestone floor. The light appeared to have landed just inside a small alcove surrounded by a mound of stones. She'd started toward it when Jason called her attention to where he was shining the beam of his flashlight. The ceiling they'd been standing beneath, directly above the back, was crumbling. Chunks were already missing, showing gaping black holes.

"Just a second," Laura said, intent on retrieving her expensive spotlight first, praying it wasn't broken beyond repair.

Jason moved a little closer to get a better look through one of the holes in the ceiling. "I'll be," he said. Look's like another cave above this one. Damn place is honeycombed with them."

"While you're over there so close to the wall, would you pick up one of those rocks we saw? I'd like to confirm that those markings are tool marks." Laura went down on her knees and carefully began dusting the powdery sand off the light. Her hand bumped against a part of the mound of stones, knocking some out of place. As they tumbled onto the floor, she yanked her light out of the sand before it could be smashed. Relieved that she'd managed to save it, she began blowing off the dusty coating when she became aware of a dark object in the sand by the fallen stones.

She turned the beam of her flashlight on it and sucked in a breath of excitement. Carefully she laid down the broken light and began inspecting the alcove and the mounds of rocks and stones inside. Her heart was suddenly in her throat. "Jason," she called.

Jason heard the excitement in Laura's voice and quickly turned to where she was sitting on the floor. When he started forward, she yelled at him and he froze.

"Take care where you walk. There might be something else lying around. Look." She held up the object she'd spotted on the floor by her knee and waited for Jason to say something. "Do you have any more Ziploc bags in your pocket?"

"Sure." He gave her one and watched as she placed the object in the bag and closed it. "What is it?" He didn't like the feeling he got looking at the object and moved the beam of his light to the mound in the alcove.

"It's a bone, Jason, a human finger bone, and I think there's a hand, too."

He shivered. "How do you know it's human?"

"I'm trained to know these things."

"Is it old?"

Laura saw his reaction and smiled. "I don't know—won't know until I have it carbon-dated. Besides, with the conditions in this cave, the dry cold...it could be very old and not look it." She reached inside the alcove to remove some of the stones. "Ah, the hand is attached to a wrist." She carefully removed a few more stones. "And here's part of an arm. This has to be a burial mound, Jason." Her excitement increased. "What with the wall carvings and now this..." Her words trailed off in a dream of academic acclaim.

"That's what I'm afraid of." He reached out, grasped her arm and hauled her to her feet. "I think we should leave it alone."

"Jason, no!"

"Have you forgotten the condition of the cave back here? You start digging around, displacing rocks, bumping into walls, and there's no telling what could happen." She gave him one of those steely looks, and he sighed. "Listen, he or she has been here for a long time. A little longer won't make a difference now, will it? Have the bone dated then we'll tell Matt and see what he wants to do."

"But—"

"Laura," he said, touching her cheek. "I know this could be a big deal and important for you, but if we blurt this out, if Matt thinks there's going to be hordes of people tramping in and out of the wine cellar, he'll come down here and close off the caves permanently."

Jason was right. She knew full well how Matt felt about his wine, and rightly so. It was his life and his family's livelihood, but it was hard to agree to wait when she itched to get to work. At least she nodded. "We should stop for now and go, because if I stay a second longer, I'll regret agreeing with you." She looked around, feeling elated and defeated at the same time. "I don't deal well with losing. I guess your head hurts too bad to do any work on your place today."

"Absolutely not." The thought of having her back in his bed was too much of a temptation to let a little pain interfere. "A couple of aspirins, and I'll be in top form again."

As she gathered up her equipment, she paused and cast him a suspicious look. She didn't trust his brilliant smile or the gleam in his eyes. There was an explanation for that look, and she knew what it was. Not a moment had passed since they'd made love that she hadn't thought of returning to his house—his bed. Jason Van der Bollen was like a lovely habit, and she understood now that the craving only increased with each passing moment.

Jason talked her into skipping eating with the rest of the workers and let him fix them lunch at his place, but only after they fed and talked to his girls.

When finally they entered the house, she was touched and amused at his neatly made bed and his attempt to clean and straighten his house as much as the mess would allow. As he set up a card table and folding chairs, she made numerous trips to the small office-type refrigerator in his bedroom upstairs to gather what he wanted. Exhausted after a few trips, she started dropping the items to him over the railing.

She watched, biting her lip to keep from laughing at how intently he went about his task. Obviously this was serious business. He mixed a couple of ingredients in a bowl, turning his back to her and blocking her view with his shoulder when she tried to see what he was doing. He had her laughing as he whispered incantations over the bowl, telling her it was his secret brew. Then he painstakingly stacked two soft buns with a combination of pastrami, pepperoni, Swiss and provolone cheeses, and added slices of tomato, sliced pickles and shredded lettuce. Then he ladled on his "secret" sauce. She knew he was watching her as she bit hungrily into the thick sandwich. Closing her eyes, she savored the explosion of flavors. She moaned in ecstasy, chewed and swallowed. "Wonderful."

Jason relaxed. "One of my few culinary successes."

"You could sell these and make a lot of money."

Jason shook his head. "I thought of it, but it would be too much work. Besides—" his voice lowered to a purr "—I only share my talents with special people."

He had that gleam in his eyes again, and even with her heart in her throat, she wasn't about to fall into his trap. She munched on a salty potato chip. "The hatchery was impressive." He'd taken her on a tour of the long, low building she'd thought was a series of stalls, which it had been before he'd refurbished it. More than two-thirds of the building had been remodeled as shelter for the emus.

The last stall area, however, had been bricked off and looked like a sterile operating room, with lots of stainless steel, cages and heat lamps. Inside a large incubator were six large, dark green eggs. "When will the eggs hatch?"

"Four or five weeks." He took a sip of beer and grinned. "Those five eggs are the first payback on my investment."

"You're selling them." She realized what he'd said and asked, "Five? But there are six eggs."

"Not selling—past tense—sold, and I'm going to keep one out of every six eggs to increase my flock."

It all seemed kind of iffy and mysterious to her. She didn't fully understand the significance of what he was trying to do and it must have shown.

Jason set his sandwich down and leaned forward. "Those five eggs sold for approximately fifteen thousand dollars." He grinned when she almost choked on her drink. "Eggs run anywhere from two to five thousand dollars apiece."

"Heavens, Jason. That's a fortune—for eggs." Then she said without thinking, "God, how much do grown birds cost?" Her rudeness embarrassed her, and she held up her hand to stop him from answering. "I'm sorry. Please don't answer that."

After lunch Jason told her he wanted to finish the kitchen so that he and Matt could install the cabinets. He ran the how-to video for her, which illustrated how to tape and float the Sheetrock, then explained texturing, how to apply a primer coat and, finally, painting procedures. She wanted desperately to laugh when he pulled over a large piece of Sheetrock he'd obviously been practicing on and proceeded to show her how it was done.

When he handed Laura the roll of tape, a couple of tools, a slab of gray Sheetrock mud and pushed the practice piece in front of her, she hesitated. Should she or shouldn't she? She'd never played coy or the helpless female before, and she wasn't about to start now.

Jason watched, waiting to correct her if she made a mistake, but she worked so expertly and fast that he was left standing behind her with his mouth open. "You've done this before?"

Laura grinned and tilted her head way back so she could see his face. "Summer jobs. A couple of friends banded together and worked summers hiring out to building contractors. Drywalling, finishing, painting, wallpapering—things like that.''

He struggled between feeling foolish at being the butt of her private joke and relieved that he had experienced help. He swallowed his wounded pride. He was a lot of things, but a simpleton wasn't one of them. He knew a good thing when he saw it.

What amazed Laura, she thought an hour later, was how well they worked together. She'd worked with a group of girls who were always bumping and tripping into and over each other. But with Jason it was different. They worked in unison with every move as if they'd been doing it for years. When they finished taping and floating the Sheetrock in the kitchen in record time, they stood back, side by side, to admire their work.

He never could have put into words the way he felt at that moment, the contentment and satisfaction. The fact that Laura was mixed in with those feelings gave him pause. He gazed at her and smiled, then pulled the rag from his waistband and wiped a chalky gray streak from her cheek. Dragging over one of the folding chairs, he sat down, pulled her onto his lap and kissed her long and lingeringly.

When she came up for air, she asked, ''What was that for?''

''Because you're the best.''

If he'd said she was beautiful or he was crazy about her, she would have moved out of his reach, frozen him out. But the sincerity of his seeing her as ''the best'' made her pulse race. She wrapped her arms around his neck. ''You're not so bad yourself.''

Jason ran his fingers through her hair, smiling against her lips. ''Let's go upstairs.''

''Is this part of my job description?''

"I hope so," he murmured as he planted tiny kisses on her mouth.

"No strings attached, right?"

By this point he had only one thing on his mind, and it took a moment for the question to sink in. "Strings? I don't know anything about strings."

"I thought you were going to take me upstairs?" she breathed, nipping the corner of his mouth and rubbing against him in a manner he couldn't ignore.

Still holding her, he stood up, laughing when she wrapped her legs around his waist and locked her arms around his neck. He turned toward the stairs, but just as he was about to put his foot on the first step, he heard voices and froze.

Laura heard them, too, and leaned back in his arms. When the voices came again, calling their names, she unlocked her legs. Her feet had just touched the ground when Austin and Ginny burst through the front door. She barely had time to put a couple of inches between them before Austin spotted them.

"Hi, Uncle Jason. Laura. Ginny said she needed an afternoon walk and suggested we come see the progress you two have made." He looked at the kitchen. "You're almost done with the walls, huh?"

Ginny glanced at Jason and Laura, noting Laura's bright red cheeks, and smiled. "You're a fast worker, Jason."

"Now, Ginny," he pleaded, sensing a lecture. "It's not like that."

"Like what?" Austin asked.

Ginny was about to explain when the emus set up a racket that sent them all running out the door.

Jason skidded to a stop, curious as to why the birds were all crowded together with Elvis making threatening noises.

He spotted Dog calmly sitting at the fence, his head resting on the lower rung as he followed every move the birds made and grinned that savage grin of his. "Don't even think about it, buddy," Jason growled like the canine he was talking to. When Dog ignored him and his threats, he looked at Ginny and implored, "Tell him I'll turn him into a eunuch if he so much as sets a paw through my fence."

Dog's gleeful attention was only diverted when Ginny spoke his name. She shook her finger at him and said sweetly, "The males in this family do not prey on innocents."

Dog sighed, turned and walked dejectedly away.

Jason got the message, sighed, too, and followed Dog.

CHAPTER ELEVEN

LAURA PULLED HER VAN into the gas station in Two Rivers and waved to Ron, Annie's son, as she waited for him to approach the door. "Fill it up, will you, Ron?"

"Sure thing." He leaned his shoulder against the door frame and crossed his arms over his massive chest. "What in the world are you doing out before the sun's up? Not another all-day shopping spree like the one you and Ginny dragged my poor old mom on, is it?"

Laura laughed. Ron was referring to the day about a week ago when she and Ginny took Annie with them for a return trip to the barn that had been converted into an antique store. They'd planned to just pick up the antiques Ginny had bought a few days before, but had spent hours there browsing and buying even more irresistible items. "Old, indeed," Laura said now. "Annie nearly killed me."

"She can do that, can't she."

There was no point telling Ron she was in a hurry. She had quickly learned that everyone in town always wanted to talk. "Yeah, she's quite a gal," Laura said.

Ron flipped off his baseball cap and rubbed a large hand through his shock of carrot red hair, just like his mother's. "Well, Matt came to town that day hunting for Ginny. He was mad as a hornet when he found out you all had sneaked off."

Laura nodded while trying to look serious and truly chastised. "He's driving Ginny nuts, you know. Won't let her out of his sight or go anywhere without him tagging along.''

"So you and my mom planned the great escape?"

"Guilty."

"Heard that after Matt went to all that trouble to supply everyone with a cellular phone in case they saw Ginny having a problem—even gave Doc Augustine one—you ladies turned yours off."

"No, no. They shorted out or something."

Ron laughed and pushed away from the van. "All three? At the same time?" He settled his cap back on his head. "Fill it up, you said?"

"And check the oil. This old thing sucks it up like water."

Ron patted the van. "It's a real honey. If you ever want to get rid of it ..."

"You'll be the first to know." She watched him walk away and marveled at his grace—he was such a big man! But then Two Rivers seemed to grow their men large. She'd met Sheriff Gillespie and quickly saw where his two boys got their height.

"Where you off to this early, Laura?" Ron asked as he took her credit card.

"Austin." There was no use not telling him why she was going because she knew it would be his next question. "I have some university business to take care of."

The mention of business was the magic word. Ron quickly finished up and she was on her way. She glanced in the rearview mirror and gave him a wave. Ron, his wife and three children had recently moved back to the booming economy of Two Rivers. Ron had opened the filling station, and his wife was in the process of opening a bakery across the street.

By the time Laura passed the town limits sign for Two Rivers, the sun was breaking through the dawn sky. It was hard to believe two weeks had passed since she'd come to Two Rivers. Actually, she thought, counting more accurately, two weeks and five days. On numerous occasions she worried about overstaying her welcome. She'd pestered Ginny, telling her she'd be happy to take a room in town. Two of the women she'd met at the general store had offered her accommodations any time she needed them.

When she thought about just how long she'd been at the Bolts', and how much she'd come to feel part of the family, it gave her the strangest feeling, one of hope that it could last forever and that she belonged. Then she'd face reality. Her happiness was about to come to an end. Not only was she almost through with her research in the caves, but late last evening one of her colleagues had called about the results of the carbon-dating test of the finger bone. He wouldn't give her the results over the phone, but insisted that she come back to the university.

JASON STROLLED up the driveway of the vineyard, whistling a tune he couldn't put a name to and thinking what a wonderful day it was going to be. The sky was clear and the early-morning sun didn't seem quite as hot as it had yesterday. A cool breeze ruffled the grape leaves, bringing with it the scent of mimosa and the jasmine Ginny had planted in pots.

The thought of Ginny brought him to an abrupt stop. He glanced at his watch. Laura and Ginny should have been sitting on the fence having their morning talk as they did every morning. Matt should have been leaning against the gate, bare feet crossed at the ankle, sipping his cup of coffee and laughing at the antics of his wife and Laura.

Jason hastened, wondering if something was wrong. Ginny was, after all, close enough to her delivery date to have the baby now. But then, Matt would have called him if it was Ginny's time.

Dog's bark warned the occupants of the house that they were about to have company. Jason opened the screen door, but before he said his good-mornings to the family he eyed the mutt. "You remember what I said to you about my girls?"

Dog's grin widened, and a growl rumbled deep in his throat.

Jason pulled out a chair, frowning because there was no third coffee cup sitting on the table. "Where's Laura?"

"She's gone," Ginny said.

"Gone? Gone where?" There was a sudden sinking feeling in the pit of his stomach. Jason looked at Ginny, then at Matt, wondering why they were so watchful and quiet. "Einstein?"

Austin stopped shoveling his cereal into his mouth. "She went to Austin early this morning."

Jason sat digesting the news a moment, trying to hide his disappointment. At last he said, "She didn't say anything to me about leaving. We were going to start putting down the flooring today." Pretending unconcern, he got up and poured himself a cup of coffee. "How long did she say she was going to be—a couple of hours?"

"She said she wouldn't be back until tomorrow," Austin answered.

The coffee burned a trail down his throat. "Spending the night, huh?"

"I think she has a date tonight." Austin picked up his toast and took a bite. "Jim Chapman called her last night."

"Chapman?" Jason said softly as he stole a piece of toast from Austin's plate and nibbled at one corner. "Who's this Chapman guy?"

"He's an assistant professor in the anthropology department. I've met him a couple of times—even went to the movies with them once."

"He's a good friend of hers, then?"

"She dates him. He's real neat. Funny and smart, too."

"Smart and funny," Jason mused out loud, and took a savage bite of the toast. "That's nice, isn't it."

Ginny was fascinated by Jason's lack of expression, though his eyes simmered with anger. She bit her lip and glanced at Matt. Her husband seemed just as intrigued with his brother's reaction as she was.

Jason pushed back his chair and stood. "Well, folks, I have work to do."

Austin swallowed a mouthful of orange juice too quickly, coughed and cleared his throat. "You're not staying for breakfast, Uncle Jason?"

"I'm not hungry, Einstein."

When the screen door slammed shut, Austin looked at Ginny. "Uncle Jason never skips breakfast. Is he feeling bad, or is he mad at us?"

Ginny managed a sad, solemn expression. "There's nothing wrong with your uncle, Austin, but a dose of his own medicine."

"I don't understand."

Matt patted his son on the shoulder. "It's an adult thing and more important to females than us."

He was still puzzled, but when his dad said a female thing, he understood all to clearly. Austin frowned. "What does a female thing have to do with Uncle Jason?"

"Exactly!" Ginny snapped, and glared at Matt. "Ask your father to explain." She left the kitchen in tears.

Austin glared at his father, too. "What have you done now, Dad, to make her cry?"

Matt shoved his chair back and stood up. "Nothing." He followed Ginny but paused long enough to say, "It's your damn uncle."

Austin glanced around the empty kitchen, wondering what had happened. He felt light-headed from it all. His gaze rested on Dog curled up on his bed in the corner, and when he received a snarl just for looking that way, he shrugged. "It's going to be one of those days, Dog." He shuddered. "I can feel it." He stuffed the last bit of toast in his mouth and left the table. "Think I'll get dressed and spend the day with Jericho."

JASON FED, petted and talked to his girls, then wandered into the house. He started to take off his shirt, ready to go to work, but suddenly he dropped his hands. She should have told him she was leaving. After all, it would only have been common courtesy. Damn, of all the days for her to run off, just when he needed her help the most.

Granted, the kitchen was almost finished. The walls were perfect, not a seam or screw showed, and there were no missed painted areas. It was a testimony to their team-work, their ability to work together in harmony. They'd had fun trying out the ice maker on the new refrigerator, too, and had ended up in a wrestling match to see who could get the most ice down the other's jeans. He'd lost the game but won in bed later.

With Laura and Matt's help the cabinets were installed. The man from the appliance store had been and gone, and he now had a bright, shining, steel commercial stove, a separate oven, dishwasher, trash compactor, microwave and a side-by-side refrigerator that dispensed chilled water and crushed or cubed ice. The only things left unfinished were the granite countertops and island. Those needed to be installed by a professional and he expected it to be a two-day job.

As he looked around admiring their work, he wondered why Laura never mentioned this Jim Chapman. After all, she knew about *his* women, not because he'd told her of course; he'd had to disconnect the damn answering machine after she'd heard some of the messages they'd left. Not once had she said anything about leaving. Jason rubbed his stomach. He felt a bit sick and decided he'd better go back to Matt's house and get something to eat.

Dog warned Ginny of Jason's arrival.

"I'm in the family room, Jason," she called. Then she watched, feeling both amused and sorry for him as he ambled in, glanced around and flopped in a chair with a long, mournful sigh.

"I'm taking the day off. Actually—" he studied his fingernails and frowned, realizing he needed a manicure "—I'm bored with the whole mess. Thinking about selling the damn place."

Ginny couldn't look at him without laughing. She rolled to one side, pushed herself into sitting position and struggled to her feet. "Want something to eat?"

Jason picked up a throw pillow, gave it a few hardy punches and set it back in its place. He brightened. "My stomach is a little shaky," he said, but followed her to the kitchen.

"Shouldn't skip breakfast." Her voice came out in a squeak.

"You catching a cold?" Jason asked.

Ignoring his question, Ginny made a fresh pot of coffee and slapped some bacon in a skillet, all the while watching from the corner of her eye as he pushed around the salt and pepper shakers.

"Where're Austin and Matt?"

She winced when he knocked over the salt and threw a pinch over his shoulder. Dog snarled, shook the grains from his head and moved away. "Matt's in the wine cellar. It's *remuage* today."

"He'll be down there hand-rotating the champagne bottles all day. Maybe I'll give him a hand."

She was just about to nix his idea when he said, "Nah. That's a one-man job, something about the right rotation. Where did you say Austin was? Maybe he and I can go fishing."

"I didn't, but he's gone to Fredericksburg with Jericho and the Gillespie boys." She patted the excess fat off the bacon and quickly scrambled a couple of eggs as the bread toasted.

"When did she tell you she was leaving?"

"Jason, her friend didn't call until late." Ginny glanced at him and immediately turned away to add some grated cheese to the eggs. "It must have been around ten. She was helping me put together the stroller."

"Dammit, Ginny, you should have let Matt or me do that."

"I would have, if I wanted to wait forever. I wanted it done then."

He knew better than to argue and only thanked her as she set his plate in front of him. After a moment of pushing his food around, he picked up a strip of bacon and munched it thoughtfully. "Thanks for the food, but guess I wasn't hungry, after all. Maybe I'm coming down with something. Feel my forehead. Do I have a fever?"

Any second, she figured, she was going to explode with laughter, and she struggled to keep a straight face. When he leaned toward her, she pressed her hand to his forehead. "You're cool as can be." The ringing of her cellular phone, attached by a long strap around her neck like a dog collar, was her salvation. She talked to Matt a moment, assuring him she was fine. Then she sighed and pushed the off button.

Jason picked up his plate and headed for the sink. "I'll clean up the kitchen while you go back to the family room and relax. Then we'll see if there's anything else I can do for you."

"Really, Jason, there's nothing."

"Maybe some dusting."

"Lupe does that. You'd hurt her feelings if you did her work for her." As she struggled to get out of the chair, Jason dropped the plate in the water and rushed to give her a hand.

"You're really big. You sure you're not having twins?"

"Positive," she said. In the past week it seemed her tummy had doubled in size. "Look. If you want to help, Laura and I had trouble getting the wheels on the stroller." She watched in amusement as Jason dried his hands off on his jeans and started to follow her. "The dishes first, then bring me a glass of orange juice."

Jason's eyes narrowed. Matt had warned him she was getting crafty in her advanced pregnancy. "You mean cranberry juice, don't you?"

She laughed. "No. But I'll take it. Just put in lots of crushed ice."

"Ginny—" Jason stopped her as she was just about out of the kitchen "—did Laura say anything about this Chapman guy?"

"Only that he was doing her a favor."

"She should've told me she was leaving."

Ginny leaned against the door frame. "Did you tell her when Judy Burns called and you ran off to meet her for lunch? Did you tell her when you took off to San Antonio to meet April Silverstein for half a day?''

"Judy Burns is an architect. She did the design for the barn.''

"But you used to date her. She calls you love and darling.''

Jason shrugged. "That's her way. And I went to San Antonio to meet April because she's an interior decorator and was generous with her ideas.''

"I bet,'' Ginny mumbled. "And you date her.''

"Used to.'' He stacked the dishes in the dishwasher, clamped the door shut and started to turn it on.

"Put some soap in, Jason.''

He did as he was instructed, then shut the door. "I stopped seeing April about a year ago.''

"By the way, while we're talking about your women, why are they calling here for you, instead of your place?''

"I had to turn off my answering machine. Anyway, what does this have to do with Laura?''

She frowned and was about to ask the logical question, but decided Jason had deliberately changed the subject. "Well, Jason, Laura took most of your calls to keep me from having to jump up and down all the time.''

"I see. She thinks I'm seeing a few other women?''

"Well, aren't you?''

He glared at her. "No.''

Ginny wanted to ask him how he felt about Laura, was actually trying to work the question out in her mind so he wouldn't know she was being nosy, when she remembered Matt's warning her not to interfere. "How's the work in the cave going?'' she asked, instead. When he continued to glare at her, she wondered what she'd said wrong.

"Laura's about finished.'' He handed Ginny the glass of cranberry juice and walked with her to the family room.

"Has she said anything to you about when she's leaving here for good?"

Ginny settled on the couch and glanced at him as he pushed the stroller back and forth until all four wheels fell off. "I told you we didn't put them on right. And no, Laura hasn't said when she'll be leaving, but I'd imagine soon. What with her work all done and nothing to keep her here."

Jason sat cross-legged on the floor and pulled over the toolbox and the stroller. "She's cute, isn't she?"

Cute! Ginny would have used a lot of words to describe Laura, but "cute" wasn't at the top of her list. Then she realized that Jason was working his way around to what he wanted to ask her, but didn't want her to know. "I think she's very pretty."

"Of course she is. Why would you think she wasn't?"

"I . . ." Anything she said wasn't going to be right. She clamped her mouth shut, figuring the best thing she could do was just agree with everything Jason said.

She thought she might go stark raving crazy after an hour of watching Jason take the stroller apart until it was reduced to a pile of nuts and bolts and pieces of metal. Then she had to endure watching him put it back together again and listen to his chatter as he seesawed between griping over Laura's disappearance, then praising her talents, her looks, her intelligence and her sense of humor—all, it seemed, without stopping. When she heard the slamming of the screen door and Dog's yelp of recognition, she slumped back in an exhausted heap.

It didn't take Matt more than a minute to sum up the situation. As much as he wanted to laugh, he couldn't help but be sympathetic. He could easily remember how he felt when he fell in love with Ginny. Fate could be exceptionally cruel and unrelenting on strong, arrogant men who thought they had all the answers where love and women were concerned. Love tended to bring the mightiest to their knees, he thought, then grinned—literally to their knees.

Jason rolled the stroller toward Matt and frowned as it wobbled a little. "I think I know where I made my mistake." He scooped up a couple of screws and bolts and stared at them.

Ginny covered her face with the instruction booklet and moaned pathetically. "Jason, they print these things to be used."

"Those don't make a damn bit of sense. I can do this." He started for the stroller.

Matt grabbed the shaky little thing. "Not now, Jason. Why don't you help me put some lunch together?" He watched his brother head toward the kitchen, and when he was out of hearing he moved to Ginny's side. "Are you all right?"

Ginny lowered the booklet so only her sparkling eyes showed. "Make him shut up, will you? He's talked nonstop since he found out Laura left."

"I warned you, didn't I? I said when it hit him, he was going to make everyone around him as miserable as he is."

Ginny buried her face in the book in an effort to muffle her laughter. "Don't you dare leave him here after lunch."

"Hey, I don't want to hear his troubles and woes."

Ginny picked up one of Matt's hands, kissed the palm and laid it against her cheek. "All this dissension's not good for the baby, Matt."

"You don't play fair, Red."

"Then you'll take him away with you after lunch?"

"I'll send him home."

"Don't hurt his feelings. They're kind of tender today."

JASON KICKED the tangle of covers from around his legs, raised himself on one elbow, glanced at the bedside clock and groaned. He couldn't understand it; he was usually a sound sleeper. Nothing bothered him. But here he was at one in the morning and his eyelids felt like they were taped open. The thought of a drink flitted through his mind, but after a moment he shook his head. He'd just end up a wide-awake drunk.

He rolled onto his back and stared up at the skylight, then his gaze caught on the dream catcher that hung from the chain pull of the ceiling fan. Dream catcher, he thought, was a crock of crap. It didn't work, because he was having nightmares. Visions of Laura with another man.

The sound of a car pulling to a stop in front of the house brought his thoughts to a halt. He threw back the covers, stepped into the jeans he'd thrown across the foot of the bed and was halfway down the stairs when the knocking started. He yanked open the door, and Laura all but fell into his arms.

"Laura, what's wrong?"

"Nothing, you pulled open the door too fast, that's all." She pushed him aside and walked in. "Jason—"

"What's the matter, did something go wrong with your date?"

"Date? What date?"

Jason slammed the door and stood his ground, his arms folded across his chest. "With Chapman."

"I didn't have a date with Jim." She found her way to a lamp sitting on the floor and switched it on. "Jason, we have a problem."

"If you didn't have a date with this guy, then how come the minute he calls, you rush off without telling a soul?"

For a moment she thought he was teasing, but one look showed her he was serious and angry, though he tried to hide it. "I told Ginny and I'm sure she told Matt and Austin."

"But you didn't tell me."

"It was late, and I didn't think I had to check in with you when I wanted to go somewhere. Jason, you're not my keeper. I come and go where and when I please."

He backtracked a little after realizing just how possessive he sounded. "Well, it would've been nice to know I wasn't going to have to get up early and freeze in the damn caves. I could've been working."

"Did you?"

He sensed a trap but neatly fell in, anyway. "Did I what?"

"Work around here?"

"Well, no. Ginny needed me to help her."

He was lying; she could tell by the way he kept scowling. "Listen. This isn't important right now."

"I think it is. Why did you run off to this fellow the instant he called?"

"That's what I've been trying to tell you."

"Are you in love with him?" He braced himself for the worst.

He obviously wasn't going to let her tell him her news until she set him straight. "Jason." She grabbed his crossed arms and steered him to the folding chair, then pushed him down and straddled his lap. "Now, listen to me. Jim is the one I sent the finger bone to. He called to tell me he got the results of the test, but he didn't want to talk about it over the phone."

"Why?" Jason refused to be moved by her closeness and the fragrance of her perfume.

"I asked the same, but he only said it was important I come back to the university."

"And that took until one in the morning."

"What burr have you got under your butt, Jason? Just hush and listen. Jim thought it best to tell me in confidence and give me a chance to tell you and Matt before it has to be reported. That finger bone is approximately forty-five to fifty years old."

"So, the poor bastard was in the prime of his life when he died. Did you have a date with Chapman?"

She had the most absurd urge to kiss him. It hit her suddenly that all his questions were because he was jealous. "Yes, but I was only supposed to have lunch," she murmured, her mouth closing in on his. "Something came up for him, and I ended up waiting all day. But you don't get it about the bone, Jason. The body in the cave has only *been* there for forty-five to fifty years. Jim estimates the person was about thirty-five or forty when he died."

Jason threaded both hands through her hair and pulled her mouth against his. It was in the middle of that kiss that he realized what she'd just said. He pulled his mouth from hers. "God almighty, is he sure?"

"Absolutely. Jason, someone buried a body in the cave fifty or so years ago. And if that person was trying to hide him, it could mean that the death might not have been from natural causes."

Jason planted a quick, hard kiss on Laura's lips, lifted her off his lap and stood up. "You haven't answered my question. If you only had dinner with this guy, how come you're so late getting here?"

"Are you jealous?"

"I don't know. Maybe. Answer my question."

He sounded confused and she smiled sweetly. "I had things to take care of at my place." That explanation got an arched eyebrow and a disbelieving frown. "Jason, I've been gone almost three weeks. I had bills to pay and the place needed cleaning." He was still scowling, knowing she was leaving out something. "Okay, Professor Hadley got wind of my find, and there were a dozen messages for me to return his call. He's in France, and by the time I tracked him down and explained what was happening…well, you get the picture."

"How'd he take your little deception?"

"Not very well. I told him he was welcome to call Matt to see about sending a team in."

Jason grinned. "You know the answer to that."

Laura returned his smile. "Yes, but Hadley is a bore, a chauvinist and a bully, and I'd love to be a fly on the wall when he butts heads with Matt." She ran her hands over Jason's bare chest, loving the feel of hard muscle. Then she remembered what she'd rushed home for. "Jason, we have to tell Matt. Hadley talked to Jim, and they're not going to wait before calling the authorities about the body in the cave. There's going to be questions."

"We'll call Argus, but you're right. Before we make that call we have to go tell Matt."

"He's not going to like this one bit, is he?" She watched as Jason plucked his shirt from the back of the chair and slipped it on. She could see he no more wanted to wake his brother than she did. "I think I'll stay here. You tell him."

Jason laughed and seized hold of her arm. "And have him kill one messenger when he can have two to slice and dice? I don't think so, Professor."

CHAPTER TWELVE

LAURA STAYED in the kitchen while Jason clamored up the stairs, making as much noise as possible. She grimaced. If his intention was to wake the dead, then with Dog at his heels, snarling and barking with every step, he was sure to achieve his goal.

The sudden silence unnerved her, and she moved to the bottom of the stairs, staring up into the darkness and wondering if she should go up and add her explanations to Jason's. When she heard the rumble of voices, she returned to the kitchen table to wait.

Jason was the first to appear and immediately took a seat next to her. Matt followed more slowly as he helped Ginny down the stairs. Ginny smiled to take the sting out of Matt's fierce frown. Austin, it seemed, had slept through the din. There was no sign of him.

"This better be good," Matt said, looking at Jason as if he was ready to strangle him. "Not, I hope, a replay of a certain evening."

Laura didn't understand what Matt was talking about. Some male thing, she guessed, but she wasn't about to let him take the blame for her. "This is all my fault," she said, grabbing Jason's arm when he started to protest. "And I'm sorry to wake you, but it's important you know what's happening." She knew Ginny would understand, but Matt was a different kettle of fish altogether.

Ginny tugged on Matt's hand. "Stop hovering over us like some gargoyle, sweetheart. Sit down and relax. No one's hurt or dead."

Laura winced. That wasn't exactly true. She faced Matt and said, "It has to do with the cave. Jason let me photograph the back wall." Matt's dark gaze cut like a laser toward his brother. Jason shrugged and would have said something, but she waved him to be quiet. "We didn't go there at first because the cave spirits didn't seem to want us back there."

"Cave spirits," Ginny whispered, shivering with excitement.

Jason refused to keep quiet. "Spirits. Ghosts. Personally, I think it was just our own clumsiness that kept hanging us up. Every time we tried to go back there, things happened. Either the lights would blow or we'd trip and fall over each other. Then there was the moaning and drums."

He was enjoying himself a little too much. Laura stepped in. "When we were back there a couple weeks ago, we had another accident." She ignored the raised eyebrows.

Jason slipped in again and said, "When we were leaving, Laura stumbled on a grave mound and found a bone."

Matt snorted. "A bone? When I was a kid I found all sorts of animal bones down there."

"Try human finger bone, brother." Jason grinned when Matt's eyes widened.

"Matt," Laura said, "I asked Jason not to say anything until I had it carbon-dated. Then I—we—would have something more concrete to tell you and decide what to do. Surely you see that an ancient burial mound would make archaeology news, and I didn't want the place swarming with people asking questions and trying to get into the cave.''

"That was thoughtful," Ginny said, "wasn't it, Matthew?"

"Oh, I don't know, Red." He gave Laura a hard look. "Was it thoughtful, Laura?"

"Back off, Matt," Jason said, annoyed.

Laura shook her head. "Jason, don't get into a fight over this. He knows full well I was being selfish. I haven't tried to hide my ambition. But, Matt, things have gotten out of my control and progressed beyond my ability to keep quiet." She paused, waiting for him to explode.

But Matt was only intrigued, and somewhat amused. Laura was so serious, so upset. What she obviously didn't understand was that this was his land and no one could or would invade his property. "Go on. What's going to happen?"

"The bone was estimated to be from a person who was between thirty-five and forty years old, probably a male. And it's only been buried for about fifty years. You see the problem, don't you?"

"Yes."

"Well, I don't," Ginny said.

"Jim—he handled the carbon-dating for me—has to report the body and location to the authorities. Someone went to a great deal of trouble to bury the body. The wall to the alcove had been blocked up to hide it."

"I see," Ginny murmured. "You're thinking murder, aren't you?"

Jason glanced at Matt. "If the bones are around fifty years old, it was way before our time, but do you ever remember anyone saying anything? Any old stories?"

"No," Matt said thoughtfully.

"Me, neither."

"And it couldn't have been a migrant worker. They wouldn't have known about the caves and certainly would never have dared enter the wine cellar. Dad would've shot them on the spot." The last sentence sent them all into a contemplative silence. "Do you think Dad knew?" Jason asked.

Matt shook his head. "He didn't have the guts to kill anyone, much less hide the body." He glanced at the kitchen clock. It was almost three in the morning. "How long do you think we have, Laura, before this friend of yours calls the authorities?"

She was suddenly embarrassed. "Not long. He was very angry with me, and I wouldn't put it past him to call the dean first, then the news media as early as he can."

"Why was he angry?" Jason wanted to know.

"Well, for one thing, I've lied and kept this all a secret. Professor Hadley isn't happy with me, either." That brought to mind another problem. "Matt, Professor Hadley wants to call in a special team to investigate the caves. I told him he better talk to you first." She couldn't help the savage smile that lit up her eyes.

Matt laughed. "I don't think we have any worries there. My main concern is the authorities. I can't keep them off my property if there's a possible murder victim buried down there." He glanced at the clock again and smirked. "Let's wake Argus up and see what he thinks."

SHERIFF ARGUS GILLESPIE sipped coffee and listened to Laura and Jason intently. Laura had heard of the strong, silent type, but this was ridiculous. Sheriff Gillespie was at least six foot five and appeared to be rock solid. He said nothing upon being introduced to her, only gave her a brief nod. Mostly he just heard everyone out, watching and evaluating. When she finished telling him about the finger bone and attached body she'd found, he leaned back in his chair and took a sip of coffee.

Then he surprised everyone by reaching behind him and picking up the telephone. "I'm going to get Doc in on this. He'll have a better idea as to the cause of death and what to do with the remains." As he dialed the number, he glanced at Matt. "You might want to lock the gates and secure the vineyard."

"Seems like old times, doesn't it?" Jason chuckled, then his smile faded when he glanced at Ginny. "What did I say?"

Sensing the tension, Dog lifted his head from Ginny's leg and snarled at Jason.

"Some of the *old times* I try to forget, Jason." She rubbed her stomach, but thought of another little girl whom she would never again hold in her arms, never hear her voice. Tears pooled in her eyes and spilled down her cheeks. Like lightning, her mood shifted and she glared at Matt. "And don't you even suggest that I go back to bed."

"Wouldn't think of it." Her tears still had the ability to make him come unglued. At that moment he would have given her anything, done anything for her, to take the pain of the past away.

"I want a cup of coffee."

Well, almost anything, he thought. "Cranberry juice," he said, trying to placate his wife with his most charming smile.

Laura got up and poured Ginny her juice. She waited until the sheriff had finished his conversation before she slid back into her chair. Jason wrapped his arm around her shoulders for comfort, and she felt a lump in her throat.

"Doc's on his way," Argus said as he hung up. "I told him to bring a body bag. We'll get whoever's down there out. I'll take some pictures of the body's position and location so there won't be any reason for anyone to come sniffing around.''

"What about the authorities from Austin or elsewhere?'' Jason asked.

"I think I can handle them.''

Jason knew Argus didn't have any answers and wouldn't until he'd seen what was left of the remains and Doc had made his examination, but he needed to reassure Laura and his family. "You know of anyone disappearing back then? Better still, do you have any files that go back that far?''

"If the bones are only around fifty years old, I was just a gleam in my father's eye then. As for records dating back that far, there're some old boxes stacked in the storeroom at the station. You'd think someone might have filed a missing-persons report?''

"If he or she was from around here,'' Jason said, "but what if it was a migrant worker?''

"If it was, then how the hell did he get himself buried there?'' Matt ventured. "Knowledge of the caves isn't widespread.''

"So who buried him in our cave?'' Jason asked.

They fell silent, each lost in thought. After a moment Laura asked, "Could I take another look at the bones before they're disturbed?'' Over the sudden din of protests, especially from Jason, she noticed that the sheriff only stared at her and waited until the commotion died down.

"She's an archaeologist, Jason,'' Argus said. "Her experience could be useful. She could give us a pretty good idea about the victim—whether it's male or female, the condition of its remains, which might reveal a lot. Am I right, Laura?''

"Yes. But to be honest, Sheriff, your doctor can probably tell you more than I can. I just wanted to get another look and take pictures."

Jason took a sip of coffee to hide his smile. "She's scrupulously honest, Argus."

Laura felt a deep flush of shame. If he only knew. She glanced away, and in doing so caught Ginny studying her curiously.

Matt could see he was going to be overruled by Argus. "Maybe it would be a good idea. Laura's got enough high-tech camera equipment with her to photograph the moon, and from the quality of the pictures I've seen, you'd be far better off using her camera than depending on that rinky-dinky rig of yours."

Argus nodded. "Save me a trip back to the station for my gear." He picked up his Stetson and settled it on his head. "That'll be Doc."

No one had heard anything, though Dog had raised his head from Ginny's thigh in interest.

As Argus pushed open the door to allow the doctor to enter, he shook the man's hand. "Sorry about the hour."

"Liar. It made your day to drag me out of my bed. Ginny, how you feeling? Don't answer that, I can see you're blooming. Ready for the little one to get here, aren't you. And you, Matt? Ginny tells me you're going to participate in the birthing. That's great." He patted the pale father-to-be on the shoulder. "No need to worry. I'll be right there."

Laura stifled a giggle. It wasn't only Matt's reaction to the mere mention of the birth that she found amusing, but also the doctor—he was the type who asked a million questions but didn't allow anyone to answer them. She had to admit she was surprised, though. She'd thought, by the way everyone talked about him, that he'd be an old man.

But Dr. Augustine Harper wasn't a day over forty, and among the giants of Two Rivers this man's lack of stature was refreshing. Doc was only her height, though stocky, and he was also totally bald. He wore wire-rim glasses that tended to slip on his small nose, and as he talked he was forever either pushing the glasses in place or rubbing his shiny head as if the action helped him think.

"Well, let's move it, people. Do you think I have all day?" Doc said impatiently. "Let's go see this body."

As everyone but Ginny started to leave, Matt halted the procession by blocking the doorway. His gaze settled on Dog, and he whistled softly to get the animal's attention. "You take care of her." Dog twisted his head around and showed a full mouth of gleaming teeth. "If she needs me, you come fetch me, okay?" When Dog barked, Matt, to everyone's amusement, nodded as if he and the animal understood each other and had made a pact.

Jason and Laura used her lights to guide everyone through the tunnels to the cave. The group was silent until Doc and Argus saw the cave paintings and exclaimed over them. Laura gave her theories as to how old she thought they were.

"You really believe these could be Anasazi markings?" Matt asked. "I didn't think they migrated this far east."

"I didn't, either, but I'd swear that some of the older paintings are from that period. They're almost identical to the Anasazi paintings in Arizona."

"How old are you talking about?" Doc asked as he stood almost nose to nose with one of the wall figures.

"Archaeology has dated the cliff dwellings of the Anasazi people in Canyon de Chelly in Arizona from A.D. 348 to about the eleventh century," Jason said. When he noticed they were all staring at him, he shrugged and said, "So shoot me—I did a little reading."

Laura couldn't explain the way she felt on hearing that Jason was interested enough to learn something of what she loved. She cleared her throat and continued to answer the doctor's question. "Mind you, evidence of the Anasazi ranged from Arizona, New Mexico, Colorado and Utah. There's even been some artifacts found in West Texas, so who's to say after the invasion of the Spanish that, like so many tribes, they didn't spread out, seeking safer places to live. But that's just my theory, you understand."

"Sounds pretty logical to me," Argus commented as he inspected the wall. "I've seen the cave art in Canyon de Chelly, the Pueblo Bonito at Chaco Canyon and the cliff dwellings along the San Juan River basin in New Mexico. These all look very similar."

"For a very long time," Laura continued, "this cave was sacred to the Indian tribes in this area. There's evidence of later markings of Apache, Comanche, Cheyenne and Kiowa. But the oldest and most exciting are on the back wall."

Jason led the way as they all followed the moving glow of his light, then halted when he did. Jason, determined to make the showing as dramatic as possible, waited until they were lined up before he slowly lifted the light.

"These are much, much older than the paintings."

Doc rubbed his head, pushed his glasses up on his nose and started to move closer to the wall when a dusting of shifting sand and pebbles rained down on his head. He quickly stepped back. "All those figures look as if they've been cut into the rock. How old are these?"

"They're what's called incised, pecked and stippled art," Laura answered. "As to how old they are? I don't dare even guess. I'd rather have a second opinion, plus get an anthropologist and a paleontologist to take a look at them." Her enthusiasm overcame reality, and when she glanced at Matt, all her promises came back like a slap in the face. She was never going to be able to verify her find other than from her pictures, drawings and her written descriptions. "Sorry—" she directed her apology at Matt "—I got carried away."

Matt said only, "It's too dangerous."

Laura took one of the lights from Jason and began working the beam across the floor until she located the alcove. After a brief discussion as to who was actually going to unearth the body, Argus decided that he and Doc would do the manual labor together, and that Matt and Jason would hold the lights while Laura helped them in between taking her pictures.

After a half hour of carefully removing the mound of piled rocks from the alcove, Argus stood up and held one of the stones from the broken alcove wall to the light. "Laura, get a couple of close-up shots of this. It's got mortar along the edges."

Jason shivered, causing the light to bounce somewhat. Suddenly it seemed colder in the cave, and the dark had a menacing feel to it. "Please, don't tell me this person was buried alive."

Doc continued to dust the deposit of powdery sand off the skeletal remains when he made a loud, long, hissing noise. The sound made everyone jump. Laura knelt down to see what he'd found and immediately started taking pictures. "You better tell them, Doc."

Doc didn't stop his examination as he felt everyone crowd in around him. "Our victim is a male, and as Laura said, he was probably around thirty-five or forty when he was placed here."

"Get to the good stuff, Doc," Jason whispered in a gravelly voice strained with excitement.

"Well, first things first." He moved to one side to allow for Laura's next photo. "The man was shot." Doc held up a piece of metal that resembled a tiny black mushroom. In his white limestone-coated hand, the dark, irregularly shaped piece looked menacing. "I'd say from the broken ribs that there were at least three shots." He continued to pick up pieces of lead. "Let me revise that." He dropped them one by one into the Ziploc bag Argus held out to him. "This man was shot at least six times."

Jason leaned over the seated doctor. "Overkill, isn't it?"

"Someone wanted to make damn sure he was dead," Doc said.

"A woman's method," Matt added, and everyone turned to look at him. "Fact—women usually empty a gun, and men tend to take careful aim."

"Interesting," Argus mused out loud as he held the bag to the light. "You're probably right, Matt. Anything else, Doc?"

"Yep. The man was buried naked. That's telling in itself—whoever did it was very smart and knew what he—or she—was doing. I'll find even more when I get him laid out on a table and do a professional examination." He motioned for Laura to kneel down beside him. "Take a look at his right hand."

When the Doc held up the bony hand by the wrist and the fingers wiggled, Jason flinched. "Don't play around with him for God's sake. Just put him in the body bag and let's get the hell out of here." When Doc glanced over his shoulder at him, the light reflected off his glasses, making his eyes appear like two black holes. Jason gulped.

Matt murmured, "Amen."

"Don't rush me," Doc said. "What do you think, Laura?"

She inspected the hand and the missing little finger. This wasn't the same hand from which she'd taken the finger bone. "There's a buildup of calcium and cartilage on the stump. I'd say he lost that finger at a very early age."

"I agree," Doc said. "Get some more pictures, then we'll bag him up." While Laura worked, he turned to the three men. "From what I can tell right now—you have an estimated thirty-five to forty-year-old man murdered some fifty years ago. The only identifying feature so far is a missing little finger on the right hand. He was shot six times, and from the broken ribs and shattered spinal cord, I'd say most of the six shots were fatal."

"That all you can tell us?" Jason asked.

"There are no clothes for identification," Matt said. "No fingerprints left. Doc might be able to trace any dental work, but fifty years ago... who's to say." He smiled at his friend. "Argus has his work cut out for him, a fifty-year-old mystery to solve. I don't envy him."

Argus watched as Doc and Laura carefully began transferring the bones to the body bag. "You're a liar, Matthew Bolt. You're just dying for me to ask you to help."

"Maybe," Matt said.

"Well? *Are* you going to help me?"

"If you insist."

When they were ready to leave the cave, Jason made sure he kept a couple of feet in front of everyone, not only to make sure they had sufficient light to see where they were going, but to make sure he stayed as far away from the sound of bones knocking together as possible. To his way of thinking, Doc was entirely too careless with the bag.

He was never so glad, he thought, to face the morning sun and its warmth. Shrugging out of his jacket, he sighed, caught Laura's smile and pulled her away from the rest of the group. "I can't help it. That bag of bones gives me the willies. Besides, I'm starving."

Laura's rumbling stomach was the only answer she needed. As she and Jason started toward the house, she looked back and saw Matt and the others talking to Jericho. "If he's been around here so long, maybe he knows who the bones belong to."

Jason's only answer was to quicken his steps and tighten his hold on her shoulder. "Let's put the light away and go get some grub."

Laura crawled into the back of the van, emptied her camera, placing the canister in her pocket with the others, and carefully packed all her equipment away. She was backing out when Jason grasped her around the waist, lifted her out and stood her on the ground in front of him.

"You never told me just how close you and this Jim fellow are. Friends? Lovers? What?"

"Are you still jealous, Jason?" Her laughter died when she realized how serious he was.

He brushed a smudge of white dust from her cheek, letting his fingers linger there a moment. "Surprise, surprise, but I believe I am."

She was shocked, and it must have shown because he smiled and pulled her against him. "What are you up to, Jason?"

"Oh, ye have a suspicious mind."

"You've been reading about Native American petroglyphs, haven't you. Why?"

He kissed her to make her stop asking questions, and to prevent his having to answer them. "First, tell me about your anthropologist friend."

"I used to date him, that's all."

"Not a lover?"

"Jason," she said, her tone half serious, half amused. "I haven't asked you about all, and I do mean all, your girlfriends."

"They don't matter because I'm not in love with any of them."

Her heart felt as if it had stopped, then started again by thumping hard against her chest. She gazed at him, noting how pensive he was, as if he was trying to say something. "Jim was never more than an interesting and fun date. He wasn't my lover."

Jason was so relieved he sighed and visibly swallowed. 'I'm crazy about you, you know that?"

"No. How crazy? As crazy as you are about the girls? Or that new commercial stove you keep polishing?" She was well aware of Jason's teasing nature and didn't want to read too much into his statement, but that didn't stop the twinge of hope.

He laughed. "Okay, get all your digs in. Make fun of me." He sobered and began again. "Laura—" But before he could finish, they both heard a loud, high-pitched voice coming from the kitchen. "That's Austin's indignant caterwauling. My guess is he's just gotten up and been told what's happening. He's not going to be a happy camper for being excluded." He threw an arm around her shoulder as they walked away from the van. "And Ginny's probably worried herself into an eating frenzy by now."

Ginny was, in fact, doing all she could to keep Austin from joining them in the cave. When Jason and Laura entered the kitchen, she sat down with a show of relief.

"Thanks for waking me up," Austin snarled. "I would've liked to see the bones, too, you know."

Jason managed to keep a straight face. His nephew's fierce temper fought with the sleep-tousled hair, the sheet imprint on the left side of his face and the crookedly buttoned pajama top. "Hey, Einstein, don't get mad at me. Do you have any idea what it takes to wake you from a sound sleep? It's like shaking a stone to life.

"Now, you're a big boy, and if you want to see the bones—" he held the screen door open "—then go to it. Doc's not even at his car yet." He'd barely gotten the words out of his mouth when the blur moved past him, Dog at his heels.

Laura looked around, took in the situation and quickly began gathering up the array of candy wrappers and an empty Coke can. "Shame on you, Ginny. You know you're not supposed to eat this stuff. Matt's going to be ticked off."

"I got a sudden little sweet tooth."

"More like a monster craving," Jason replied as he picked up a couple of wrappers from under the table and handed them to Laura.

"Better put those in your pocket, Laura. You can ditch them later." Ginny glanced out the window and hurriedly swished water around in her mouth. "My husband's gotten into the habit of checking the garbage can lately."

"Is this crap good for the baby?" Jason asked.

"If it's good for me, it's good for her." She could see Matt and Argus getting closer. "Don't be a tattletale, dear brother-in-law."

"Me? Never."

"Never what?" Matt asked as he came in, but he only received innocent looks from all three. He poured Argus a cup of coffee and stepped aside as Jason did the same for himself and Laura. He knew by the silence that Ginny had been up to something and they were covering. Before he sat down, he wiped the corner of Ginny's mouth with his thumb. "Snickers or M&M's? I know I smell peanuts." He looked from one to the other, waiting. "I see. She's sworn everyone to silence."

Jason caught Matt eyeing Laura, and noticed, as he was sure his brother had, the bulging front pocket of her jeans. He tried to distract the approaching one-sided argument between Ginny and Matt by offering to cook breakfast.

Austin returned just then, and he leaned against Laura's chair, striving to appear nonchalant. He spoke to her out of the corner of his mouth. It took her a moment to decipher the mumbled words, and when she did, she asked, "Now? I thought you were going to wait."

Austin gave up all pretense of subterfuge. He cupped his hand around Laura's ear and whispered, "Ginny was feeling pretty low when I came downstairs. You can tell because she always eats candy when she's down. I think she feels left out, like a prisoner, and needs some cheering up. Don't you?"

Laura slipped him the keys to the van. It was amusing to watch everyone try to hide their curiosity about what she and Austin were up to. It wasn't long before Austin returned, carrying a large box. She watched as he handed it to Ginny.

Ginny looked at the box, and suddenly everything was clear to her. She covered her mouth as tears slid down her cheeks. "This is the car seat I was talking about, isn't it?"

Austin grinned proudly and nodded. "The best and safest."

Ginny yanked a tissue from her shirt pocket and loudly blew her nose. "But how? This child's car seat is so expensive!" She had the typical horrible thought of all mothers. "Oh, Austin. You didn't skimp on your lunch to save money for this, did you?"

Matt struggled to swallow the lump in his throat. "He'd have been skin and bones if he'd done that. That's why you were tutoring that football player, wasn't it? For the money?''

"Sure, Dad. Can you think of any other good reason to try and teach chemistry to a jock other than for money?''

Food, tears and laughter seemed to be the answer to everyone's jittery nerves. And Jason, Laura thought, had other talents besides being a great lover. He most certainly had a way with bacon and eggs. She munched the last piece of bacon as she divided her attention, rather absently, between Ginny and Austin, who were going over the benefits of the car seat compared to others, and Matt and Argus, who were discussing what avenue to take on the investigation. Then abruptly, the sheriff changed the subject. He looked at Jason.

"The company trying to buy up your twenty-five acres is M.M. and Lloyd,'' Argus said.

Suddenly Laura's attention was riveted to Sheriff Gillespie and what he was saying. Her skin turned icy cold, but she could feel perspiration break out on her forehead.

Jason shook his head. "Never heard of them.''

She couldn't breathe as she was plunged into a nightmare of her own making.

Argus touched a napkin to his mouth. "The man I got the name from is a real-estate agent in Fredericksburg. Mark said he thought this M.M. and Lloyd was a dummy company and wanted to do a little more research. Before I left the house this morning, I checked my answering machine. I had five calls from Mark, and he seemed frantic to reach you, said your phone was out of order.'' He handed Jason a folded piece of paper. "Here's his number. Give him a call, will you?''

"Right now,'' Jason said, and reached for the telephone.

Laura couldn't sit there any longer, but she didn't dare draw attention to herself by jumping up and running from the room. She couldn't have, anyway, because her legs felt like frozen lumps stuck to her chair. When she finally forced them to straighten so she could stand, she found she had to hold on to the table to maintain an upright position.

She was taking too long and knew that any second someone, like the observant Ginny, was going to see she was about to collapse. Everything seemed to be moving in slow motion. She was dizzy and sick. She was hot and cold at the same time. Then, planting one weighted foot in front of the other, she managed to square her shoulders and walk from the room. When she finally got to the stairs, she hit them running. The only thing on her mind was to reach the bathroom before she was sick all over the floor.

She made it. She wiped her face with a damp cloth, then rested her head on her folded arms. She should have known better. She'd let her happiness overcome her good sense, her good judgment. Now everything was falling apart. Jason was going to find out who she was, and then he'd remember what she'd done. For eight years, she'd lived with the nightmare of one day having to face Jason Van der Bollen with the truth.

Her nightmare was finally reality.

CHAPTER THIRTEEN

LAURA KNEW ALL TOO WELL what and who M.M. and Lloyd was, and that knowledge sent a chill through her.

What was she going to do? Confess and take the consequences on the chin? Tell Jason who she really was and see the distaste in his eyes as recognition dawned?

She didn't have anyone to blame but herself. But who would have thought in a million years that events would take the turn they had? And, of course, in her desire to hide her head in the sand, she'd let things get out of hand. Up until now, it was only her secret, her embarrassment and shame. Yet, with that one telephone call Jason was making, probably at that very moment, she could now add *liar* to her list. Well—she strived to reason it out to her advantage—not exactly a liar. After all, she'd just omitted almost everything about herself to keep Jason from discovering her real identity.

Laura soaked a washcloth in cold water, wrung it out and covered her face. The only alternative to her problem was to run. The thought of leaving was too much to bear. She had to come up with a better option. What was the worst thing that could happen? Lowering the damp cloth, she stared at her reflection in the bathroom mirror. Jason could throw her out on her butt for lying to everyone. Ginny and Matt wouldn't speak to her. Austin would hate her for deceiving him and his family.

She groaned.

She hadn't actually openly, deliberately lied to anyone; she just hadn't volunteered anything important. Her attempt to rationalize didn't work very well. The minute she'd realized that Jason was Austin's uncle, she should have reminded him of the past and their meeting. "Damn," she whispered. Did she have the courage to tell him now? The fact that he had no memory of who she was, after all, was to her advantage. "Isn't it?" she asked.

The threat of something jogging his memory about another name connected to the May family was the razor edge of the sword that hung over her. Jason was a smart man. She couldn't continue hiding behind his lack of memory. Taking the towel from the rack, Laura patted her face dry. Her only deliverance was that eight years ago Jason was skunk-drunk. If he hadn't remembered her up to this point, maybe the odds were in her favor. Because of his condition then, he would never remember. "And," she said softly, "there have been a lot of women between then and now. Could an overindulgence in sex over a period of time affect a man's memory?"

Oh, who was she fooling? As much as she wanted to forget, she had more then just one sword edge to balance on. Her problem was twofold, two-edged. She felt sick all over again. If she'd just come to Two Rivers, done her work and left, nothing would have come of it. But no, she had to get involved with Ginny, Matt and Austin. Then to make matters worse, and even with that little voice of reason screaming foul, she'd done the most asinine thing since that act eight years ago—she'd fallen in love with Jason all over again.

No matter how hard she tried, there was just no getting around it; she was going to have to tough it out. She squeezed her eyes shut. She was a coward, and as hard as she argued with herself to come clean, the more that inner voice kept saying, *Not yet, not yet.* She thought of Jason and the others sitting in the kitchen probably wondering where she was. She would have to rejoin them and find out what was happening before she could make up her mind what to do.

As she returned to the kitchen and reclaimed her chair, no mention of her absence was made, and her tense muscles relaxed a fraction. Jason absently put his arm around her shoulder as if to reassure himself she was back. Then he continued to talk. Paying attention to what was being said wasn't easy—her mind kept racing ahead to the inevitable confrontation. Her fear had made her almost deaf to what was being said, and she only managed to catch bits and pieces, but they were enough for her to realize her secret was still safe. But her relief was short-lived when she heard Matt's question.

"Holcombe May?" Matt asked.

"Of May Market Corporation," Jason said, "the monster superstore magnate."

Laura's blood froze in her veins at the mention of the May name. She didn't know how she managed to turn her head and look at Jason, waiting for his reaction as recognition of the May name struck. But she didn't see so much as a twitch of response.

"I've heard of Holcombe superstores," Argus said, "but what does that have to do with the company that's making the offer for your land?"

"Your friend Mark found out that Holcombe May wants to expand his empire into Texas. He's targeted my twenty-five acres outside of town. Mark says the Fredericksburg Merchants Association, the Civic Club and city council want to meet with me immediately. Actually, they want to make an offer on the property to keep it out of May's hands."

Ginny had been quiet until now. She struggled to sit up straight and said, "Oh, my. I know who you're talking about." She whistled softly under her breath. "No wonder the businessmen of Fredericksburg want a meeting. Holcombe's are the super of superstores. They carry everything under the sun, from fresh produce and farm equipment, to seeds and potted plants. They have their own bakery and their own name brand of soft drinks to outprice all the big companies, and a huge pharmacy.

"And Holcombe's builds these connecting buildings, like barns, where they pride themselves on selling antiques, folk art and country arts and crafts from every state in every one of their locations. That's the type of merchandise that Fredericksburg, Two Rivers and a lot of other towns around here thrive on. I've seen what these stores do to small towns. It's frightening. They come in, build their monster stores in strategic areas and dramatically undercut the local merchants' prices. After a few months they manage to turn every midsize small town within a hundred miles into ghost towns."

She paused and met Jason's gaze directly. "What are you going to do?"

"Not sell to them of course!" he snapped, surprising everyone. "Two Rivers is just getting back on its feet again. Have you noticed how many of our age group are dropping out of the stress of the corporate world and returning home to a simpler life-style? Home businesses and services are what's happening. But what's more important, there's a big movement to get back to the basics of living and raising children in a better environment. Returning home to small towns has become very attractive. Can you imagine what would happen if a Holcombe's is built outside of town?"

"They're big, Jason, and tough," Ginny said glumly, then brightened. "If you're serious about not selling, then we need to have our own town council meeting, start the wheels to rezone all the property around here for only residential or farmland."

Matt jumped in before his wife got too carried away. "Argus can handle the town meeting. But tell me this, Jason. You laughed when you first mentioned M.M. and Lloyd. Why?"

Laura prayed the floor would open up and suck her in, she was so scared.

"M.M. is Monica May. The Lloyd part is her twin brother, Lloyd May. They're Holcombe's oldest children. Both of them are a real piece of work."

"Monica May?" Ginny frowned, then gasped. "Isn't she the Monroe-ish movie star? And just how do you know them? You *do* know her, I take it?"

Laura swallowed hard and waited for the ax of his memory to drop on her head.

"I had a couple of dates with Monica."

Everyone laughed, and Matt said, "We all assumed that, Jason. Who *haven't* you dated?"

He chose to ignore the remark and go on with his story. "When I was at university, I had a bitch of an advanced business course, plus a professor who took a dislike to me—just because his wife and I shared a few drinks. Anyway, I thought I'd curry favor if I picked a tough subject for a term paper—the history and economics of the May Market Corporation. I even flew out to Ohio and managed to meet and interview the man himself. Actually, he's a pretty down-to-earth guy. We got along quite well, for some reason.

"You know the May Market empire started with a chain of feed stores in the Midwest. Then they added a general store. It was old Holcombe's grandfather who started the business by providing everything he could think of to farmers who were too far from a town to make even weekly trips. Holcombe's father and Holcombe himself just kept expanding on the idea.

"Anyway, Holcombe invited me to spend the weekend at the family estate with his family. That's where I met Monica and Lloyd. Monica and I kind of hit it off, but Lloyd—he's spoiled, arrogant, mean-spirited and was instantly jealous of the way his father and I got along. My last evening there, Holcombe threw a party in my honor, and Lloyd—I can't prove this, mind you—deliberately tried to get me falling-down drunk so I'd make a fool of myself. Almost succeeded, but Monica realized what her brother was up to and rescued me."

Laura closed her eyes and waited for recognition to hit. When nothing happened she couldn't figure it out. Surely he should have remembered. But then she hadn't known what Lloyd had tried to do, nor that Jason had been so drunk. She shivered with hope and a deep sense of relief. Maybe there was a chance for her to rectify the situation before Jason found out.

Jason felt her shudder. Concern softened the hard edge of his voice. "Are you cold? You look pale."

She couldn't have pried her cotton-dry mouth open with a crowbar, so instead, she vigorously shook her head.

"I'll say this," Jason went on. "I don't think Lloyd has changed in the past eight or so years. He's used to getting what he wants, and he's ruthless. He wants my land, and I expect a legal battle is out of the question. The May Market Corporation must have a hundred lawyers and an entire department dedicated to steamrolling over individuals and small towns who oppose him. Argus, the sooner you get the town together for a special session of the council, the quicker we can start putting the brakes on Golden Boy's juggernaut and maneuvering. I'm going to call in a few favors from some movers and shakers in Austin. See what they can tell me. Plans would have to be filed, permits requested."

It took a moment for Laura to realize what the cause of the silence was about. They were all stunned by Jason's take-charge know-how and his business acumen. It seemed the family tomcat and playboy had more on the brain than his personal pleasure, women and sex. They were used to his wild comings and goings, irresponsible behavior and his rash schemes, always soon abandoned. She could have told them Jason was no longer the same man—if he had ever been all those things they accused him of being.

Jason took a second to enjoy the shock. He knew full well what people, even his family, thought of him. It always amused him to play games with people's heads. The misconceptions were usually to his advantage. He'd made a huge profit on the sale of the buffalo herd and long-horns, pulled off a ten-year grazing lease for the land and was in the process of allowing a drilling company to tap off gas wells they'd located on the same grazing land. He'd sold his interests, also at a profit, in his advertising agency and the wine-and-cheese shops in Austin.

Granted, he'd blown almost every penny, but his dreams were close at hand now, and all the worry and sacrifices were worth it. "I need to get some work done at the house and make some calls." He kept his arm firmly on Laura's shoulder and leaned toward her. "Are you going to help me?"

Laura's answer was to push the chair away from the table. "After Austin and I clean up the kitchen." She mussed Austin's hair and smiled as he grumbled about dishpan hands and women's work, which only got him a few stern words from his father. "Why don't you go on, Jason, and I'll be there as soon as I'm finished here and change clothes." She needed some time to deal with her relief that Jason didn't remember, didn't know her at all. A ton of guilt immediately lifted off her shoulders.

IF THERE WAS ONE THING Jason was an expert at, it was seduction. The problem now was the setting: his unfinished bedroom walls, with the wiring visibly hanging, insulation drooping and the air-conditioning ducts that looked like a long silver snake didn't exactly make for seductive atmosphere.

But then, he was always up for a challenge. He draped and tacked designer sheets around the walls. He changed the bedsheets and neatly and invitingly turned the covers back. Even though the morning sun streamed through the skylight, Jason placed scented candles around the room. He carefully picked through his CD collection and stacked them in the player next to the bed.

The only fly in the ointment was that most of his things were packed away and stored in a room at Matt's. He was forced to ice the champagne in a plastic bucket he'd used to mix joint compound, and instead of crystal flutes, he had to be happy with the jelly glasses he and Laura had been using. Standing back, hands on his hips, he glanced around with a sense of pleasure. He'd done pretty well, considering his limitations. Now all he needed was Laura.

LAURA FELT as if she was walking on air. She was free! She'd even convinced herself she'd blown her fears way out of proportion, anyway.

She was almost at the end of the drive when the emus spotted her. They set up a welcoming racket as all ten of them rushed the fence. Veering off the drive, Laura climbed the fence and balanced on the top rail. Attila was the first to reach her, and he cooed as he rubbed his head against her leg and batted his long eyelashes at her. "You're a terrible flirt." The others crowded around, each wanting their share of attention. Even shy Joan seemed to be coming out of her shell and vied with pushy Helen to be talked to and petted.

Laura never heard Jason coming up behind her, and when he placed his hands on her shoulders, she shrieked, lost her balance and fell against him. His arms closed around her, and he laughed. The birds screamed and flapped their stunted wings in shock, or was it laughter, too?

"Damn you, Jason." Laura twisted around to face him. "If you think I'm going to help you after that, you're nuts."

"Never crossed my mind," Jason said. "You're not one to take the blame for anything you might be responsible for, are you."

For a split second she wondered if there was a hidden meaning in what he'd said, then decided it was just the residue of her guilty conscience. She couldn't help but notice the way the sun caught his blond hair, making it shine like gold, and the way his eyes looked even bluer, more intense, in the light. Most of all she loved the shape of his mouth and the way one corner curved upward when he was amused and fighting not to show it.

His breath caught in his throat when he saw the way her gaze was all over him. "You could get into real trouble looking at me like that."

"Like what?" She was a little embarrassed at being caught with her emotions plastered on her face. "Don't make a mountain out of a molehill here. I'm a little tired, that's all. I haven't actually had much sleep. And what you think you saw was exhaustion.'' She pulled away from him and stomped off.

"Liar," Jason whispered. "It wasn't exhaustion I saw." He followed her, then reached out and grabbed her, loving the way she threw her head back and laughed, really laughed, not some simpering giggle. "I know what I know, and you want me so bad you can hardly wait." Slowly he pulled her against him, pinning her arms to her sides.

"There goes that overinflated ego of yours again."

Suddenly he slid one arm down her body and behind her knees, and before she knew it, she was swept up and being carried toward the house. "Stop squirming. This is the only way to keep you from falling all over me. You've got my full attention now, Professor."

"You're being ridiculous again," she said stoutly. "I never planned . . ." She totally ruined the sternness by the way her lips curved ever so slightly. She laughed, wrapped her arms around his neck and soundly kissed him.

"I dare you to kiss me like that again when my hands are free."

Laura clucked her tongue and made noises like the emus. "What's the matter, can't take it?"

"Oh, you're all talk now, but we'll see just how brave you are when we get inside."

"I'm capable of walking on my own, Jason. Put me down."

"No. Not after yesterday." He pushed open the front door, went in then kicked it shut. "I'm not letting you out of my sight. You might take it into your head to run off again without telling me." He paused at the bottom of the stairs to catch his breath. "Or maybe one of your boyfriends will lure you away."

"If you don't let me down, you're liable to have a heart attack—then where will we be? Jason!"

"Maybe you're right." He dropped his arm from under her legs but kept her pressed against him while her body slid down and her feet touched the floor. Then he kissed the tip of her nose. "Besides, I'm going to need my strength, aren't I." He took hold of her hand and started to lead her up the stairs.

She was suddenly nervous under that electric blue gaze of his but couldn't have looked away if she'd tried. It wasn't until they were at the top of the stairs that he stepped aside. Her eyes skimmed the room. "Oh!" was all she could say when she realized the effort he'd gone to.

Other than the obvious transformation, something major had changed. For the past few weeks, they'd been working together, spending hours talking, making love when the mood hit them and just being close. Now, all of a sudden, Jason had decided to change their routine and make this time together special.

Jason handed her a jelly jar of Matt's special stock of champagne, and as he did, he kissed the back of her neck. "Do you like it?"

"The champagne?" She sipped. "Of course." For some silly reason she felt the sting of tears when she noticed the jelly jars. Her pulse sped up. "Why, Jason?"

He took the jar from her hand, led her to the side of the bed and began working at the knot of her shirt, tied at her waist. "I had a hell of a day yesterday, Laura. I realized something, too. Not only was I jealous thinking of you and Chapman together, but I missed you."

"I missed you, too." Her fingers trembled with expectation and excitement as she quickly unbuttoned his shirt.

Jason stilled her hands. "I want the truth. No lies."

For a moment she froze, fear eating at the edges of her desire for him.

"I'm not just an easy make?" he asked. "You're not just using me for sex?" He playfully slapped at her hungry hands. "I'm not a sex object, you know. You can't have me on demand."

She loved his sense of humor, his sense of the ridiculous. "I could never take advantage of you." Jason was a never-ending delight, and it was obvious he wanted to play. "You know how I feel about you."

He'd carefully led her into his trap. He tightened his grip on her arms, lifted her a little and gently laid her back on the bed. As he leaned over her, he said, "Actually, Laura, I don't have the slightest idea how you feel about me. Why don't you tell me?"

It wasn't so much his question, but the way he looked at her, the seriousness of his gaze, that took her breath away. She was about to give him a glib answer, but he placed a finger across her lips.

"I know you. You have an honest nature, honest to a fault, maybe. You've also got a soft heart and wouldn't want to hurt my feelings. But I need you to be truthful about this."

The mention of honesty jabbed at her conscience. For a moment she strove frantically for an answer. Then she relaxed under his weight, deciding to give as good as she got. "I'm crazy about you, Jason."

Clever, he thought, and smiled. Then he quickly undid the front clasp of her bra, and lowered his lips between her breasts. "I'm to be satisfied with that?"

"I was—" she sucked in a breath of air as his mouth found an already sensitive nipple "—when you told me the same." Laura closed her eyes, loving the way he touched her, the way his hands were gentle as they slipped off her shirt and bra completely, then unzipped her shorts and slid them down her legs.

Her fingers were playing with the buttons on his jeans fly, slowly undoing each one and brushing against him. His greedy desire for her suddenly overcame his need to worm out answers. There was a buzzing in his head, a warning that he was losing control. When he tried to move away, put only enough distance between them to call a mental time-out, she wasn't having any of it. The knowledge that she wanted him with the same depth as he did set every cell in his body humming. He claimed her mouth in a hungry kiss, full of emotions that neither of them was willing to openly discuss.

They spoke their feelings for each other with their lips and hands and finally their bodies. The heat of desire consumed them as the flames licked at their very core, an uncontrollable craving that only each other's touch could quench. She dug her nails into his back, arched, gasped and whispered his name on a breath she thought was her last. When the next climax came, he slammed into her, taking her with him on his own ride for release.

They lay entwined, hot and spent for long moments. At last Jason eased his weight off her, and said, "Have you thought what you're going to do when you're through at the caves?"

She was still floating in the erotic world of release, her body tingling and sensitive, so it took a moment for Jason's question to sink in. If she'd learned one thing about Jason it was that he was not one to give up easily or quietly. Whatever he'd had on his mind earlier was still an itch he needed scratched, and he wasn't about to let go. For a moment she lay staring up at the dream catcher swinging gently above them, then she smiled and pulled the sheet up over her nakedness. "I'll go back to Austin for a while, and maybe home before classes start again."

Jason crossed his hands behind his head. "You'll go visit your family?"

She nodded, too tired to speak and a little scared at his line of questioning.

He felt, more than saw, her nod. "Have you thought... Would you think about staying here?"

"In Two Rivers?" Her heart started beating faster and she strived to stay calm.

"Yes. But not with Ginny and Matt or in some room in town, but—" the word stuck a second in his throat "—here with me."

For a moment she didn't move or speak, then she rolled on her side to face him, a glib remark on the tip of her tongue—until she saw the nervousness and uncertainty in his eyes. She smiled sweetly. The time was right to tell him. "Jason, there's something I think you should know."

He was suddenly up on one elbow, gazing down at her. "Laura, I don't want you to walk out of my life, and I can't move back to Austin, not with the emus and this." He waved a hand at the room. She looked as if she wanted to say more, but he hushed her with a kiss and said, "I don't want to rush you into anything you might feel uncomfortable with, but think about staying, okay?"

He reached across her and picked up the two jelly jars from the table, then handed one to her. She felt shell-shocked. She kept running his question over and over in her mind. Then she smiled up at the ceiling. The silly goose, she thought, he was scared. Scared she'd turn him down. She seriously doubted if he'd ever asked any woman to actually live with him before. Now it was her turn to have a little fun.

She sipped at her warm champagne. "Are you asking me to come live with you, Jason?"

"I know you wouldn't have classes every day. You could commute between here and the university easily enough. We've got a long way to go to finishing the place."

He was talking fast from nervousness, she knew. "You didn't answer my question." she said. "Do you want me to live with you? Is that what you're asking, or do you just want cheap labor?"

In his blind panic about being turned down, he hadn't realized she was playing with him. Now it dawned on him, and he chuckled. "You want your pound of flesh."

"Yes, indeed." What she really wanted was a marriage proposal, but couldn't bring herself to say the words. He grabbed her, and she started laughing.

"What will your friends and parents think?" he asked. "You'll have to tell them."

The mention of family brought on a deep dread. "I haven't said yes, Jason."

"But you will."

She stroked his rough cheek. "You're so sure of yourself?"

He was suddenly serious. "No. Just wishful thinking. But you will?"

"I don't know." A thousand reasons to turn him down raced through her mind, and an equal number urged her to give in. But life wasn't that simple. She wanted a home, children and the security, as far as it went nowadays, of marriage. But she couldn't agree, couldn't say yes or no to anything until she'd come clean with Jason. She took a deep breath. The moment was right to tell him what she'd been hiding, but Jason kissed the words away, and by the time he let her go, the moment had gone.

"Just think about it, Laura."

Spent and happy, the effects of the sleepless night took hold of them, and they drifted off in each other's arms. It was Jason who awakened with a jerk, knowing something wasn't right. He sat up and glanced at the clock. He was about to throw the covers back when he remembered Laura curled up beside him. For a moment he enjoyed just looking at her, then he kissed her warm, bare shoulder.

"Laura," he whispered against her skin, moving his lips up her neck. "Laura, we have to get up. Matt and Ginny will be expecting us for dinner." He chuckled when she snuggled down deeper in the bed and pulled the sheet over her head to shut him out. "If we don't hurry up, Austin's going to come get us."

"Go away, Jason. I'm not hungry."

He had a grump in his bed. This was a side to her he'd never seen. He grinned, lifted one edge of the sheet and said, "You promised Austin you and he would make peach ice cream after dinner. You know he's *not* about to forget anything that has to do with his stomach."

Laura sat up, yawning, and ran her fingers through her hair. "I was having the most unusual dream in which you said you were crazy about me and wanted me to live with you. Weird, wasn't it?"

Jason whipped the covers back and vaulted over her. He had grasped hold of her arm in the wild leap so that when his feet hit the floor Laura was pulled out of the bed.

Her laughter died as he led her to the shower. She wondered how she was going to get herself out of the mess she'd made. The longer she let the truth lay unrevealed, the more it was going to fester into a major problem.

Tonight, she promised, and felt a deep sense of relief. Tonight, after dinner, when Matt, Ginny and Austin went to bed, she'd sit Jason down and have a long talk with him. She'd tell him everything.

CHAPTER FOURTEEN

"WHAT DO YOU MEAN I have to crank it?" Austin demanded, his face still with shock as what Laura was telling him sunk in. He set the plastic bag full of crushed ice down, jammed his hands on his hips and leaned over the old-fashioned ice-cream maker, eyeing it with a mixture of curiosity and distaste. Then he glanced at Matt. His dark eyes narrowed as he realized Laura and his father had played a trick on him. "Where's the motor?"

Laura bit her lip, ducked her head and poured salt around the big cylinder. "Austin, I need another layer of ice, please."

Austin did as he was asked, but his attention was elsewhere. "You're joking, aren't you, Laura? There's a motor, right?"

She reached over and felt the muscle in his right arm. "That's the motor."

"Man," Austin grumbled, "this isn't fair. How long do I have to crank the stupid thing?" But there was a resigned tone to his griping.

"Probably about thirty minutes," Laura said. "Then, of course, it will have to sit another thirty minutes or so to harden. But your uncle Jason told me on the way over here that he'd spell you."

Austin huffed in exasperation. "That's a relief."

Jason grinned and ruffled his nephew's hair. He was feeling too happy and magnanimous to argue with anyone. "What I used to do, Einstein, is when I thought my arm was about to fall off, I'd think real hard of all that cold ice cream and I'd crank faster."

"I never would've asked for homemade ice cream if I'd known the machine was an antique with no motor." Suddenly Austin brightened. "Couldn't we hook some kind of harness on Dog and let him crank it?"

Dog, sensing trouble, lifted his head and growled, but he'd heard his favorite word—ice cream—and wasn't about to leave the kitchen. He sidled closer to Ginny, rested his head on her knee and gave her his most pitiful look.

"Damn mutt's become an actor," Jason said. "But it won't work with me, Dog." He realized everyone was staring at him and quickly continued, "We have an understanding. I explained what was going to happen to him if he ever upsets my girls."

"And what did Dog say to that?" Ginny asked.

"Well, he didn't grin when I explained the details of the operation." He watched with interest as Laura topped off the ice-cream machine with ice, then locked the top on and inserted the crank. "Ever since Ginny's been here, Dog's become a lazy, good-for-nothing mutt. He doesn't even tomcat around at night anymore."

"Sounds like someone else I know." Matt looked at his brother.

Laura listened to the good-natured family banter, even joined in—until she remembered what she'd promised herself to do that evening.

At last the ice cream was done. They retired to the family room to enjoy it, eating until there were moans and they'd scraped the large cylinder spotlessly clean.

Ginny rubbed her stomach, then laughed as the baby kicked furiously. "I think that's her favorite. This is a million times better then the most expensive store-bought stuff." She glanced at Dog sprawled at her feet, his stomach bulging. "You see, Dog agrees." She tickled the round belly with her bare toes. "Poor baby, he ate too much, too."

Jason closed his eyes and groaned. "Well, I can't believe I ate two bowls."

Laura was in the process of collecting the bowls and spoons to take to the kitchen when the front doorbell sounded. Usually visitors came to the back door; this was such an unusual happening that for a second no one moved. When Jason said he'd get it and struggled to get up off the sofa, Laura gathered up the rest of the dishes and continued on to the kitchen.

As she placed the bowls and utensils in the dishwasher and filled the cylinder with hot soapy water to soak, she couldn't help but be pleased. The dessert had turned out even better than she'd hoped. Homemade ice cream was the one thing her mother was a master at, and even though she'd been allowed to help, she'd never actually made it. She'd panicked for a moment, trying to remember the right measurements. But it had all come back to her, and from the way everyone had oohed and ahhed and almost licked their bowls, they thought so, too.

Of course, her good mood was partly because of Jason. He'd been in high form that evening with his teasing. Ginny and Matt might not have noticed, but she certainly had—he'd seldom left her side and was never more than a touch away. She leaned against the kitchen counter and smiled. After drying her hands, she replaced the dish towel and started out of the kitchen and down the hall.

She was too far away to hear more than the muffled sound of voices, but as she drew nearer she realized they were men's voices—Jason's and another.

Premonition slowed her steps. Dread brought her to a dead stop outside the door as she identified that other voice. Fear kept her from entering the family room and confronting the people she loved with her lies. She closed her eyes as a voice in her head screamed, *Why did you wait?* She should have told Jason. She hung her head in despair and listened.

WHEN JASON OPENED the front door, his welcoming smile died a quick death. "Hello, Lloyd. I was wondering if you'd show up in person or send one of your underlings." He glanced at Lloyd May's "bookends," and though the two men were, like their boss, fashionably dressed, there was too much muscle under the expensive material for them to be anything other than Lloyd's goons.

It was still a shock to look at Lloyd, but see Monica. They were only fraternal twins, of course, but they were still uncannily alike. Both were brown-eyed blondes, both five foot ten, though where Monica's height made her tall and stately, Lloyd's made him small in stature. Their facial structure was the same, except Lloyd's was a little sharper than Monica's. It was weird standing there seeing Lloyd and at the same time remembering Monica and what they'd shared off and on for a year.

Lloyd walked past Jason and into the house, his men close behind. He'd expected wealth; his research department had done a thorough job on the Van der Bollens. But he wasn't prepared for the size, style and obvious "old money." The magnitude of the vineyard, even in the dark, had been another revelation. And Jason wasn't at all as he remembered, nor did the Texan seem to fit his background research. Van der Bollen was no inept weakling with little sense and more money than he knew what to do with. Lloyd didn't like surprises, and from everything he knew and had found out, this should have been merely a meeting for Jason to posture, hem and haw, and attempt to up the price of his land.

Jason shut the door, his smile like a sleek cougar who'd just spotted his next meal. He knew why Lloyd was here, knew the businessman had done his research. But Lloyd only thought he had the lowdown on him, the Van der Bollens and their money. Mentally he rubbed his hands together in anticipation. He couldn't wait to have his fun and turn pretty-boy Lloyd over to the oldest son and heir— Matt. Just the thought of Lloyd coming up against his brother made him smile and his eyes sparkle.

"Why don't you join us in the family room?" Jason waved his hand toward the open double doors.

Lloyd nodded, taking in the furnishings, paintings and scattered European antiques in the room before he gave his attention to the people. He didn't like the familiarity and the memories of this hick from Texas, and was forced to smile amiably at the pregnant woman and the boy. Their presence gave him a jolt. He hadn't been aware of Jason's having a wife and kid.

Jason was enjoying Lloyd's confusion immensely. "This is Ginny and Austin, my sister-in-law and nephew." He stepped aside just as Matt unfolded his height from the chair behind him. "And this is my brother, Matt."

Jason almost danced a jig when the three men turned their attention to Matt. His brother, in his opinion, looked like what he was—a dangerous man. From Matt's height and build, long black hair tied back in a ponytail, jet eyes narrowed and assessing, to the curve of his mouth expressing his mild amusement at the two bodyguards, there was no mistaking the feel of an unspoken threat. Tension hung thickly in the air. Maybe it was the law of the jungle, the predators sensing there was a meaner, more menacing beast close at hand, but Jason didn't miss the way Lloyd's men sized up Matt and immediately recognized a professional. One of them mumbled a few words to Lloyd.

"Brother?" Lloyd said, and winced as he shook hands with Matt. "I didn't realize there was more than one Van der Bollen heir."

Matt sat back down, and Jason realized he was letting him handle this. He saw the way his brother captured Ginny's hand so that if she decided to interfere he could give her a warning squeeze. Ginny smiled and nodded, understanding Jason's need to control the situation. Jason's gaze shifted to his nephew, noticing the way the kid was curled up in a large wing chair, striving to go unnoticed so he wouldn't be sent from the room.

Jason had to think a second to recall what Lloyd had just asked. "You're right, there is only one heir—Matt. He's the firstborn."

Another surprise, Lloyd thought. He didn't like it. "Then you don't own the vineyard and the land I'm interested in?"

"The vineyard, this house and the surrounding land—no. But the land you're interested in is mine." By not inviting the men to be seated, he'd set the tone he wanted.

"You live here?" asked Lloyd. Surely his research department had totally screwed up. It hadn't escaped him, either, that he hadn't been offered a seat.

"No. I have the house across the highway. You want to introduce your two...assistants?"

Lloyd shrugged. His confusion had made his manners slip. "Paul and Booth."

"So, what can I do for you, Lloyd? I thought I'd made myself crystal clear to your agent and you. The land is not for sale."

Lloyd smiled, his tone arrogant and confident. "Everything's for sale, Jason. It's just a matter of price."

"My land's not." Jericho had taught him to play poker, how to bluff and how to be on the lookout for an opponent's little tricks that would give his hand away. Lloyd's intentions were evident in the way he shifted his weight, the way his hands in his trouser pockets tightened into fists. Jason continued leaning against the wall, his arms crossed carelessly over his chest, his smile at its most charming.

"Listen, let's not dance around this," Lloyd snapped. "I came here as a courtesy to you, and because of your friendship with my sister and father, to make a face-to-face offer, instead of sending some eager executive. I'm willing to double my offer, but that's it, old man. It's more than enough for the twenty-five acres."

"Oh, I agree. Actually, *old man,* your *first* offer was more than enough for nothing but rocks, scrub and trees. But *you* didn't make the offer, Lloyd. You hid behind a blind company. You tried to sneak into a community, buy up the land, were going to start construction of a Holcombe Superstore without even considering what it would do to Two Rivers and any other town within a fifty-mile radius." Jason pushed away from the wall and dropped his arms to his sides. "I don't want a Holcombe's here. That's why the land is not for sale."

"We're not prepared to change our plans. You know, Jason, when Dad said he wanted to test the Texas market, I thought of you and your little Two Rivers. I remembered how you talked about the values and families and the people. So, I decided to come here.''

"Just so you could make it a ghost town?'' Jason asked. He was well aware Lloyd had hated him eight years ago; Lloyd wasn't good at hiding his feelings. But it stunned him that with maturity, Lloyd still hated him.

Lloyd could see that Jason had made up his mind, and any higher offer was going to fall on deaf ears. He nodded, made as if to leave, then stopped. His gaze drifted to the pregnant woman and the kid. "I'm sorry to hear that, Jason. I always get what I go after—but I think you know that. We do what it takes, and sometimes in the process innocent people end up getting hurt. If that were to happen, the blame would, of course, fall on your head.''

Matt had been carefully monitoring the conversation and gauging the subtle nuances in Lloyd's tone. He didn't miss the threat or the way the man looked at his family. Before Jason could stop him, Matt was blocking Lloyd's exit and at the same time giving a hand signal to a growling Dog to stand guard at Ginny's side. He'd had a lot of pent-up frustrations over the past couple of months, his fuse was short, and this guy had just pushed all his buttons at once.

Matt was close enough to see the masked fear in Lloyd's eyes, and it gave him a savage pleasure. "That's your first and last mistake.'' He sensed Lloyd's men move closer to intervene, but he stopped them with a quick turn of his head and a single look, one reserved for putting blood-chilling fear into the most hardened of criminals. The two men understood and froze.

Matt returned his attention to Lloyd. "I don't think you fully realize what trouble is, but you're perilously close to finding out. When you're older and wiser, you'll learn to hold your tongue. Until then, let me give you your one and only warning. If I ever see you or your men around here again, I'll tear out your tongue and feed it to you. You don't come in my house and threaten my family." Matt calmly turned around and joined Ginny on the couch.

Jason wondered how Matt had managed to stay so cool. Following his brother's lead, he took a deep breath and grinned at Lloyd. "I think that about says it all, doesn't it."

Lloyd shrugged, striving to appear unmoved, but Matt's eyes had shown him a side of human nature he'd never seen before. Fear wasn't natural to him; he could either bully his way through something or buy it. One way or the other he never lost. Anger began to replace fear, and he leaned close to Jason. "I think after a time you'll be willing to sell."

"I won't change my mind. Get out, Lloyd."

"We'll see." He started to walk toward the open door when he stopped in surprise.

"You never change, do you, Lloyd?" Laura said, stepping into the room. "You're still the same mean-spirited bastard. But this time you've gone too far. You've threatened people I care about, and I won't allow you to get away with it."

All through the conversation Laura had stood glued to her position outside the family room, paralyzed with fear. She was appalled at the seemingly effortless threat that Lloyd had made, and even though she believed Matt would do as he said, it didn't stop the terror from squeezing her heart. They didn't know what Lloyd was capable of doing, of who he could hurt before he could be stopped. But she knew all too well.

"Daisy!" Lloyd was, once again, thrown off balance and his anger soared. "What the hell are you doing here? Are you in on this effort to stop me?"

Laura flicked the question aside like a pesky insect. Her attention was riveted on Jason. The name Lloyd called her by should have been like a two-by-four slammed between his eyes, but Jason didn't seem to have made the connection. She felt relief, but knew it would be fleeting. "I swear this isn't what it looks like, Jason." She was taken aback by his serene smile and the twinkle in his eyes. Then she glanced at Ginny, saw the confusion and hurt. Matt's expression was noncommittal and watchful as he kept his attention on Lloyd's men.

"Dammit, Daisy!" Lloyd snarled.

"Shut up, Lloyd." She knew he wasn't used to being talked to like that, especially from her. "Jason, I haven't lied to you. I just couldn't tell you. Please, you must believe me—I never lied."

Jason continued to smile. "I know that."

"Why the hell are you talking to him when I asked you a question?" Lloyd demanded. "I want an answer."

Laura looked at Lloyd with contempt. "Well, what is it?" She was all too acquainted with the changes in his expression, and watched the shock slip into outrage.

He took a couple of steps toward her. "Listen, you little bitch. Tell me what you're doing here."

"I could ask you the same thing, but from what I just heard, it's obvious." He took another step toward her, placing her within his reach. She was aware of Ginny's gasp of fright and the urgency in her whisper to Matt. Jason moved close to her side and inflamed Lloyd's anger even more by placing his arm around her shoulders.

"Tell me something, Van der Bollen, isn't one May sister enough for you? You seduced Monica and walked away. Now you're after my little sister. Isn't she too young for your tastes?"

"You leave Jason out of this." Laura stepped directly in front of Jason as if to protect him from Lloyd's nasty insinuations. "I'm not your sister, Lloyd!" she shouted, losing all patience and the tight hold she had on her temper. "Get this through your thick head. I'm not Daisy *May*. I'm Laura Daisy Ghant. My mother married Holcombe. He did not adopt me."

"Only because that fool of a father of yours wouldn't have it."

She ran her fingers through her hair, wanting to pull it out. How many times since she'd lived with the Mays had she heard that same argument? "You're wrong, as usual. I didn't want to be a May, thank you very much. I made that clear to my father and to Holcombe. And my father is not a fool, he's a noted paleontologist." Lloyd had always had the power to trigger her temper, and the attack on her father was just the start. But she wasn't going to fall into his trap this time.

The intimacy between Daisy and Jason hadn't gone unnoticed by Lloyd. The target of his rage shifted. "Is seducing Daisy your way of payback, Jason, for what I did?" He hesitated for a heartbeat as a thought hit him. "Or did you do that, too, eight years ago? I always thought Daisy was infatuated with you. Maybe you have a taste for fifteen-year-old girls. Did you—"

"Shut your filthy mouth!" Laura moved so quickly no one was expecting, nor could they have stopped, the slap that resounded loudly in the quiet room.

It seemed to Laura then that everyone jumped up in the same instant.

Austin bounded out of the chair, rushing one of the bodyguards with the intention of tackling him around the knees, but Matt pulled him away.

Dog clamped his teeth firmly on the other bodyguard's calf, and the man was smart enough not to even twitch.

Lloyd drew back his fist, ready to slug Laura, but Jason caught it, gave one hard, quick twist and had him on his knees as if he was praying. Jason liked the analogy and smiled. As much as he wanted to break Lloyd's neck, and could have easily, he kept calm, his voice even. "This has become too ugly for my taste, old man. We don't try to punch women in this house. Apologize."

Laura grasped Jason's arm. "I'm used to his rages and tirades." She was also aware of Lloyd's vicious vindictiveness. He was a maniacally dangerous man when crossed. The only person she'd ever known who could handle him was his father. "Let him go, Jason."

She watched Lloyd closely as he got to his feet and brushed his pant legs. She recognized the murderous calm. "Lloyd." She said his name twice more before she got his attention. "Get out, now, and don't come back here."

Tight-lipped and silent, Lloyd signaled his men with a movement of his head and would have walked past her, but Laura stopped him with her next words. "I'm going to call Holcombe. I'm going to tell him everything you've done. Go home, Lloyd."

He left, and she shivered at the hate she'd seen in his gaze.

She stayed where she was until the door slammed shut, then continued to stare at the empty space for a moment. Slowly she turned and faced the room. "I'm sorry. Lloyd thinks anyone with a Southern accent is mentally challenged, and if they have a Texas drawl they immediately drop about a hundred points in IQ. He figures that gives him the right to treat you all like morons.'' She burst into tears. "I'm so sorry."

Jason tried to embrace her, but she shrugged him off. "I hope you believe me when I say I had nothing to do with all this mess. I've never liked what my stepfather does, how he rides roughshod over small communities. Since his semiretirement and Lloyd's increased power and position, it's gotten worse.

"I came to Texas to get away from Ohio, the May name and, as you can see, Lloyd. He always thought he could run my life." She laughed on a sob. "And most of the time he managed to do just that."

Women's tears had never bothered him before, and other than being mildly sympathetic, Jason usually paid them minimum attention. But he couldn't stand to see Laura cry. It hurt, like a knife twisting in his gut. He wanted to hold her, but she kept inching away until he was forced to grab her and pull her against him. He held her tightly as she struggled to stop crying.

Ginny kicked Matt's shin and held out her hand. He grasped it and hauled her to her feet. "Men," she mumbled, and included Austin and Dog in her condemnation. She crossed to Jason and Laura. "I'm not going to pry your hands off, so let her go, Jason." Jason didn't release Laura until Matt clamped a hand on his brother's shoulder.

"Come on, Laura," said Ginny. "Sit down and tell us what's going on."

Laura moved to the couch, then thanked Austin for the tissue he offered and blew her nose. She turned to Ginny.

"That's just it. I don't know...didn't know...couldn't have known. They never discussed business with me." She wasn't sure she was making any sense but couldn't stop babbling. If she did, she'd have to look at Jason and ask that one question she'd shied away from the moment Lloyd had called her Daisy May. That was what the family called her. They thought it was cute. She hated it with a passion. "I had no idea the company was even thinking of moving into Texas, and certainly not Two Rivers. That's Lloyd's doing. I never lied to any of you—I couldn't do that."

"We know. Take a deep breath," Ginny said, rubbing Laura's cold hands. "How old were you when your mother married Holcombe? Has your stepbrother ever hit you before?"

Laura took a deep breath. "I was eleven when we went to live with the Mays. Lloyd's always been a bully. He couldn't push Monica around because she knew how to push back." She shrugged. "So he picked on me. For a while Mother thought it was cute, assuming Lloyd was only being overprotective, but I didn't think so. Holcombe and Mother, when they were home, could control him."

"How old is that cretin?" Austin demanded. "He acts younger than me."

She wiped her eyes and managed a smile. "He's thirty and he *is* a child, a mean-spirited and vindictive one." She glanced at Ginny and Matt, then finally forced herself to look at Jason. "We humiliated him, and he's not one to forget that or let it go."

Ginny had to ask—all the signs were there. "Laura did he ever abuse you—sexually?"

"No. I'd have killed him first." Her answer was expressed so vehemently no one doubted her. "He was into mind control, and he'd go ballistic when he realized I was smarter at the game than he was. Like all bullies he'd revert to brute strength." She sat up and pressed her fingers against her mouth as she thought of something. "I have to call Holcombe and tell him what Lloyd's doing. He won't give up, and it can only get worse if he's not stopped."

Ginny tried to stop her, but Jason shook his head, knowing more than anything that Laura needed to feel she was doing something to make up for the trouble and embarrassment her stepbrother had caused. He also knew she desperately wanted a moment alone to compose herself. When she'd left the room, Matt was the first to speak.

"That was a pretty slick move you pulled on Lloyd, Jason. Where'd you learn it?"

Jason shrugged. "I picked up a little here, a little there."

"You don't think Lloyd is going to stop after what happened here tonight, do you?"

"No," Jason said. "He's not the type to give up that easily. Besides, I got the better of him, even humiliated him, and he's not about to forgot that."

Matt looked at Ginny, then Austin. "I'd like to know one thing. What happened to the town security? Either Tom or Foster should have been alerted when Lloyd's car didn't continue on through town. It should never have made it here without us being warned." Once again the fear for his family rose up. He looked at Ginny again and realized she was avoiding his gaze. "What's wrong, Ginny?"

"It was when I was talking to Annie, going over the legalities of rezoning for the town." The more she talked the deeper Matt frowned and the sweeter her smile became. "I told her to call off the security. Everyone was getting tired of it, and I'm perfectly safe now. Besides, did any of you catch the evening news or see the paper? No? Well, the story of the body found in the cave hit the media, and Annie says some of the townspeople were already getting telephone calls. Annie got one from a Houston television station. They'd aired the story but wanted to come to Two Rivers to follow up on the bones and the caves." Matt still hadn't said anything. "My security is putting too much of a burden on our friends. I'm safe."

"Of all the…" Matt's voice rumbled like a freight train, the volume increasing.

Ginny dropped her gaze to her stomach. "Don't raise your voice—it's not good for her, Matthew. You don't want her to be afraid of you, do you?" Ginny rubbed her stomach as if to emphasize her point. She'd learned early in her pregnancy just how to manipulate Matt, and she thoroughly enjoyed doing it.

Matt sat down beside his wife and clasped her hand in his, but he kept his fierce frown of displeasure. "I'm going to give Jericho a call and have him wake the others. A little extra protection couldn't hurt."

"I'm taking Laura home with me tonight," Jason announced.

"Why?" It was Austin who asked. "She's safe here. Dad won't let anything happen to her. Will you, Dad?"

"Yes, why?" Ginny said as she folded her arms over her stomach, then jabbed Matt in the ribs with her elbow.

Jason scowled at them. He wasn't ready to say anything until he and Laura had settled a few things. "Because, nephew mine, she's going with me." He held up his hand. "Don't ask any more questions. Just take my word for it that she belongs with me."

Matt struggled to keep his expression stern, even with Ginny poking his ribs. Jason's tomcatting days were over. "But does Laura know she belongs with you?"

"She will after tonight," Jason said, his attention divided between the doorway and the persistent questions of his family. He was aware they were speculating, but wasn't about to satisfy their curiosity.

"Eight years ago Laura was fifteen," Ginny said. "Did something happen between the two of you back then?"

"Not what you're thinking." He heard Laura's footsteps and met her at the doorway. "Were you able to reach Holcombe?"

She let out a long, exhausted sigh. "Yes. Matt, Ginny, Holcombe asked me to give you his profound apologies. He said he'd take care of Lloyd and the project and not to worry about it anymore."

"Do you believe him?" Matt asked.

"Holcombe? Yes. But you have to realize that since his heart attack a couple of years ago, he doesn't have the control over the company he'd like to believe he has. I wouldn't be opposed to any legal plans to drive them out."

"And his control over Lloyd—how's that?" Ginny asked.

"I don't know. He says he can stop him, and he has before." She moved to Ginny's side. "I'm so sorry this happened in your home. You know I wouldn't have upset you for the world."

Ginny smiled. "This has been more fun than I've had in months." Cutting her gaze sideways, she said, "I heard that groan, Matthew Bolt. You know very well I've been good lately."

"Except for the candy you talked Austin into buying."

Ginny shared a conspiratorial wink with Austin. "I don't know what you're talking about. Laura, don't worry about this brother of yours. The men here are capable of protecting what's theirs." She suddenly yawned. "And I'm going to bed."

Jason took Laura by the hand. "C'mon. We're heading back to my place." He glanced back at his family. "We'll see you later."

She dug in her heels, suddenly reluctant to be alone with him. "I'm a little sleepy myself."

"Too bad." He refused to let her go, and as he opened the back door, he whispered, "We need to have a long talk, don't we."

There was no doubt in her mind that he remembered now who she was and what she'd done.

CHAPTER FIFTEEN

LAURA DIDN'T KNOW what to say, where to start, so she kept silent. Perhaps the best thing was to let Jason do all the talking. Then she'd know what and how much he really remembered. But that was being a coward, which she fully admitted she was at that moment. "The moon's beautiful tonight, isn't it?"

He'd been lost in his thoughts, trying to figure out a way to broach the subject without making Laura feel embarrassed. They were halfway down the driveway before he slowed enough to glance around. The night was indeed beautiful. A big, bright lovers' moon hung low in the sky. A soft breeze teased the jasmine, mimosa, roses and cedar, picking up their fragrances and mingling them together like an expensive perfume. It seemed almost sinful to talk about anything but love on a night like this, he thought as he glanced at Laura walking so quietly and grimly beside him.

Laura took a breath and stiffened her resolve. "You remembered who I was, didn't you."

He had to be careful, so he stalled for time as they stopped at the vineyard gate. Once they were through, he dug into his pocket for the key and locked it. He touched the center of her back as a nudge to cross the highway. "The Daisy May I met eight years ago was an elfin creature, a delightful young girl with beautiful waist-length brown hair shot with gold from hours in the sun, lots of freckles across her nose and cheeks, serious—too serious—hazel eyes and a beautiful mouth so full of shining braces that when she smiled it almost blinded me.''

She was touched, and swallowed around the lump in her throat, but he still hadn't really answered her question. They were across the highway and had started up the drive to his home when Jason abruptly stopped. ''What's the matter?'' She followed the direction of his gaze and thought she saw something, but couldn't quite make it out. ''What is it, Jason?''

''Quick, help me get the gate closed.'' They both struggled with the rickety old gate, half-lifting and half-dragging it, but it wouldn't close all the way, leaving a gap of about two feet. ''I've been meaning to fix that. Damn, it will have to do.''

''Jason, what's wrong?''

He grasped her arm and hurried her up the lane. ''I've got a funny feeling. There's a car parked down the highway. It's too far away for me to make out the model, but I'd bet it's Lloyd and his associates. I don't think they're just there to enjoy the moonlight. If they haven't already made their move, then they're waiting for something.''

Laura glanced around, noticing for the first time how close the trees were to the lane and how deep and dark the shadows were. ''Oh, God. He's waiting to see if I left with you, isn't he. He's going to come here?''

''Well, he can certainly try, can't he.''

The moonlight captured his smile and the gleam in his eyes, and she caught her breath. ''Oh, Jason, I don't think you realize just how ruthless Lloyd can be.''

Jason checked to make sure her van, parked at the side of the barn, was okay. Then he hustled Laura inside and locked the door behind them. He picked up his cellular phone and punched in Matt's code. "I think Golden Boy and his merry men are parked on the highway and planning trouble. I'll wait."

"Wait for what?" Laura asked. While Jason spoke into the phone, Laura didn't leave his side. His arm wrapped around her shoulders, he finally pressed the disconnect button.

"Jericho spotted the car, too, and went to investigate. Matt's waiting for him to call back and doesn't want me out there."

"I guess Ginny shouldn't gripe about all the cellular phones he handed out to everyone—they've come in handy. I just hope—" She didn't finish, interrupted by the trill of the phone in Jason's hand. When he smiled at her as he listened, she knew she could relax.

He pitched the phone on the table, put his arms around her and pulled her against his chest. "When Jericho got to the place they were parked, the car was gone."

"You sound way too disappointed."

He ran both hands through her hair before grasping her head firmly and holding it still. Then he gazed in her eyes and his smile changed to a grim line. "If Lloyd had hit you, I think I'd have killed him. I could kill him for hitting you in the past." When she opened her mouth to speak, he kissed her words away. The kiss was soft, sweet and full of tenderness. When he pulled away, he still held her head in his hands. "Did no one protect you from him when you were little?"

"No. But I learned to take care of myself. Jason, we must talk."

"Soon." The corner of his mouth curved upward. "Right now I have other things on my mind, and they don't require words." He dropped his hands to her waist and started gathering up her T-shirt, hiking it higher and higher. "Well, maybe one or two words. Like the way you say my name, 'Ja-a-ason,'" he mimicked, "and that little giggle at the end. I'd like to hear that again. Right now, as a matter of fact."

As much as she knew they were both avoiding the issue, she didn't have the willpower to turn him down. She wanted Jason as much as he wanted her, judging from the hardness pressing against her stomach. Her jeans slid down her legs and pooled around her feet. "I don't giggle," she said, her voice raspy with desire.

"Oh, yes, you do. Right at the end, after you've said my name. It's the most erotic sound, like pure joy." He was about to kiss her again when he jerked his head up, listening. "Someone's out there."

"I don't hear anything." Before she could even attempt to stop him, Jason had picked up the nearest weapon he could find, a large screwdriver, and was out the front door. Stunned and left standing there in only her T-shirt and bikini panties, she took a moment to gather her wits. Then she sprinted into action, trying to cram her feet into the sandals she didn't even remember stepping out of. Failing, she kicked one across the room and ran for the door.

The moon was more brilliant then she'd ever seen it. Or maybe it was her heightened sense of danger. She could easily see Lloyd's car parked halfway up the long lane. What she couldn't see was Jason, and she started to move cautiously out the door. Then the urgency of the situation hit her and, unconscious of her bare legs and feet, she began running, only slowing when she saw Jason appear from around the back of the car.

Jason jogged to Laura's side, grasped her arm and turned her around. "Get back in the house."

"They're not in the car, are they?"

"No." Jason, still gripping Laura's arm, raced to the back of the house. One of the rooms was stacked with cardboard boxes, and he began moving them around haphazardly in his frantic search. Finally he found the box he was looking for and tore it open. He reached inside, brought out a leather rifle case trimmed with long fringe and balanced it under one arm as he searched inside again, stacking items on the floor.

As she watched, Laura didn't know whether to be horrified or amused at the arsenal. It looked as if he was preparing for a war as he carefully placed a pistol, a hunting knife and a couple of boxes of shells on the floor. "Jason, what are you doing?"

He glanced over his shoulder and smiled. "I'm going to teach your stepbrother a little lesson about the Texas law of No Trespassing." He picked up the pistol, quickly loaded it with bullets, double-checked the safety, then tucked it in the waistband of his jeans at his back. He tied a leather scabbard to his leg just below the knee and slipped the hunting knife into it. Then he slid the double-barreled shotgun out of its case and picked up the box of shells.

She'd been so fascinated watching him, the quick, sure movements, the concern for safety and the way he handled the weapons, that it took a moment for her to realize his expertise. "This is crazy, Jason. You're not going to shoot Lloyd...are you?"

"Of course not." He gave her a wounded look. "I'm going to scare the hell out of him and his men."

He would have rushed past Laura if she hadn't grabbed his arm. "Listen to me, Jason. Let's just lock the doors. He'll go away."

Jason kissed her hard, then said, "No, he won't." He tried to move away, but she wouldn't let go, and instead of dragging her with him, he stopped and said, "Listen to me, Laura. They didn't come here to have a friendly conversation with us. They parked down the lane and sneaked up here with one purpose in mind—to get you and cause me as much physical grief as possible. Lloyd intends to take you with him when he leaves." He ran the back of his hand across her soft cheek. "But I promise, the only way they're leaving here is on foot and without you."

Jason was right. She'd made it obvious earlier how she felt about Jason. The best revenge for Lloyd would be to forcibly take her out of Jason's reach. "Jason!" she shouted, and followed him as he took off toward the front of the house. "Don't do this. You don't know Lloyd like I do."

She found him in the living room, or the area that was designated to be the living room, standing beside one of the huge windows that faced the front of the property. The skylights afforded her plenty of light to dodge around the debris-strewn floor. "I'm going to call Matt."

"If you're going to walk around in front of the windows you might think about putting some clothes on." He motioned for her to move, and when she didn't, he snapped, "Get away from in front of the window, Laura."

"What do you plan on doing?"

"Wait and let them make the first move."

She never totally took her attention from Jason as she found her jeans and pulled them on. Then anger replaced her fear, for Jason had opened a window and was leaning out, surveying the area. He was having entirely too much fun.

Suddenly the emus set up a commotion the likes of which she'd never heard before. They were screaming, all ten of them at the same time, a high-pitched sound full of fear and confusion. A chill crept up her spine. Surely Lloyd wouldn't hurt the girls!

"Stay here," Jason hissed, and disappeared out the window.

Laura rushed across the room, almost tripping over the old running shoes she'd left in the room. She pulled the shoes on and rapidly tied the laces, all the time praying Jason would be careful.

She jumped up and vaulted through the open window. Landing neatly on her feet, she took off at a run, keeping low and as close to the shadow of the house as possible. As she rounded the corner, she paused to get her bearings. The emus were still screaming and running frantically around their enclosure. Then she spotted movement around the shelter and hatchery.

With a feeling of dread, she ran to the hatchery, calling Jason's name to let him know it was her. Just as she reached the open door, he stepped directly in front of her. His expression, a mixture of sadness and disappointment, quickly melted away, leaving only anger. His blue eyes glowed, a muscle along his jaw twitched and his mouth was a straight, grim line.

"They destroyed everything. All the equipment."

"The eggs?" she whispered.

"Smashed to bits." He flicked the lever on the shotgun, broke it open across his thigh and loaded it with two shells. In the distance they heard a car engine start up. Jason grinned.

She shivered. "I'm going to call the sheriff. He can catch them as they're leaving town."

Jason's grin grew. "They're not going anywhere. I punched a hole in all four tires with the screwdriver." He pointed the barrel of the gun in the air and pulled the trigger.

"What are you doing?" She made as if to grab for the gun, but Jason stopped her.

"Giving them time to run," he said.

She didn't understand what was happening, but she knew she didn't like it. "Jason, let's go call Sheriff Gillespie and Matt."

Jason balanced the shotgun under one arm and placed his other around her shoulders. "Help me round up my girls and secure them in their shelter."

His eerie calm made her nervous. Jason wasn't one to hide his feelings. "Jason, please," she begged, but he wasn't listening.

"They're scared, Laura, and might hurt themselves."

Jason began calmly talking to the emus as he approached the gate, then, holding it open so they could pass through, he called all their names. Laura followed his lead, copying his composure but feeling anything but composed.

One by one the emus quieted, and one by one they edged closer, seeking comfort and reassurance. It was Elvis who snuggled up to Laura's side, and when she put her arm around his soft, trembling body, he laid his head on her shoulder and blinked his ridiculously long lashes. "Poor baby," she cooed. She noticed that shy Joan and even standoffish Bessie were crowding Jason for reassurance and comfort. They continued to talk to the birds, easing their fears as they herded them into the shelter. Then Jason closed and secured the door.

"Jason," she said as they headed toward the house, "I want to call Matt."

Jason was still as calm as ever. "Sure." He led the way around the front of the house. Before entering, he stopped and stared for a long moment at the car down the lane. He chuckled. "They're on foot."

"They'll just catch a ride on the highway. We need to alert Sheriff Gillespie."

Jason opened the door for her. "No. Lloyd knows full well the local law will be looking for him and he wouldn't take that chance. They're heading for the highway on the other side of Two Rivers and the county line. Do you see that tree there beside the car?"

"Barely. Why?"

"Because one of the bigger branches is broken off. Someone lost their balance and grabbed hold of it. That's how I know which way they're heading."

Laura dashed into the house and searched for the cellular phone. When she found it, she started to dial, then Jason's next question made her pause.

"How good a hunter is Lloyd? I remember eight years ago he bragged about being somewhere on a level with big-game professionals."

His question and his tone sent another set of chills up her spine. She put down the phone. "He hunts in Wyoming and Montana, or he used to. He's a good shot."

"Did he have a guide on his trips?"

"Yes. Jason, what are you going to do? He's like a vicious dog. Corner him and he'll turn on you."

"Lloyd's made this into a game. I intend to teach him not to play with the big boys ever again."

"He's dangerous. Please." She thought he was going to leave her, and she snatched hold of his belt. "Don't go without me!"

"Don't be ridiculous." Jason pried her fingers off his belt. "Stay put. Lock the door. Call Matt and Argus if it'll make you feel better. I'm out of here."

He was as good as his word and left her standing alone, her mind racing with doubts and fears. Taking a deep breath, she tried to think what to do. Suddenly she snatched her backpack-style purse, dumping everything out of it onto the floor. She gave it a good shake to make sure it was empty, then rushed to the refrigerator. She stuffed a couple of plastic bottles of water into the purse, picked up a flashlight and put that in, then added the cellular phone.

Laura went to the front door and stepped outside, then turned and double-checked the door to make sure it was securely locked. She began searching for a sign of Jason. The night was so beautiful it almost hurt to think of the ugliness that was going on. Laura gazed at the lovers' moon, thinking that was what she wanted to be—a lover—with Jason.

She looked around, feeling lost and unbearably lonely and scared. How could he have gone off after three men? Two of them bigger than he was and one a whole lot meaner. Jason had bitten off more than he could chew and was going to need help, certainly more than she could contribute. She decided to head down by Lloyd's deserted car, to where Jason had pointed out the broken tree branch. Logic told her that was the point Jason would more than likely have started from. As she moved out along the edge of the lane, she dialed Matt and Ginny's number.

Matt didn't ask a lot of questions; instead, he let her tell him everything first. "I warned him, Matt, that Lloyd is dangerous when he's crossed, but he wouldn't listen to me." Leaving the lane, she sidestepped down the incline until she was even with the broken tree limb. The more she talked to Matt the angrier she became. "Is it some testosterone-driven thing, Matt, that he had to go off on his own like Daniel Boone without waiting or asking for help?"

"Probably." Matt laughed.

Ducking under a couple of low branches, she found herself out in the open. "I have no idea where he's gone." She asked the one question that had been nagging at her since Jason took off. "Matt, Jason's..." She didn't know how to put into words what she wanted to say without being unfair to, perhaps even belittling of, the man she loved. "Can he take care of himself out here, Matt? I mean, Jason's expertise leans toward women, parties... and women." Glancing around, she lowered her voice. "You and I both know how he's nurtured his playboy image with passion—no pun intended—but does he know what he's doing now? God, he's carrying a knife, a pistol and a shotgun. Does he even know how to use them?" She waited for an answer so long that for a moment she thought they'd been disconnected.

"Laura, I honestly don't have any answers for your concerns. Until over a year ago, I didn't know Jason at all. But keep in mind that no one thought he could do what he's done to the barn. As for his playboy days, I think those are behind him, and maybe we ought to give him the benefit of the doubt. Listen, Ginny's got Argus on the other line. She say's he's on his way to the vineyard, and as soon as he gets here we'll start out after Jason. Go back to the house or come stay with Ginny. You'll be safer here, with Jericho and the men guarding the place. Try not to worry about Jason or Lloyd. Argus and I will find them." With those words, Matt hung up.

"Isn't that just like a man," she grumbled as she looked around. "Send the women somewhere safe and then let them worry while they have all the fun." Though the moon afforded her enough light to easily see, the shadows were dark and all around her. As the light breeze stirred her hair, she became aware of the vast emptiness and the quiet, and of the futility of taking off on her own. The valley stretched in front of her and beyond. The rolling hills suddenly looked more like mountains. She knew that beyond them was another highway, which was where Lloyd and his men were heading. Damn, she needed Jason, and without thinking she called his name. She waited. When he didn't answer her or appear, she raised her voice and screamed his name.

"I'm right behind you, Laura."

She whipped around and almost lost her balance. Then she rushed to him, threw her arms around his neck and said, "I was worried. Matt and the sheriff are coming. You'll have help." With her arms still locked around his neck, she leaned back to get a good look. "I'm glad you came to your senses and returned, Jason."

"My good sense had nothing to do with returning. It just took me a while to realize you weren't about to go along with what I told you to do. I knew you'd be out here searching for me, and I couldn't let you wander around alone worrying."

She dropped her arms and stepped back. "You're not going to wait for your brother or the sheriff? Jason, Lloyd and his men have had a lot of time to get far ahead of you."

Jason laughed, took hold of her arm and entwined it with his as if they were going for a Sunday stroll. "I was almost upon them when I had this picture of you out here lost."

"But you came all the way back, and they're that much farther ahead now. Look. Let's go to the house, get my van and meet them when they get to the highway." She tried to pull away, but he wasn't having it and kept her walking forward.

"Laura, as expert as Lloyd thinks he is, he's a novice out here. Once you get past the cleared farmland and into the hills, it's pretty rough going. Lloyd's wearing expensive handmade Italian loafers. Paul and Booth are wearing dress shoes. They're not going to cover a lot of territory. If we move quickly, we can catch up with them in no time."

"And what happens then?" Once again, she tried to stop, but he wouldn't allow it. "What do you think you're going to do, Jason?"

"Take them back to town. Deliver them to Argus."

Any argument she might have, she knew, would be like reasoning with a brick wall. At least if she went along, she might be able to keep him from getting seriously hurt. "Okay. I'll go."

Jason laughed. "I never thought you wouldn't, Professor. What did you bring with you?"

Laura shrugged off the straps of the backpack and handed Jason a bottle of water. When he drank his fill, she finished off the bottle and replaced the empty in her pack. They continued to walk and fell into a long, companionable silence. After a while Laura glanced at what she'd considered the distant hills and realized how close they loomed now.

"Jason, have you ever used a gun or pistol before?"

"Not on humans."

She didn't like that answer or his almost gleeful tone, and she shivered. She tried to examine his expression in the moonlight. "But you've hunted before?"

"Are you concerned about my abilities?" He fumbled with the shotgun tucked under his arm, almost dropping it.

"No, no, no." She glanced away to keep him from seeing her doubts.

"Do you think I can't handle this or protect you? I'm good at most things I do."

"Well, you're certainly good at being a playboy."

He laughed, and when he saw the scowl of annoyance on her face, he said, "I'm sorry, Professor. But I never thought of myself as a playboy. Others gave me that label."

"Ah, but you never denied it, nor—mind you—did you ever stop chasing women."

"I never chased a woman in my life." He pretended to be outraged at her suggestion, then added, "Until now, that is."

"Stop splitting hairs, Jason. You know very well what I mean. You can't blame me for having doubts about your hunting skills. If we were at a cocktail party or a fancy restaurant, I would never question your abilities to charm the pants off all the women there, order the correct wines for a five-course dinner, know the difference between a diamond and a flawless fake, or guess the name of every woman's dress designer." Her arms flew wide as if to encompass the world. "But this is different." Lowering her voice, she tried to imitate Jericho's sonorous tones. "It's dangerous."

Jason stopped and touched her arm to get her full attention. "See that rock there?"

She followed his pointing finger and nodded at the plate-size rock. "What about it?" It was amazing how bright the moonlight actually was. Looking around was like viewing a black-and-white photograph in which every minute detail stood out; the white and light gray rocks and boulders were highlighted against the dark shadows of the trees and the dense, impregnable bushes.

"There's a long, dark mark along the side of the rock made by a leather shoe. I'd say the wearer wasn't watching where he was stepping, landed on the edge of the rock, and his shoe slipped off. Lloyd is leading that way. He's about eight or ten feet in front of his men. Do you see the way the grass is crushed—" he pointed out another area "—and how that wildflower at the edge of the depression has been snapped off at its stem?

"From the size of the area, I'd say Paul and Booth walked there, and one or the other of them likes flowers and snapped the top off the bluebonnet. Of course, picking the state flower is just another crime to add to their list."

If he hadn't pointed out the tracks Lloyd and his men had left behind, she would have walked past them without notice. His ability and knowledge left her speechless with a mixture of delight and embarrassment for ever doubting him. He'd started off again and she had to jog to catch up.

"As to your concern about my ability with firearms— I've hunted all my life and am a pretty fair shot."

She stopped, making him do the same by grasping his arm. "I'm sorry. But you're awfully adept at hiding your true self, aren't you. Why?"

Jason grinned and ran his finger over her cheek. "Maybe for the same reasons as you. All my life I've only been able to depend on myself for what I wanted and needed both physically and emotionally. That careless kind of independence spills over into everything, doesn't it." He motioned for her to continue walking. "Then maybe it was the fact that my father never had a moment to spare for me. He was too wrapped up in the vineyard and hating Matt. My mother had three passions—her social standing, traveling and, last on the list, my father. It's easier to let people think what they want, instead of beating your head against a wall trying to change their minds. Then again, who cares? I know what and who I am. It's always served my needs."

Now was a good time to come clean and tell him the circumstances of their meeting eight years ago, but she couldn't bring herself to do it. Instead, she said, "How did you learn to track someone and read all the signs?"

"Jericho taught me." When she made a face, he chuckled. "I know you don't like him much, but when I was growing up, he was the closest thing to a father I had. He taught me how to shoot and track. How to live off the land if I had to. He taught me how to take care of myself no matter where I was. Now, don't laugh, but it was Jericho who taught me about women, too."

"What did he tell you—they're dangerous? It's all I've ever heard him say." She skirted around a boulder, and as she glanced over her shoulder, she became aware they'd left the valley and were beginning up the gentle incline of a hill. She could no longer make out Jason's home.

"One of the things he said that's always stuck with me is that women are what keeps men from reverting to animals and killing each other. Jericho and my father were always at each other's throats over the harsh way Dad treated my mother, and women in general. And, of course, I'd always heard gossip of how miserably Dad treated Matt's mother, too." Jason shook off the darkness of his black thoughts and smiled suddenly as he remembered a happier part of his childhood. "Jericho told me that a man's life isn't worth two cents unless he's loved by a woman, and he didn't mean sex. Said a man just isn't a whole person until he can love back. He believes women have gentle souls and a great need to share their love and themselves unselfishly.

"I'd listen to Jericho talk about tenderness and respect and the cardinal rule that a man never raised a hand to the opposite sex, then I'd see my father and mother going at each other. Believe me, she was no wimp and gave as good as she got. But Jericho wouldn't let me believe that's what a relationship should be—he kept me pretty straight."

Laura blinked away the blur of tears from her eyes. "Isn't it awful the baggage we carry around from our childhood?" She had a little better understanding of the playboy, ladies'-man image he'd been labeled with. Jason was one of those rare men who truly liked and enjoyed women. He understood them and genuinely cared about their thoughts and feelings.

"Holcombe tried, when he was around, to love me," Laura said, "but I was too butt-headed and bitter with my mother for divorcing my father. Besides, how can you have any sort of relationship with people who are always walking out of your life?"

"Who walked out of your life?" Jason asked quietly, wanting to know, but still determined to control what she said. He didn't want the conversation to get too close to the past, specifically eight years ago. It wasn't the time or place to bring that up.

"For one, my father. Oh, I understand. He's a well-known paleontologist, even famous in Europe where he lives and works now. I'd get to see him a couple of times a year, but he was always leaving. After mother married Holcombe, they traveled a lot. Then I was always going back and forth to various schools." The ice, she felt, had been broken, and she was ready to tell him about eight years ago. "Do you remember—"

Jason hushed her with a chopping motion of his hand, then pulled her down into a squatting position beside him. She glanced at her watch and was surprised to see they'd been walking for more than two hours.

Then she heard the voices ahead of them and froze.

CHAPTER SIXTEEN

THE NIGHT stood still. The delicate breeze halted, even nature's evening noises hushed. But the night was a liar, deceiving the listener, as voices traveled the distance with deceptive clarity only to end in a garble of sound. Laura strained to decipher what the men ahead of them were saying, but finally gave up. They weren't as close to Lloyd and the others as she'd first thought.

"What are we going to do now?" she asked, keeping her own voice to a whisper.

Jason gazed at her. She was worried and scared but wasn't about to give up. "*We* are going to do nothing, but *I* am going to sneak up to that stand of trees they're in and see if I can make out what plans they have in mind for the rest of the evening."

Exasperated with his cavalier attitude, she kept her voice low even though she had an overwhelming urge to scream. "Stop playing games, Jason," she hissed, then bit her lip to keep from laughing when he made a cross with his fingers and held them in front of him as if to ward off evil. "If they catch you, it'll be three against one."

Jason pondered a moment. "True. But I have the firepower and I know the terrain." He placed a finger against her lips. "Plus, I can sneak up on them and they'll never know I'm there, and I fight dirty."

Laura grabbed his shirt to keep him from leaving. "Maybe we should wait for Matt and Argus. Do you think they can find us?"

"Laura, my love, stop worrying. Jericho taught Matt the same as me. He told me my brother was the best tracker he'd ever come across, that he had a natural ability, maybe because Matt's half-Indian. Some talents just come naturally. Believe me, if Matt's out there, he knows where we've been, what we've done and where we're going."

She liked being called "my love" and savored it a second before she started digging in her backpack. "But you're not sure, are you. Not one hundred percent sure that if you sneak off and they catch you that help will arrive in time to keep them from beating the hell out of you." When she pulled out the flashlight, Jason tried to snatch it away, and in doing so knocked her from her squatting position.

"Don't turn that on," he said. "Lloyd or his men might see it and then they'll know our position."

Laura rolled a foot or so away, then sat up. When he reached for the flashlight again, she held it out of range. "I'm going to point it down the hill toward the house, to let Matt and Argus know where we are." As she was telling him this, she actually began the signaling before he could say anything. "There—three dots, three dashes, three dots—that's the international SOS."

Jason buried his face in his hands to smother a laugh. When he looked up, she'd put the light back in her bag. "Do you feel better now?" he asked.

"No! Because I know it won't stop you." She crossed her legs and punched the leather bag in her lap. "Those two men with Lloyd are bigger than you, Jason." She gave him a wave of impatience. "Oh, hell, go on. I'll sit here alone and wait—and listen to your screams of pain. Then when they beat you senseless and come after me, I'll still be sitting here, worried and waiting for you to rescue me as Lloyd carts me off."

"Guilt doesn't set well with me." Jason leaned over and kissed her. "I love you."

"I love you, too, Jason." She was lost in the tenderness of his gaze and unable to say anything else.

"Do you?"

"Yes, dammit. Now, go on before I change my mind." She grudgingly accepted another kiss, then listened to him leaving, waiting until the stillness of the evening closed in around her. Slipping her hand into the backpack, she retrieved the flashlight and began frantically sending signals.

Jason's footfalls were as silent as a snake moving through water. He made it to the stand of trees, then crawled beneath the scrub oaks and cedar until he was only a few feet away from the men. He watched and listened as the trio bitched about being hot, tired, thirsty and lost. They squabbled over which direction to go until Lloyd called a halt to the bickering.

Carefully, silently, Jason backed out of his observation position and made a wide berth around the men to a more open area, clear of trees and obstacles. He knew they'd take the easiest route out, and he squatted beside a boulder to wait. He didn't have long to ponder his next move because just then the three men walked by him, not sensing his presence. They walked in single file, leaving a good distance between one another. Lloyd was in front, his two men behind.

Jason waited, giving them time to spread out a little farther, before he left his position. Laura was right, it was a game. The old game of stalking and hunting, where the strongest didn't necessarily end up the victor, but the smartest and fastest walked away with the kill.

As the second man passed him, Jason rose to his feet and stepped out behind him. When he could feel the man's body heat, he pinched a nerve at the side of his neck. Jason slid his hands under the man's arms as he went limp and gently lowered him to the ground. He recognized this one and whispered, "Good night Paulie." Then as he stood over him, grinning, he brought the butt of the shotgun down on the side of the big man's head with a satisfying thump. He wouldn't be waking up too soon, and when he did, he'd have a hell of a headache.

Jason moved off, slipping in and out of the shadows as he took up the trail of Lloyd and Booth. Once again he gave the men a wide berth, circling around so he could take up a position in front of them. The land was giving way to thicker vegetation, overhanging trees and larger boulders that had to be skirted. Jason found his spot in the deep shadows of an outcropping of rock and stunted brush, and became one with his surroundings.

Again he let them catch up to him, and still keeping in the shadows, he took a step forward. His attention was centered on Booth, who was just passing him and only an arm's length away. He took another step, reached for the back of the neck.

Suddenly a solid force slammed into him from behind. Before he could react, the shotgun went flying through the air. He managed to twist his body around to cushion the fall as he was being knocked to the ground. But he hit hard rock, and roots dug into his back as his breath escaped his lungs in a choked off gasp.

He should have known.

THE INSTANT Laura replaced the flashlight and sat alone, she knew she'd made a mistake. The night wasn't as welcoming as before. Actually, it was damn frightening being all alone. Shadows moved, and there were sounds she couldn't identify. She scrambled to her feet, telling herself she'd just follow Jason's direction for a while. If she got lost . . . well, he was an expert tracker. He'd find her.

Her decision to leave her position wavered when she tripped over one of her brother's men. Terrified that Jason might have killed him, she stopped long enough to make sure he was breathing. She started off again, and the more she warned herself to slow down, the faster she ran.

Then, as she entered the deep shadows from the overhang of trees, her eyes tried to adjust to the darkness—but not in time to stop from running smack into a solid and all-too-familiar object.

"Jason," she hissed, and started to scramble to her feet only to end up straddling his body as he grabbed her arms. "Jason?"

He couldn't get his breath, couldn't speak, and shook his head to warn her, at the same time shaking her. When she pounded on his chest he was able to catch a breath, then another. But it was too late. As his vision cleared, he found himself looking past Laura to Lloyd and Booth. "You didn't call out," he managed to say on a strangled breath of air.

Her smile disappeared as she felt someone grab her from behind. Before she could scream in shocked surprise, she was hauled to her feet and facing her brother. She tried to twist out of Lloyd's grasp and at the same time keep her gaze on Jason.

Jason attempted to sit up, but Booth placed his foot in the center of his chest, shifted his weight and forced him back onto the ground. The pistol stuck in his waistband jabbed into his back. He gave Lloyd a grim smile. "You're out of your depth here. Don't make it worse than it already is."

"Keep still." Lloyd glared at Laura and shook her like a rag doll. "Or I'll let Booth break your lover's neck. Where the hell is Paul?"

"Taking a nap." Jason grinned.

"Lloyd, stop this, this instant!" Laura demanded. "I called Holcombe. Ouch!" She flinched at the vicious pinch to her arm. "I told him what you've—" The slap landed across her mouth, cutting off her words, smashing a corner of her mouth against her teeth and splitting her lip.

The sound of the slap was like the stab of a hot poker in Jason's brain. The sight of Laura's bleeding mouth made him go wild with hatred. Jason wrapped his hands around Booth's ankle and twisted, rolling his weight into the move and bringing the big man down with a scream of pain. He was on him before the man could react, his fist connecting solidly with the other's jaw and causing his head to bounce off a rock. When Booth went limp, Jason got to his feet, his pistol pointed at Lloyd.

For a second Laura watched the big man being felled like a tree. Then she started struggling, fighting Lloyd as he attempted to assist Booth. She punched and kicked, landing a fist in his stomach and a good whack to his shin. Lloyd wasn't shy about fighting a woman. He yanked her arm hard enough that she tripped and fell, then he started dragging her across the rocky ground.

Her position put her at a disadvantage. It wasn't until she spotted Jason's shotgun in the moonlight that she realized Lloyd was trying to get to it and was determined to take her with him. She screamed Jason's name. She fought harder, grabbed Lloyd around the leg and bit it as hard as she could.

Laura sagged in defeat when she felt Lloyd pick up the gun. It was like some old western on television. The showdown with guns drawn, two gunfighters waiting for the other to make a wrong move. She would have laughed if it wasn't so deadly serious.

"Put the gun down, Jason." Lloyd held the shotgun, the butt balanced on his thigh, his finger on the trigger and the barrel pointed at Jason's middle. In his other hand he held Laura's arm in an iron grip. "You're not going to shoot and take the chance of hitting Laura. Jeez, Daisy May, I can't believe you'd fall for this creep's line."

"Lloyd, please." She tried to twist her arm free and winced when he tightened his fingers. "What do you think you're going to do—kill him? That's crazy and you're crazy. Put the gun down and walk away." Her plea was like spitting in the wind. Lloyd had let his vicious temper get control of him and wasn't willing to listen to sense.

"Put your gun down on the ground in front of you, Van der Bollen."

"Why don't you do the same, May?" A voice came out of the shadows, a voice deep and soft but so full of power and authority that Lloyd froze. Matt appeared as if he'd been born from the very earth at their feet. He rose between them tall and dark with a gun trained on Lloyd's head. "Now."

Lloyd laughed, a maniacal sound. "What's this? Big brother comes to the rescue. I could put a shot in Jason before you can blink."

Matt shrugged. "He's just my half brother, Lloyd. We're not very close. But think about this—before Jason drops, I can put one between your eyes."

Jason put his gun back in his waistband. "He's off his nut, Matt," he said, then watched in horror as Lloyd turned the end of the shotgun on Laura.

"What about her?" Lloyd asked with a chuckle. "You both seem pretty protective of little Daisy May here."

Matt's revolver made a cocking sound that brought all eyes back to him. "She's no kin of mine."

Lloyd laughed, but there was real fear in it this time. "You're all crazy bastards." Suddenly the shotgun was ripped from his hand and an arm was around his throat, strangling him.

Argus pitched the shotgun in one direction as he threw Lloyd to the ground, turned him over and quickly handcuffed him. "Boy, you're a real pain in the ass."

Jason thumped Matt on the back and said, "You stole my thunder."

"I saved your butt."

"But I took down two out of three, and I was handling Lloyd."

"Looked to me like he was the one doing the handling," Matt said.

Laura buried her face in her hands and wept with relief. Jason sat down beside her, but she refused to look up. "Stupid macho men. I hate this. I hate crying." She rubbed her eyes and glared at them.

Jason put his arm around her and hugged her close. "My poor professor. Did Matt scare you?"

"No. Yes. He was very believable, wasn't he?"

"Well, love, he used to be a cop. He's supposed to be believable."

Laura took a long, shaky breath. "What now?" She addressed her question to Matt and Argus. "What are you going to do with Lloyd? What about his men?"

Argus helped a silent Lloyd to his feet. "We found the first one Jason took out, and he's handcuffed to a tree, waiting for us to pick him up on our way down." He pitched Matt another pair of cuffs. "Take care of Booth, will you?"

Lloyd finally came to his senses and realized he was in big trouble. He spoke to the sheriff. "Listen, this is a family matter and doesn't concern you."

Argus stuck his thumbs in the waistband of his jeans and rocked back on his heels. "Well, boy, I have to tell you, you're in big trouble and likely to be a guest in a Texas jail for a while."

"No, sir, I think not. As soon as we get out of here, I'm going to call my attorney. He'll straighten everything out."

Laura felt any hopes of Lloyd paying for what he'd done slip away. The Mays had enough money to buy Lloyd out of any trouble. She allowed Jason to help her to her feet and stood still while he inspected her cut lip and the bruises on her arms. Before anyone could stop him he hit Lloyd hard enough that Lloyd fell and landed on his backside.

Matt gave one long, shrill whistle, and two horses galloped their way. "Lloyd, you and your men committed a felony. You were trespassing on posted land. You threatened my brother's life and, from where I stood, attempted to murder Laura. Those are serious charges." As he talked, he helped Booth to his feet, took a length of rope from his saddlebag and tied the two men's wrists together, then twisted the end of the long rope around the saddle horn.

"Trespassing is a fine," Lloyd snarled. "And all I'd have to do is convince the judge that I was trying to save my sister from a notorious playboy. I don't think Jason's reputation would stand an in-depth investigation. Not to mention the scandal that would descend on your family. As to a felony? I'm sorry, you've lost me there. My men and I accidently kicked some equipment over and broke some eggs."

"Lloyd." Argus dropped his good-old-boy game and stepped very close to his prisoner. "Those broken eggs are valued around fifteen thousand dollars. And where you come from, trespassing on posted land might not be a serious offense, but in Texas you've stepped into a real pile of trouble. Then there's attempted murder. Don't forget there are witnesses besides Laura and Jason. And finally, I don't think Jason or Matt cares one fig about public scandal." He started to walk off, leaving Lloyd with his mouth open. "Oh, I forgot." He leaned close. "Son, this is my county. The judge is my cousin. I pretty much run things around here, and right now I'm your worst backwater, hick-town, redneck nightmare. You will spend time in my jail. You will pay Jason compensation for the eggs and mental damages. Lastly, you will make a public apology to Jason, Laura and the Bolts. After that we'll see how much slack I cut you and your men."

After picking up Paul and securing him with the others, Matt and Argus led their horses with Laura and Jason walking beside them, and the three men trailing on tethered ropes farther behind. Jason kept fussing over Laura's cut lip, wanting to doctor it with the bottled water, until she snapped at him to leave her alone. When he looked hurt, she apologized.

"Did you see my signal," Laura asked no one in particular, just to take Jason's mind off her injuries.

Matt and Argus looked at each other and burst out laughing.

Matt said, "Like a beacon on a lighthouse. The SOS was a nice touch. We'd never have known you were in trouble otherwise."

Laura heard the sarcasm and was prepared with an equally sarcastic retort when they were all silenced by a sudden trilling. Laura grabbed her backpack, which Jason was carrying, as Matt dove for his saddlebag. Both cellular phones were going off and everyone had the same gut feeling. Emergency. As Matt talked he untied the rope around his saddle horn and swung up into the saddle.

Jason grabbed the reins. "What's happened? Is it Ginny?"

Matt nodded; he could barely speak with the fingers of fear clutching his throat. "That was Austin. Ginny's in labor. He's called Annie and Doc and they're both on their way, but Austin's scared and Jericho's concerned they won't make it in time."

"Get going, man." Jason stepped aside and gave the horse's rump a slap. Then he glanced back at Lloyd and his men. "If anything happens to my sister-in-law or the baby over this upset, you won't make it to court—any of you. Argus and I will see to it."

Silently, grimly, Jason set a faster pace, and even though Argus tried to get him to take the horse, he turned it down. "I'm not leaving Laura anywhere near Lloyd, and doubling up on your poor horse isn't going to get us to the vineyard any sooner."

WHEN THEY ARRIVED, Laura and Jason were met with a shocking array of lights on, everywhere. The hands and some of their wives were standing around outside. As they drew closer a sound like nothing they'd ever heard reached them. They both broke into a run, hitting the back door at the same time and getting stuck as they struggled to get through. Austin jumped to his feet, his eyes red and skin white.

"What's happened? What—" Jason was interrupted by an eerie howl. He looked at the ceiling and swallowed, then made for the stairs.

Austin stepped in front of him. "It's all right, Uncle Jason. Don't go up. Annie and Doc are there, and Dad doesn't want anyone else there."

Laura grabbed Jason's arm, pulled him over to a chair and made him sit down. "Something's wrong, Austin, or Dog wouldn't be howling like that."

Austin collapsed in his chair. "Oh, that. Every time Ginny has a pain, Dog howls at the door. Dad won't let him in the bedroom. He even tried to drag Dog down the stairs and put him out, but Dog turned on him. He won't let anyone come near him."

"Matt won't let anyone come near him?" Jason asked, dazed by the noise, fear and events.

"No, Dog."

"How's Ginny? Do you know anything?"

Austin rubbed his face. Fat tears pooled in his eyes and he made no effort to stop them as they rolled slowly down his pale cheeks. "This is harder than I thought it would be. All those books Dad and I read, well . . . She's in awful pain, Laura. I was upstairs trying to keep Dog quiet and I heard her." He jumped and ran to her when Laura opened her arms to him. "I heard her screaming and moaning. I think she's dying. I can't lose Ginny, Laura!"

Laura bit her lip to keep from smiling. The usual male panic over a woman's labor. "Has Annie or Doc come down and said anything?"

"Oh, sure. Yeah," Austin mumbled.

"What did they say, Austin?" She never thought she'd ever have to prompt him to talk. But like his uncle, he kept his gaze riveted to the ceiling as if it might open up and show them what was happening upstairs. "Austin, tell me."

"They said everything's going just fine. But I heard her, Laura. She's in terrible, terrible pain!"

"I'm sure she is, Austin, but that's normal under the circumstances." She glanced around. "Where's Jericho?"

"When he saw you, Uncle Jason and Sheriff Gillespie coming, he said he had to take care of something. Did you catch the men? Dad didn't stop to tell us anything."

Jason nodded. "We got them. Argus is taking them to jail."

"I'm sorry about the eggs, Uncle Jason. But the girls are fine. Billy Bob, Wayne and I went over to check on them. Then when we told Gomez about it, he took Roberto and they cleaned everything up." Austin gulped and said, "The eggs were close to hatching. They were just little baby chicks." The evening had been such an emotional roller coaster he couldn't talk about baby anything anymore.

Dog howled again, and they all shivered and fell silent. They heard a door shut, footsteps on the stair, then Matt stood in the doorway. His face was as white as flour, but his eyes were a mixture of joy and exhaustion. "Austin, you have a sister."

"Da-a-ad, everyone knew it was a girl months ago. Is the baby okay? And Ginny. What about Ginny?"

Matt collapsed in the nearest chair and suddenly his hands starting shaking. "Ginny's fine. Baby's fine." So like his son, he made the gesture of scrubbing his face, then tears filled his eyes and slipped silently down his cheeks. He dropped his arms on the table and lowered his head and wept for a moment. Then he sighed and looked up, nodding his thanks as Austin furnished him with a tissue.

A moment later they all noticed Dog standing in the doorway. He looked as bad as Matt—unsmiling, his coat stuck out in all directions, his head hanging, his tail drooping and dragging along the floor. His steps were shaky as he made his way toward Matt, then rested his head on his master's thigh.

"Well, look what the cat's dragged in. You're a fine one to show your sorry face down here after the racket you kicked up," Matt scolded him softly, but he was stroking Dog's head. "I held out better than you, old boy."

"I hope the baby looks like Ginny, Matt," Jason said. "When and what are you going to name her? You can't keep calling her 'the baby.'"

"Ginny's thinking of a name."

After a long wait Annie finally came downstairs with a small blanket-wrapped bundle. They all jumped to their feet.

"Sit down, everyone," Annie said quietly but firmly. Everyone sat. "Don't crowd her." She handed Matt the bundle. "Ginny said her name, if you agree, is Antonia Mia Bolt."

Matt nodded in agreement to the name as tears stung his eyes. His big hand engulfed the infant, and he handled her like a rare china cup. Austin edged out of his chair and stood beside his dad as Laura and Jason, defying Annie's order, got up and peered over his shoulder.

Jason whispered in Laura's ear, "Antonia is Ginny's middle name. Mia was Matt's mother's name." He cleared his throat and said, "I think I'll call my niece Tony."

"Hey, she sure has a lot of black hair," Austin said. "She looks just like you, Dad."

Matt glanced at his tiny daughter and grinned hugely. "No, Austin. Like you. She looks just like you did when you were a baby."

Austin stood straighter and smiled proudly. "You think so? I thought she did, too, but I didn't want to say anything."

Jason punched Laura and they started laughing. Matt and Annie joined in, and soon everyone was laughing, though trying to keep it down. Then they all watched, stunned and unable to move, as Dog stuck his nose close to Antonia. For a moment he stared, unsmiling, his ears forward and alert. The baby turned her head and appeared to look straight at Dog as if sizing him up. A tiny fist thumped him on the end of his nose. Dog grinned his weird toothy grin and his tail thumped loudly against the floor, then he headed for his bed in the corner.

Annie pried the baby from Matt's hands. "I'll take her back up to Ginny." When Matt started to rise, Annie touched his shoulder. "Ginny's doing real good, Matt. Doc needs to finish up with her, then you should let her get a little sleep—she's exhausted. I won't leave her side, I promise. Have a drink and celebrate. Oh, by the way, Ginny told me she'd like to have a couple more." Her parting words left Matt speechless.

Laura and Jason served a glass of champagne to all the workers still gathered outside, and once Matt had made a short speech and they toasted the baby's arrival and health, they left. Jason was opening another bottle for them when Argus knocked on the back door.

He pulled off his Stetson and congratulated Matt. "Everyone in town knows about Antonia's arrival." When Jason offered him a glass of champagne, Argus shook his head. "We have a problem."

He was looking at Laura when he spoke, and she asked, "What's Lloyd done now?"

The sheriff shook his head, pushed open the screen door and pulled Jericho into the kitchen. The old man's hands were cuffed behind his back, and he wouldn't look at anyone. "I locked May and his men up and was headed back here when I saw the vineyard truck speeding by. With what was going on here, I couldn't think why someone would be heading out old Post Road toward Doc's clinic. If there was a problem, I thought I could help. Anyway, by the time I'd made up my mind and pulled up in front of Doc's, I spotted the truck parked off the road and half-hidden. I had a bad feeling. The feeling didn't go away when I found Doc's back door pried open, either. Then I caught Jericho coming out of that door carrying the body bag full of the old bones we found at the cave."

For a long moment no one spoke, too shocked to comprehend what the sheriff was telling them. Finally Jason said, "Why, Jericho?"

The old man's mouth grew grimmer and he shook his head.

Laura saw the obstinacy, but she also saw how Jericho was shaking with fatigue. "Did you have to cuff him?"

"He tried to fight me," Argus said, still surprised at what had happened. "When I asked him what he thought he was doing, he took a swing at me."

"Well, take them off now." Laura pulled over a chair, while Argus reluctantly removed the cuffs. "Here, Jericho, please sit down." She poured him a cup of hot coffee. His hand trembled so she had to help him until he got a couple of sips down. She glared at Argus. "You should be ashamed of yourself, treating an old man like this."

Jason chuckled. "He's an old con artist and a faker. Stop trying to get our sympathy, Jericho, and tell us what you were up to."

Jericho shook his head, smiled and remained silent.

"Well, I'll tell you what I think he was doing," Argus said. "I think he was trying to get rid of evidence. But that won't help you, old man. Doc and I know who the man in the cave was and that more than likely you killed him."

While Jason and Matt's mouths fell open in surprise, Laura looked at Jericho and smiled. "You tried to scare me and Jason away from the caves to keep us from finding the body, didn't you." Jericho still wasn't talking, but she caught his wicked wink and the sparkle in his eyes. "You did a good job. We thought it was really haunted when we heard the drums."

"I didn't make no drum sound. Just moaned and groaned a little."

Jason poured Argus a glass of champagne, and even though the sheriff shook his head, the glass was pushed in front of him. "You said you think Jericho killed the man in the cave?" Jason asked. "But you don't know for sure? By the way, do you have a name to put to the bones?"

"Thomas Herbert. He and his wife had a small farm on the other side of the river. I've been talking to a couple of old-timers around town and they remember Herbert. Said he was a drunk and a real mean son of a bitch. One day, fifty years ago, his wife reported to the local sheriff that her husband was missing. According to the records I found, Herbert never turned up. Then a couple of months later the wife ups and disappears.''

"So what does this have to do with Jericho?" Jason asked.

"Gossip says Jericho was having an affair with Herbert's wife, Sabrina. I think the husband found out and went after Jericho, and Jericho killed him. How's that sound so far?" he asked, but Jericho refused to answer.

"You can't keep your secret anymore, old man."

The voice, deep and soft, came from the opposite side of the screen door and startled everyone. "May I come in?" Without waiting for an invitation, a man stepped inside.

Dog lifted his head and snarled, then to everyone's astonishment, when the man returned the stare, Dog settled down and closed his eyes.

CHAPTER SEVENTEEN

LAURA COULDN'T HELP but gawk.

She knew the man was aware of her stare, but it didn't seem to faze him in the least, as if he was used to it. She thought that was probably true.

If Jason was drop-dead gorgeous and Matt ruggedly handsome, this man fitted somewhere in between, but the difference was the aura of mystery about him. Maybe it was the way he moved with the least amount of effort, quite an accomplishment for a man his size. She estimated he was about six-three. He had raven black hair, skin deeply tanned from the sun, and the coldest green eyes she'd ever seen. She doubted that under the beautiful three-piece suit there was an ounce of excess fat.

"Who the hell are you and what do you know about anything?" Jericho asked.

The intruder's gaze moved over everyone, assessing and calculating. Laura figured those cold eyes hadn't missed a thing. Jason moved closer and his arm tightened around her shoulders. She loved him for being so protective, but could have told him that the man had no interest in her other than to make the usual male tally of female attributes. But she bet if he saw her on a crowded street five years from now, he'd know where he'd met her.

The man couldn't seem to make up his mind between Matt and Argus, and because the sheriff wasn't wearing a uniform he asked, "Which one of you is the law around here?"

Before Argus could acknowledge the question, Matt said, "Since you barged into my home, why don't we start by you telling us who the hell you are."

The man nodded. He'd found the authority he was searching for. "I'm Joaquin Brightstone."

Laura noticed the way Jericho sat up and stared at the younger man. She whispered her observation to Jason.

"Your name doesn't mean a whole hell of a lot," Jason said. "Would you like to embellish on it?"

Joaquin relaxed. He couldn't seem to keep his gaze from returning to Jericho. "I was on business in Houston earlier this morning and caught a news story about some fifty-year-old remains found in an Indian cave on the Van der Bollen vineyard at Two Rivers." He had their attention, especially the old man's.

"Can you shed some light on the bones or the man?" Argus asked.

"Better than that. I can tell you the killer."

Jericho started to rise. "I think—whoever you are—that you know nothing about anything." His strength seemed to seep out of him and he sat down heavily. "I killed Thomas Herbert."

"Liar," Joaquin said, his voice rough with emotion. "Sabrina's long dead, Jericho, and she wouldn't want this."

"Who the hell *are* you?" Jericho and Matt asked in the same breath.

Laura watched the struggle Joaquin Brightstone was having, and like everyone else, she felt the tension.

"Well, old man," he said, "I'm your grandson."

For a moment she thought Jericho was going to have a heart attack, and she moved toward him, but Argus got there first and stepped between the two men. She realized that Argus, no matter what Jericho had done, was still his friend and willing to protect him.

"That's a hell of a thing to blurt out to a man his age."

"Wasn't any easy way to say it." Joaquin pulled a yellowed envelope out of his pocket and handed it to the sheriff. "After I heard the news this morning, I flew home to New Mexico and picked this up. Then I came directly here.

"The letter was written by my grandmother, Sabrina Brightstone Herbert. In it she tells how, after her husband found out she and Jericho were having an affair, he got mean drunk and tried to kill her. She shot him, then ran to Jericho for help. It seems Jericho went to Joseph Van der Bollen." He paused, waiting for an explanation.

"Joseph was our grandfather," Jason said.

Joaquin nodded. "Seems your grandfather helped Jericho get rid of the body, then gave Sabrina money to disappear. She was to wait a decent amount of time after reporting her husband missing, then quietly leave town. But she was scared and skipped, telling Jericho she'd write and tell him where she was, but she never contacted him again, did she?"

Jericho shook his head, his shoulders slumped with the weight of memories. "I waited," he mumbled. "Still waiting."

"The reason Grandmother left so quickly was she was pregnant with your child and couldn't take the chance of sticking around. She went to Santa Fe and did pretty well as an artist. My dad, Peter, inherited her talents. He's famous for his silver works and Indian jewelry."

Jericho's head snapped up, his eyes suddenly bright. "You mean I have a son and a grandson?"

"Yeah, I guess that's about the size of it." Joaquin started to leave, then stopped. "You might want to read the letter. Sabrina wrote it to my father when she was dying. She loved you and knew if she stayed you'd take the blame for killing her husband. She couldn't stand the thought of your going to jail."

As he pushed open the screen door, Jericho jumped to his feet. "Wait. Don't leave." Suddenly he didn't know what to do and could only stare at the handsome young man who looked so much like his dear Sabrina.

Laura got up and hurried to Jericho. "Why don't you take him to your place and talk?" It seemed to be the push they both needed, and they agreed. But just as Jericho was almost out the door, he stopped and asked Argus, "Am I free to leave?"

Argus slipped the letter back in the envelope and handed it over. "Free as you've always been."

LAURA GAZED at the full moon and marveled at all that had happened in the span of a few hours. "Do you think Jericho will go meet his son?"

"Most certainly. He's always wanted a family, and I've never understood why he waited."

"He loved Sabrina and was waiting for her to contact him. That's sad, Jason."

They strolled up the lane to his house and fell silent as they passed Lloyd's disabled car. "Did the sheriff say anything about Lloyd? With everything that went on, I didn't think to ask."

"He and his men are still sitting in jail. Don't worry about him." Jason stopped and grasped Laura by the upper arms. For a moment all he could see was her puffy bottom lip and the bruises on her arm where Lloyd had manhandled her. "I don't want to talk about Lloyd, Ginny, the baby, Jericho or his grandson. I want to talk about us." She was staring at him with that look of dread.

Jason grasped her face in his hands. "I asked you to think about moving here, living with me, but I've changed my mind."

He'd remembered and was disgusted, she was sure of it, and she felt her heart sink to her toes.

"I want you to marry me, Laura. Nothing temporary. We get married or stop seeing each other." He could see the inner struggle going on inside and knew she desperately wanted to say something, but he was equally determined to have his say. "I know I don't have a reputation for staying power, but I've never been in love before. I want a home, Laura, and children. I want *you.*"

Her happiness almost overwhelmed her, then she remembered what she had to do and her heart again plummeted. "Jason, don't you remember me? I mean, really remember me from eight years ago? Do you know the awful things I did?"

If she hadn't been so serious, he would have laughed. It was strange, he thought, what people can drag along with them through their life. And the more they cart guilt and shame around, the bigger it gets, until it's all out of proportion to what actually happened. "I remember everything about eight years ago."

Laura groaned and tried to move away.

He held on to her firmly. "Lloyd was jealous of how Holcombe and I got along, the rapport we had. Holcombe had even asked me, when I got my degree, to come to work for the May Market Corporation. Lloyd couldn't take it and set out to make me look bad in front of your stepfather, his family and friends. He had one of his girlfriends slip something in my drink. When it was clear the drug had taken effect, she led me into the den, where he always took the men after dinner for cigars and brandy. Then she stripped me naked and left.

"The problem was I didn't drink as much as they thought I had, and then Monica found out what her brother was up to and rescued me. She sneaked me out of the house and left me in the cabana by the pool to sleep it off."

Here it comes, she thought, and wanted nothing more than for the ground to open up and swallow her whole. "I found you in the cabana."

Jason kissed her to shut her up. When he pulled away, he said, "Let me tell you what I remember. I was lying on a chaise longue and this angel with long, beautiful hair, curious hazel eyes and a smile meant to melt hearts—when she wasn't trying to hide her mouthful of braces—came to me. She must've thought I was cold because she covered me with a blanket. Then she kissed me, the sweetest kiss I've ever had. I always remembered."

"You must have been drunker than you thought," Laura said. She could no longer hold the truth back. "I took that blanket off you."

"Yes, and you touched me. You ran your hand over me, and I thought I was going to die of ecstasy."

Laura laughed. She couldn't believe what he was saying. "I tried to seduce you, dammit. I was fifteen years old and acting like some bitch in heat."

"No. Never. I remember soft, inquisitive hands that just wanted to know what the male body looked and felt like.

That sweet young girl would never have gone any further. What she did was as normal as breathing."

"Well, what about the kiss?"

"Ahhh. The kiss. How could I resist those tempting lips? No more than than I can now." So saying, he proceeded to kiss her again. "Besides," he said breathlessly, "did you know I fell in love with that girl? That's why I became a hopeless tomcat. I kept looking for my sweet Daisy May and no one measured up," he said sincerely. "But then I found an enchantress named Laura Ghant."

"You're a fake, a liar and a fraud, Jason Van der Bollen. You could charm the pants off a stone statue."

"Really."

She pushed him away and started walking fast toward the house. "There's nothing for me to do but marry you and straighten you out." She stopped sharply and started to spin around, only to slam into him. They grabbed for each other, and when they regained their balance, they began to laugh and kiss at the same time.

THE SUN STREAMING through the skylight woke her. She listened to Jason's even breathing, felt his arm around her waist and smiled into her pillow. She thought back to that girl eight years ago and smiled with understanding. Because she hadn't had anyone to talk to about her inquisitiveness and sexuality, she'd been mortified at what she'd done. Even being an adult and knowing her actions had been utterly natural didn't diminish the shame that revisited her at important moments in her life. Somewhere along the journey to adulthood she'd lost a piece of herself, a portion of her self-respect. Jason hadn't minimized or tried to lie about what had happened; he just made her see the experience differently, as something special. He'd seen the doubts in her even as she'd denied it and tried to hide behind her anger. Besides loving her, he'd given her the most wonderful gifts—her dignity back, and his friendship.

She'd always loved him.

She always would.

EPILOGUE

LAURA LEANED against a partition behind one of the art exhibits. The crowd at the gallery was as thick as flies, and she needed a chance to catch her breath. She could hear the buzz of the crowd, the Austin society and the archaeology enthusiasts, all around her.

Who would have thought that, when Matt closed the Indian caves and she went to him with her proposal, he'd agree. All her photographs of the caves had been enlarged, mounted, framed and put on exhibit. *The Van der Bollen Caves* was such a hit that people in all fields were coming to see her work.

She closed her eyes for a moment, knowing she was going to have to leave her safe haven and return to the endless questions and congratulations.

"Where's that gorgeous Jason?"

Laura heard the question from the opposite side of the partition, smiled and continued to eavesdrop shamelessly.

"You've been out of the country too long. He's married, Mary."

"Sue Ann, when has marriage ever interfered with Jason's pleasures? Betty was still married when she dated him."

"Well, I hear he's changed. He seldom comes to Austin, staying mostly in that town—what was the name?—Two something. Anyway, he farms. No, he ranches. No, that's not right. I seem to remember something about birds. Surely not."

"Virginia, I think you've had too much of that Van der Bollen champagne. Something must have happened to him. Maybe he got fat and ugly. Or just fat, Jason could never be ugly."

Laura smiled and had to bite her lip to keep from laughing.

"Well, I heard he has to stay home because his wife dumped their baby on him and goes off digging up dirty bones for months on end."

"If you're right, Jennifer, that marriage won't last long. And you should know. Didn't your husband walk out on you because of all your trips to Europe? And you're wrong about his wife. I heard she went on a few digs when she was pregnant, but Jason went with her. I think she was getting her Ph.D. She's one of those brainy women. Probably ugly as a mud fence to boot."

"You're full of it. Jason would never marry a smart or ugly woman."

"Oh, shut up all of you. I want to find Jason and see what's happened."

Laura did, too. She stepped around the partition and began searching. When she spotted Austin, she motioned for him to meet her in a nearby corner. "Have you seen your uncle?"

"No. Isn't this great, Laura? Did you see all those people looking at the collage I did?" He sipped at his soda, his eyes bright and busy checking everything out. "There's Ginny and Dad."

Laura waved, then stepped out of the line of traffic after being bumped and jostled around. Ginny was pregnant again and Matt was more relaxed with this one. "Have you seen Jason?"

Ginny gave Matt a sideways glance, but he deliberately wouldn't look at her. She started to speak but ended up laughing and Matt quickly joined her. When she finally composed herself, she said, "I saw Jason coming out of the women's rest room a few minutes ago."

"What?" Laura immediately craned her neck and began scanning the crowd.

"He was ticked off because the men's room didn't have a changing station, so he and little Matthew just strolled into the women's rest room."

"Oh, God," Laura moaned.

"I don't think you have to worry. I sneaked a peek to check up on them. Of course he didn't need the help, but plenty was offered. When I left he was lecturing an enthralled group on the advantages of using cloth diapers over disposable."

Laura shook her head and kept searching the gallery.

Matt started laughing again, and when Ginny glared at him, he protested, "Hell, it's funny. My brother's wandering around in black tie, sipping champagne, charming old girlfriends. Ouch!" Ginny had pinched him. "And he has Matthew strapped to his chest and a diaper bag over one shoulder as if it's the most natural thing in the world. You have to admit it's a sight to see. And low and behold, here comes the party animal now."

Laura spotted him and her eyes softened. The overhead light made his blond hair look like sunlight, and his electric blue eyes gleamed with laughter when they met hers. "I hear the women's rest room will never be the same." She peeked at Matthew and stroked the thick golden hair as he slept peacefully against his father's heart.

"Hey, I got a few good tips on diaper rash and gas." He kissed Laura and asked, "Have you seen my mother?"

Laura shook her head. "About an hour ago I saw her with Holcombe and my mother, cornering the governor." Jason's mother hadn't come home for their marriage, but when Matthew was born, she showed up and had managed to return every month. Laura had been ready to dislike Barbara Sellers Van der Bollen after what Jason had said about the woman's cavalier attitude toward motherhood, but she'd been surprised. She and Barbara were never going to be close, but they were friends.

Jason wrapped his arm around Laura's shoulders and glanced down at his son. It scared him sometimes to realize how happy he was. He had the family he'd always longed for—and Laura.

"Have I told you how beautiful you look tonight and how proud of you I am?"

"Several times, but I could hear it again."

"You know," he said, "I was thinking about a brother or sister for Matthew. Maybe we ought to go home and work on it."

COMING NEXT MONTH

#706 DANIEL • Tracy Hughes
Return to Calloway Corners
Daniel Calloway's father is getting out of jail. And Daniel's come back home to set the record straight. The last time he was in Calloway Corners—with Becca Harris, the only woman he's ever loved—a man was killed. That man was Becca's father, the town preacher, and Daniel's father was found guilty. Can Daniel and Becca rise above the past and build a future for themselves?

#707 TEXAS STANDOFF • Ruth Alana Smith
Home on the Ranch
E. Z. Winston has one love—the land her father left her. Then city slicker Colin Majors washes into her life on the tide of a flash flood. They share a night of passion that leads to a bond neither anticipated, and E.Z. soon finds herself in over her head. In more ways than one....

#708 THE MAN NEXT DOOR • Ellen James
The man next door has problems. He's an ex-cop, turned P.I., pretending to be a writer. He has a partner who's pretending she's pregnant. His son isn't pretending anything, but then, the boy's barely talking to him. And to top it off, he's becoming dangerously attracted to the woman next door, a woman he's been paid to investigate, a woman who just might be pretending that she *hasn't* murdered her husband.

#709 A SUITABLE BODYGUARD • Kathryn Shay
Family Man
Cord McKay has quit the New York police force and come home to raise his little girl in the small town where he was born. He needs a job, but the last thing he wants to do is act as bodyguard to Stacey Webb, daughter of the one man who knows why Cord fled town as a teenager. The problem is that Stacey's in real danger. And even though she doesn't remember what happened eighteen years ago, Cord does—and he owes her big time.

REBECCA

43 LIGHT STREET

YORK

FACE TO FACE

Bestselling author Rebecca York returns to "43 Light Street" for an original story of past secrets, deadly deceptions—and the most intimate betrayal.

She woke in a hospital—with amnesia...and with child. According to her rescuer, whose striking face is the last image she remembers, she's Justine Hollingsworth. But nothing about her life seems to fit, except for the baby inside her and Mike Lancer's arms around her. Consumed by forbidden passion and racked by nameless fear, she must discover if she is Justine...or the victim of some mind game. Her life—and her unborn child's—depends on it....

Don't miss *Face To Face*—Available in October, wherever Harlequin books are sold.

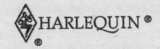

HARLEQUIN ®

You are cordially invited to a

HOMETOWN REUNION

September 1996—August 1997

Where can you find romance and adventure,
bad boys, cowboys, feuding families, and babies,
arson, mistaken identity, a mom on the run...?
Tyler, Wisconsin, that's where!

So join us in this not-so-sleepy little town and
experience the love, the laughter and the
tears of those who call it home.

WELCOME TO A
HOMETOWN REUNION

Twelve unforgettable stories, written for you by
some of Harlequin's finest authors. This fall,
begin a yearlong affair with America's favorite
hometown as **Marisa Carroll** brings you
Unexpected Son.

Available in September at your
favorite retail store.

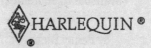

HARLEQUIN SUPERROMANCE®

Come West with us!

In Superromance's series of Western romances, you can
visit a ranch—and fall in love with a man of the West!

In September, watch for

Texas Standoff
by Ruth Alana Smith

**Let us take you to Cheyenne Moon Ranch,
in the Texas Hill Country**

Rancher Elise (E.Z.) Winston, who runs the most
successful spread in the county, knows how to stand up
for herself, her rights and her ranch. But when she
rescues Dallas lawyer Colin Majors from a flash flood,
she soon finds herself in over her head—in more ways
than one.....*A story full of Texas spunk and Texas speak!*

Look for upcoming HOME ON THE RANCH
titles wherever Harlequin books are sold.

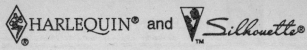 HARLEQUIN® and *Silhouette*®

are proud to present...

HERE COME THE

 GROOMS™

Four marriage-minded stories written by top
Harlequin and Silhouette authors!

Next month, you'll find:

A Practical Marriage	by Dallas Schulze
Marry Sunshine	by Anne McAllister
The Cowboy and the Chauffeur	by Elizabeth August
McConnell's Bride	by Naomi Horton

ADDED BONUS! In every edition of
Here Come the Grooms you'll find $5.00 worth
of coupons good for Harlequin and Silhouette
products.

On sale at your favorite Harlequin and Silhouette
retail outlet.

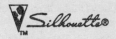 HARLEQUIN® 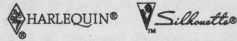 *Silhouette*®

HARLEQUIN SUPERROMANCE®

If you've always felt there's something special about a
man raising a family on his own...you won't want to
miss Harlequin Superromance's touching series

He's sexy, he's single...and he's a father!
Can any woman resist?

A SUITABLE BODYGUARD
by Kathryn Shay

Cord McKay has quit the New York Police force and come
home to raise his little girl in the small town where he was
born. He needs a job but the last thing he wants to do is act
as bodyguard to Stacey Webb, daughter of the one man
who knows why Cord fled town as a teenager. The problem
is that Stacey's in real danger. And even though she
doesn't remember what happened eighteen years ago,
Cord does...and he owes her big time.

Available in September

Be sure to watch for this and upcoming FAMILY MAN
titles. Fall in love with our sexy fathers, each determined
to do the best he can for his kids.

Look for them wherever Harlequin books are sold.